PRAISE FOR

Love WITH Noodles

"This senior version of *Portnoy's Complaint* will have readers laughing at the unspoken-sexual experience after a 'certain age' . . . highly recommended.

—*Library Journal* (starred review)

"Skates by on a breeze of light, social comedy . . . a male version of a Judith Krantz novel. For those with a yen for a kosher-style romance, this dish might hit the spot."

—*Publishers Weekly*

"I predict that Harry I. Freund's compulsively readable novel about the amorous adventures of the most sought after Jewish widower on Park Avenue will keep you reading and laughing long into the night."

—Naomi Ragen,
author of *The Convenant* and *Sotah*

"A delightful surprise, this resonant, racy debut novel is an engaging 'Sex in the Sixties' take on New York Jewish society."

—Stephen Fried,
author of *The New Rabbi* and *Bitter Pills*

Love WITH Noodles

An Amorous Widower's Tale

HARRY I. FREUND

CARROLL & GRAF PUBLISHERS
NEW YORK

LOVE WITH NOODLES: AN AMOROUS WIDOWER'S TALE

Carroll & Graf Publishers
An Imprint of Avalon Publishing Group Inc.
245 West 17th Street, 11th Floor
New York, NY 10011

Library of Congress Cataloging-in-Publication Data is available.

ISBN-13: 978-0-78671-798-9
ISBN-10: 0-78671-798-X

9 8 7 6 5 4 3 2 1

Printed in the United States of America
Distributed by Publishers Group West

This book is dedicated to my wife Matta.
She has the patience of a saint and the jewelry of a sinner.

1.

They should ban birthday parties after the age of fifty, they should pass a law. What's to celebrate in wrinkles? Why glorify the passing of another year? Besides which, if it's a surprise party, the shock alone could kill you.

I'm annoyed. It's the night of my sixtieth birthday, a cold winter's night, and I'm invited over to the apartment of my old friends, Evelyn and Bob, where I'm hoping for a quiet dinner, but suspecting that I will find myself in for a surprise. It's been only two years since Ellen died and I'm not in a celebratory mood. Walking west from my apartment on Park Avenue toward Fifth, I try to resist the urge to turn heel and retreat to the warm comfort of my home. Ellen's silent urgings push me on. "Don't disappoint our friends," I can hear her saying. "They love you. They care about you."

Besides feeling a bit disjointed by the fact that I'm facing sixty, I am also somewhat distracted by the recent news that my son Eric is in love. He has proposed marriage to a woman named Carol Hoffman, he tells me, and he'd like me to meet her. He lives a mere thirty blocks away, and he's proposed marriage to a woman he's never even bothered to introduce me to. What am I, an afterthought? When did I become so disconnected from my son that he doesn't bother to have me meet her until now? This would never have happened if Ellen were still alive. He wouldn't have treated his mother this way. I don't know what has happened to us.

A woman shouldn't die before her husband—it isn't fair to either of them. I am lost without her.

I enter Evelyn and Bob's apartment building. The doorman buzzes upstairs to let them know I'm on the way up; I can tell from his expression that something is brewing. Evelyn is waiting at the door when I leave the elevator. She gives me a warm embrace, takes my coat. We walk through the foyer together and into the living room, and I'm greeted by a crowd of familiar faces shouting, "Surprise!" I manage to give what I hope is a convincing display of shock and delight.

The living room and dining room are aglow, the chandeliers and lamps illuminating the splendid Modiglianis that Evelyn and Bob have collected over the years. All my friends are here, no one has been left out, and despite myself I can't help but be touched by all the fuss. I'm kissed, I'm hugged, I'm backslapped, I'm showered with jokey gifts: Viagra, a walker, and a carton of adult diapers. Once I regain some equilibrium, I notice that Evelyn has gone to a lot of trouble to make this party sparkle.

"Were you surprised, Dan?" Evelyn says, clutching my arm.

"Of course, of course. But what have I done to deserve all this?"

"Just being your sweet self," Evelyn coos, clearly pleased with herself.

"Dan my man," says Bob, patting me on the back. "You need a party. Everyone needs a party when he turns sixty."

Whether I need it or not, the party absorbs me. I've known these couples for some thirty or forty years. We see one another regularly at parties, events, and benefits. We've watched our kids grow up and out of the house. And now we are beginning to watch one another soften into old age. I'm touched by the wealth of warm feeling in the room. When I can, I extract myself from the crowd, the chatter, and the noise for a moment and walk over to the living room windows. They face Central Park, and the view from the seventeenth floor affords the best of Manhattan, all aglitter against the night sky. Evelyn and Bob's building may not offer the charm and detail of my prewar apartment house, but theirs is so much more open, so much airier, and I always relish the view when I visit here. I look out over the city. I count among my blessings all my good, loyal friends. Even if Eric is not here.

As I turn back to the party I realize that for the first time in at least a year I have not been introduced to a designated female. Carefully selected by the hostess, this lady is never younger than forty and certainly not older than sixty; she is Jewish like I am, she is reasonably intelligent, and she is either very pretty or very rich. She is invariably ready for a serious relationship and always disappointed at my level of disinterest. Lately, I have begun to feel a little hunted—like those women who complain of being sex objects. At sixty, I've become a remarriage object. But maybe I have been spared tonight.

With that thought I begin to relax and mingle again. Then I see Evelyn approaching with an unfamiliar woman in tow. Evidently, I am not to be spared after all. So my practiced eye evaluates tonight's offering: fiftyish; good-looking, although her face has a slightly startled look; shrewd and intelligent eyes; an impressive body, stomach flat and bosom ample, noticeably so in her clinging red evening suit. Her platinum blonde hair is piled high and fastened with what seems to be a giant diamond hair clip, which competes for attention with the diamonds on her ears, around her lovely neck, on her wrists and several fingers. She glows, her glittering diamonds in a way echoing the lights of the bejeweled city I'd been admiring through the window. Assuming those diamonds of hers are real, she would appear to be that rarity, a pairing of beauty and money. Her name is Violet Finkel. Introduced, I stand there, and staring into the eyes of this magnificent woman, I find myself mumbling, I hope not audibly, "Twinkle, twinkle, little Finkel."

"So you're the birthday boy," she says in an authoritative tone, a little loud, a little Brooklynesque, with a slight singsong intonation. "You look great for sixty. Where have you been hiding? You're gorgeous."

Just then, my old friends Charlotte and Dave Kayer join us. There's a persistent rumor that Dave is leaving Charlotte, but they're together tonight, I'm happy to see. Charlotte is a splendid-looking woman with thick dark hair and a young, taut look about her that my Ellen attributed to plastic surgery. Whatever its origin, her beauty makes it difficult to imagine Dave walking out on her.

It's difficult for Charlotte, meanwhile, to take an appraising eye off Violet's gem collection as she nervously fingers her own gold necklace. For her part, Violet has not let go of my arm, having established a not-uncomfortable body contact that reaches from shoulder to hip. And from across the room, every once in a while, Evelyn assesses our situation. She looks self-satisfied, like she has just orchestrated a good match.

Violet is treated by one and all with great deference. Women pay her compliments; men stand at attention when they approach her.

She quickly becomes the center of interest in the little groups that gather around us. In New York, that can only mean one of two things: money or power. With enough of the former, you can acquire the latter, and I get the feeling that Violet is lacking neither. I am also intrigued, as she differs remarkably from the usual compliant designated female on the lookout for a husband. For one thing, she's obviously already rich as Croesus. Of course, by relative standards, everyone at this party is well off, I suppose, including myself. But with a woman like Violet, clearly awash in money, how do I compete? It can prove to be extraordinarily expensive to mingle with the fabulously rich. You have to pay if you want to play.

The ringing of a little glass bell interrupts my thoughts. Our hostess announces that it's time for the toasts. Everyone finds a seat on one of the large beige sofas or on the floor, and Violet and I, still standing, are soon surrounded by the guests who then rise in turn to say a few words. What follows is a jumble of seemingly heartfelt toasts and carefully concocted roasts in the form of poems and little ditties. I keep a delighted smile frozen on my face, and I laugh heartily at all the appropriate moments, but what I am really feeling, profoundly, is the pain of Ellen's absence. She was the first of us to die, hers is the only missing face in our crowd tonight, and I've never missed her more keenly than right now. All this noisy celebration — it's suddenly feeling just too soon for me. If only Eric were here. I try to quell the pangs of disappointment. I smile, I laugh, on cue.

Violet continues to share the spotlight with me. We are still standing arm in arm as though we're old friends, yet I find her possessiveness more endearing than stifling. Whenever I look her way, she beams a wonderful smile at me, an amalgam of self-confidence, good humor, and the most perfect teeth I have ever seen. Occasionally I catch her shrewd eyes examining me, but I must have passed her test, whatever it was, because she's certainly hanging in there.

The toasts over, I prepare to thank my host and hostess and my friends, but before I can begin, Violet takes the floor. "I know I'm a relative newcomer to this circle of friends, and I've just met the birthday boy, but I feel compelled to say, Dan, that you must be an exceptional person to deserve such accolades. And while I would normally be very interested in your character, I have to admit that I find you so singularly gorgeous, that I don't give a damn about your character. So happy birthday, you sixty-year-old hunk." And she kisses me hard on the mouth, almost knocking me over as she lunges at me. My friends roar their approval. Afterward, as I mumble through my own little speech of thanks, I can't help feeling more than a bit distracted by the memory of that kiss. Me, gorgeous? Right . . .

Later, I take a deep breath and, claiming I have an early birthday breakfast with Eric, I begin to make my departure. The party has begun losing steam, in any case. But not Violet. She takes my arm. "I'll take you home," she says.

"Wait a minute, a gentleman is supposed to take a lady home," I protest.

"You have a car and driver waiting?" she asks. I admit that I do not. "Well, I do," she says, "so I'll drop you off." This is clearly not an offer but a command, and I obey.

Her car is waiting, her driver fast asleep at the wheel. "Wake up, damn it," she yells as she knocks her bejeweled hand against his closed window, and in a practiced and graceful maneuver he leaps out of the car, swings to attention, and holds the door for us. "Did madam have a pleasant evening?" he inquires.

"Yeah, yeah," she says, "but it's not over yet. We have to deliver

Mr. Gelder here to his apartment at Park and Sixty-third safe and sound. He's the birthday boy."

"My congratulations, sir," he says, and I thank him, feeling like a prince of the realm.

"I know almost everything about you," Violet says to me. "Evelyn did her job well, and I also checked you out with other people I know. I didn't hear a bad thing about you, not even a snide remark. It's not normal."

"I suppose I have some secrets," I say. "But I never reveal them on a first date."

"I don't do much on a first date, either," she says, "so don't get your hopes up. If there is a third or fourth date, however, you'd better watch out."

"When do I find out all about you, Violet? We'll need a second date for that alone. I know nothing about you other than that you are beautiful and that you like diamonds. That's not enough." I am surprised by my own slick audacity. Is this really me talking?

But we have reached my building. "Okay, Dan—can I call you Dan? Here's my number. Wait, I have a card in my bag, damned bag's filled with stuff. Here it is, here. Call me. Don't keep me waiting."

As I enter the building, I am smiling, almost smirking. Am I really ready for an erotic adventure? I ask myself. And yet as soon as I get into the elevator, the weight of Ellen's absence descends on me. Encased in the rich mahogany walls of the elevator, its brass gleaming to perfection, I look beside me wishing for Ellen. She would now be rehashing the evening with me, gossiping, commenting on the women, their jewels, their outfits. She would do quite a job on Violet, starting with the Finkel breasts and how natural they may or may not be, then moving on to the platinum blonde hair and the jewelry, which would put Ellen in mind of a walking advertisement for the diamond industry. Nor would Ellen fail to comment on Violet's permanently startled look—evidence of at least one face-lift. "One more lift and her eyebrows will meet her hairline," she would say. And to annoy her a little, I would act dumb. "Really?" I'd say, "I thought the woman was beautiful." She would flare, "You want me to look beautiful, shell out fifty thousand for plastic surgery, and you'll be married to Marilyn Monroe in six months' time." I'd tell her I was just kidding, I like her just the way she is, except maybe she needs just a little more breast, you know, just for show. And we would enter the apartment in good humor, together in every sense of the word.

Only tonight I enter alone.

Della has left the hall light on for me as usual; the place sparkles. I no longer need a maid five times a week, but Della is family—she raised Ellen, and she's like a grandmother to Eric. She must be in her eighties now, yet she shows up every morning at nine and stays through supper. Plain and simple: I love her. No one understands better than she what these past two years have been for me. We have been co-mourners.

I check the answering machine: no message from Eric. Could he have forgotten my birthday? My only child? I have no plan for a birthday breakfast with him; that was a small social lie. And also a heartfelt wish. Eric has been so consumed with his high-tech businesses and, I suppose, his new fiancée that he has no time for his father anymore. It's my birthday, I can feel sorry for myself.

I hang up my overcoat and go right to my bedroom. I toss my jacket and tie onto the bed, where I see a birthday card from Della on my pillow. Some bittersweet emotion propels me down the hall to the living room. I turn on the lights and stand there waiting for that particular mix of emotions I frequently feel when I spend time in this elegant and formal room. Ellen chose this apartment because of this room, and she is completely present for me here in every detail, which she designed and executed; in every item, which was carefully chosen by her before being passed by me for approval. The antique Kashan rug she loved, lying there silken with its patina of age. The sofas she chose and then covered with a fabric that was so expensive that we fought over the purchase. I'm glad in retrospect that she won the battle, and I wish I could have given her everything she ever wanted; everything—now that it's too damned late. The old Russian table with the malachite top that we bought on the Pimlico Road in London when I was feeling flush cost an arm and a leg, and what we paid to ship it to New York would have bought every stick of furniture my parents ever owned. When my mother, she should rest in peace, asked me how much we spent on that table I lied through my teeth; the truth would have killed her. The cocktail table still displays Ellen's collection of cloisonné figurines, bought one by one in shops all over the world, wherever we traveled. Holy God, how can she really be gone these two years? For two years, I've been living in a fog of sadness and grief. Of late, the pain of loss has become less acute. Now I can go entire hours without thinking of her, whereas before a minute wouldn't pass without my becoming overwhelmed by some stabbing memory of our life together. The pain is still there; it's just duller, like the worn-down blade of an old knife.

I close my eyes; I see her again: her soft brown hair hanging loosely down her shoulders, the way she wore it when we were first married, when she was a young, nervous mother. I see the three of us together; she's pushing Eric in his stroller through the leaf-strewn paths of Central Park. Then we only looked forward.

I shake my head. What am I doing standing here like a fool

dredging up memories? To what end? I can't live in the past. She would never want that. Ellen is gone, and all this stuff is . . . just stuff. I turn off the light and return to my bedroom.

Only I'm not yet in the mood to sleep. I sink into my old armchair, a little frayed despite several recoverings. It used to be my father's chair; he would sit in it to listen to operas in his bedroom. I remember a time just a few months before my wedding—I was in my late twenties, and he was a year or two older than I am now—how tired he looked even at rest in his old, comfortable chair. I didn't realize how sick he was. That was the first and only time he complained to me about his business; he must have felt his strength waning. I didn't know if he was asking for advice or just venting. I'll never know. I only know I had no idea what to say—what could I have to say at that age?—and thus I lost my last chance to speak with my father adult-to-adult, to understand him as a man. A few months after my wedding, he was dead. You treated a father differently in those days; you gave him respect, you kept a certain distance. I honored my father; even after his death, nobody sat in his seat at the head of the table in the dining room until my mother dismantled her home.

But these days . . . Almost midnight, and Eric still hasn't called me for my birthday. I'm sure Della reminded him. And how could Evelyn not have invited him to my party? He's busy, I know. He has two companies to run. He has a wedding to plan. And he's a great kid—handsome; tall and fit, he's probably in better shape than his trainer. Eric-dot-com, I call him. A total techno-wiz. Money, girls, action, travel.

Yet he could have called. He's got a phone on his belt.

He finds time to run around the reservoir in Central Park twice a day. But to call me? And he is full of advice. I should do this, I should invest in that. I tell him he can take risks, he has a rich father. I had a wonderful father, but we never had money. We had to worry about the rent. I still worry. Not that I need to. I have plenty of money, but I can't seem to shake the worry part, no matter how much I earn, save, or give away. I always feel slightly behind. Eric calls me neurotic.

The telephone rings, jarringly. "Dad?" It's Eric's voice. "Happy birthday. Sorry I couldn't be at the party. I'm in Boston, but I'll take you out to dinner next week, and we'll celebrate together with Carol. You're going to love her. Okay?" Eric speaks in a guilty rush.

"Sure," I say. I cut it short, afraid I'll blubber on the phone. The kid remembered. He still has a heart. And I was sitting here blaming him, too quick to find fault with him. After all, he is very busy.

Just as I am turning out my bedside light, the phone rings again. I look at the clock; it's after midnight.

"It's Violet," she says, "Sorry, but I knew you would still be up. I gave you the wrong card; it's my business card. Here's my home number, write it down." And I do. "Call me," she says. "I improve upon acquaintance." I don't know if I'm ready to find out.

I lie down in the dark. I hope the sadness will not return. After two years, I figure I'm entitled to time off for my birthday. Two years of posthumous faithfulness; I must be the only man in town as loyal to his wife after she died as when she was alive. Is it guilt? Or maybe I'm just nervous that in some way Ellen will know, and I fear some sort of retribution. Whatever, it's got to stop. I'm turning into a lonely old man worrying if my son is calling enough, whether I should go on a date with a beautiful woman. I might as well be in my eighties exchanging complaints with a benchmate on the boardwalk in Miami Beach.

But am I really ready for a Violet Finkel in my life?

2.

A few days later, Eric calls as promised and invites me to dinner. "Wait until you meet Carol," he says. "It'll be a nice birthday present for you. She's the one, Dad. You're going to flip over her."

The restaurant he has chosen, one of the current in spots, is jammed with people sitting too close to one another and shouting to be heard over the din. An attractive, young hostess with legs up to her ears leads me to Eric's table. As I approach, I take a quick glance at the young woman seated beside him. She is smiling tentatively. "Dad," Eric says, "this is Carol Hoffman. Carol, my father, Dan Gelder."

"Hello, Carol, I am so happy to meet you," I say and warmly kiss her on her cheek. Carol is pretty with blonde, softly curling hair that sets off remarkably blue-green, intelligent eyes. Her handshake is firm and warm.

"I've been really looking forward to this," she says, and she looks like she means it. She blushes slightly as I look her over, and I find that quite charming. She's still seated, but I have the impression that she is tall and very shapely. Eric always knows how to pick them.

We start the usual chitchat. Carol comes from Michigan, from someplace called Saginaw. "How did your family find its way there?" I ask.

She replies that her family has lived there pretty much since the town was founded. That's unusual, I think: that a Jewish family would have found its way to such a remote place over one hundred years ago; must have been peddlers and opened a store.

We order our dinner and start on our drinks. A little bit of awkwardness hovers in the air. Eric is not relaxed, and Carol, unconsciously but constantly fingering her simple pearl necklace, seems to be fidgeting.

"Tell me more about your family, Carol. How did Jewish people find their way to Saginaw, Michigan?"

There is a moment of hesitation. "Dad, Carol isn't Jewish," Eric interjects.

"But her name, Hoffman," I say, caught off guard.

"It's also a German name, Dad. Her great-grandparents came from Germany, but they were not Jews."

I am speechless, but as the waiter comes with the salads at that moment, I am spared from speaking. I am not particularly religious, yet the prospect of a non-Jewish daughter-in-law stuns me. Is this why Eric didn't introduce us until now? Was he afraid to tell me this in private? Did he bring me here to forestall a reaction? I try to eat the salad.

"She's not religious, Dad," Eric says. "She's like us, there should be no problem." A silence stifles me. I am amazed at how disappointed I am, at how deeply I am affected by this news. I can't respond. I can't eat, either, and I just sit there, holding my fork against the tablecloth.

"Look, Dad," Eric begins, "Please try to understand. We love each other. I know this sounds phony, but it was love at first sight," he says, reaching for Carol's hand. "Give it a chance, and you will love her like I do. Please, Dad, give it a chance."

I look at the young woman, who is now nervously pulling on her necklace. I want to be kind, but I still can't speak. A wave of misery passes over me. I remember my mother just days before her death, already wearing a morphine patch; in and out of a medicated stupor, for a few minutes every once in a while she'd be herself again. One of the few things she asked about was Eric and any prospective girls. "Bring me to the wedding," she said, and I wondered what she could possibly mean.

"Sure," I had assured her. "Of course, you will be there."

"I'm not so sure," she'd responded. "But remember to bring me there one way or another."

I began to understand what she meant, and I tried to lighten the mood. "Well, I hope I'll be able to be there myself," I joked. "The way Eric is going I may also be too old to attend."

She laughed. "No, no, you'll be there. There will be Jewish music, lots of food, all the relatives. Bring me there one way or another."

"I promise," I said. Jewish music, the relatives. Right, how about a Jewish bride? Images of my own wedding, Ellen's and mine, flash across my mind: the whole family gathered from Antwerp, from London, from all over New York; first Ellen, then me, lifted up on chairs, and somebody threw us a napkin that we held on each end while the fellows holding us up danced to the traditional music. I remember just before the wedding how I veiled her in the old way; accompanied by my father and by hers to make sure I was getting the right girl, I'd not be fooled like Jacob in the Bible when he got Leah instead of Rachel. The ceremonies, the grandmothers crying, my father's speech about the two grandfathers no longer alive—that's how he brought them to the wedding. But whom shall I bring to this one? Whom, dead or alive, *should* I bring? Could my mother have foreseen this event? Her only grandson marrying a shiksa.

Carol looks stricken, Eric looks furious. I still cannot speak. Suddenly, I'm unable to sit there any longer. I'm sweating, and my hands are growing clammy. I feel dizzy. "Men's room," I say, and get up, but don't know where to go. "Where do I go?" No one knows. I find a waiter . . .

Finally, to my relief, I find myself alone in the washroom. I lean against the wall. I'm sweating bullets. Then dizziness overwhelms me, and I find myself sitting on the floor with my back against the wall. I loosen my tie, open my collar. After what seems to be a long while, I feel better, less confused. The clammy feeling leaves me and I am truly embarrassed. I can hardly believe what has happened to me. I have to get hold of myself. I get on my knees, crawl across the tile floor. Using the sink for leverage, I lift myself up. Cold water, I think, and splash it onto my face, then dry myself with some paper towels. How could I have behaved this way? How am I going to face Carol? Eric? For the moment all I can manage is to just stand still.

The door opens. Eric. "Jesus," he says, "what was that all about? What are you doing? Where did this come from?"

I can offer no explanation. "Who do you think you are, the Chief Rabbi of New York?" he continues, obviously upset. "When's the last time you were in synagogue? Since when do you care so much about being Jewish?"

"It's not about how many times we've been to synagogue," I muster. "It's about being a Jew. Understanding the weight, the responsibility. How can you even think about marrying a non-Jew? I don't understand," I say in anguish. Tears brim in my eyes as I look into the startled, defiant face of my son.

I break my gaze when someone arrives to use the bathroom. Taking the opportunity to bolt, I return to Carol with Eric not far behind.

"Carol, I am sorry for leaving the table in such a rush," I begin in explanation. "But I must say, I simply was not prepared for this."

"Not prepared for what exactly?" she asks quietly.

"Well, for the idea that Eric might marry a non-Jewish woman, to be frank."

"I think I understand," she says, a question in her voice. "It's hard for you to accept, but I really believe that once you get to know us—our relationship—you will feel differently. I know you will," she says sincerely, but she looks quite shaken.

"This has nothing to do with you personally, Carol, nothing at all. You're a delightful, beautiful woman, and I am really sorry for my behavior. But this is a shock to me; I'm still reeling. While we're not a religious family, being Jewish is something much wider and deeper than that—at least, for me. We're a people with a long history, with a great tradition. I thought Eric would carry on that tradition."

"But Eric can stay Jewish, I can stay Methodist. If we have kids they can decide for themselves," she replies.

"But that's not the point," I begin to say and stop. For I'm unable to explain myself any further. "I'm really sorry for the ruckus, but . . . I'm going to need time to figure this out." Eric is quiet; he's not looking at me, but it's clear from his expression that he's angry. Understandably, Carol is uncomfortable. But I have nothing to say to placate either of them, so I get up and tell them that I'm going home.

When I get to my apartment, I sit down on the front hall bench and brace my back against the wall. I feel overwhelmed by a sense of failure. All the wonderful memories of my father's house, of my grandparents, the warm holidays, the close family, the trips to Israel—they're memories that I thought I'd shared with Eric. How could they not have made an impression on him? Evidently, he doesn't have a clue about how I feel. He wants what he wants, and to hell with me, to hell with his people and his identity. Is it my fault? It's true, we didn't go to synagogue much. I always said that I didn't need all those rituals to make me feel Jewish, but maybe Eric did. Maybe I cheated him out of his heritage. Which would make the failure mine, not his.

The next morning I awaken painfully, my head aching and my body crumpled up on the hard bench. That spell last night in the restaurant worries me: Did I lose consciousness for a few seconds when I slid to the floor in that bathroom? I'm not sure. I call Dr. Kabtzan's office and get an immediate appointment. I should be used to doctors by now, as I'm dutifully presenting my body for all sorts of examinations on a regular basis; only today I'm a bit unnerved by the prospects.

Seated across from Dr. Kabtzan in his office, I can't help but notice that he himself is looking particularly tired and worn down today, so I ask how he's feeling. "Feeling," he repeats, "how am I feeling? I'm feeling lousy to tell you the truth, lousy. You remember my little girl Stacey; remember her, she married a fine young doctor at St. Luke's Hospital, she has a beautiful baby. You remember. Well, she left him. He's not interesting enough, he's too one-dimensional,

Her Highness says. He's boring her. Now she's taken up with a woman, a woman from Albany. She wants to move to Albany to be with this woman and take the baby with her. My wife is on medication, and I should be; that is how I'm feeling. But thanks for asking."

He tells me his story, so I tell him mine. He becomes businesslike, examines me thoroughly, and declares that all is well. Only I should lose thirty pounds, and then he launches into the same little joke that he has repeatedly treated me to over the years. He tells me I am suffering from DDS, Disappearing Dick Syndrome. You know you have it when you look down in the shower and you cannot see your you-know-what. He laughs merrily. Happy to see his mood change, I join in.

"Physician, heal thyself," I say as I point to his considerable paunch.

"Everything checks out fine with you, you're a miracle for your age; you don't look a day over fifty-nine," he pronounces. "You are sentenced to a long life, enough to enjoy the many pleasures that Eric will no doubt bestow upon you. If at any time he gets you down unbearably, call me. In all probability, I won't have to prescribe anything—I'll just bring you up to date about my Stacey and you can learn to count your blessings. Misery loves company, call me anytime. I'm always good for a laugh," he assures me with an audible sigh.

And I have to admit that I feel better as I head for my office. There's something to be said for relativity.

3.

Two days later I receive a breathless call from Violet. "How have I offended you?" she begins.

"You haven't," I reply.

"So how come you didn't call? What do I have, B.O.? I told you I improve upon acquaintance."

"I intended to call, but I had a family problem."

"Everything all right? Is it your son? Is he well?"

"He's fine. He's just killing me with aggravation, no big deal." I don't feel near ready to open up to Violet about Eric.

"Tell me about it. I have one daughter, not from Finkel, but from the bum I married first. She is currently in Israel studying, but before that she was in Nepal with some lunatics meditating. Before that, don't even ask; Nepal was a plus compared. And now she is becoming ultra-Orthodox in Jerusalem, and learning Yiddish—if my Grandma Pearl was still alive, they could have a conversation. She's also now changed her name from Maria to Miriam, for her faith, which she's sharing with a young man she met through her rabbi; he's newly observant too, the young man. My whole adult life is an advertisement for birth control. So anytime you want me to hear about your son, feel free. I won't charge you for my time."

"You get what you pay for," I reply. "When is our second date?" I don't really want to think about Eric, much less talk about him.

"Tonight, if you are free and have a tux."

"What do you mean, tonight? Why didn't you give me some notice?"

"If you had called me, you would have known about it earlier. Listen, I need your help. I'm being honored tonight at a gala for an Israeli charity, and I don't have a proper escort. Rescue me, please."

This is obviously no shrinking Violet, and I doubt she has ever been in need of rescuing, but a benefit? What could be worse? And more expensive? "I hate getting into a tux," I complain.

"Oh, don't give me a hard time. It will be fun; it will give us a chance to get to know each other better. And no one will ask you for a dime. The Gift Journal is already printed."

It's sounding better: I get to see Violet again, and I don't have to pay. "Can I come in a dark suit?"

"You must wear a tux. I'm wearing a gown, not to mention the Finkel crown jewels. Please, please, help me. I want everyone to think I've got a handsome beau. I'll pick you up and redeliver you. You'll enjoy yourself, I promise."

"Oh, okay. I'll come," I say reluctantly. After all, the new me has to learn how to circulate again.

"My driver will pick you up at seven. I have to get there earlier for photographs."

A gala is a painful thing, alchemy in reverse, taking your hard-earned gold and converting it into good deeds utilizing peer pressure and a ballroom. The ancient Jewish imperative, *Tikun Olam*, the Repairing of the World, has mutated in affluent New York into this particular communal rite. And because of Violet, I am attending one, after avoiding at least two dozen others this year.

Later that evening, be-tuxed and chauffeured, resigned, and a little anxious, I am driven to the hotel. In the anteroom of the Grand Ballroom, hundreds of people are pushing their way to the laden buffet tables. Veal cutlets as hors d'oeuvres, mini stuffed cabbages on toothpicks, finely decorated little sandwiches, and, for the disciplined few, crudités. An impressively crafted chopped liver statue in the shape of a chicken is slowly collapsing in the onslaught of guests carving out chunks with serving spoons that could pass for small shovels, while a small, silent but determined crowd jostles over the sushi bar. Platters of small franks in pastry shells are rapidly emptied and refilled in unending cycles, and a great mound of gefilte fish has totally disappeared, its remains only some slices of carrot that once garnished it. Near the constantly opening and closing doors of the kitchen, groups of guests station themselves to intercept the waiters bearing fresh offerings. Only waiters trained on the football field can manage to penetrate these groups, strong men steady on their feet and unafraid of close physical contact. People yell across the tables at each other, encouraging their friends not to miss this or that treat: "Hurry up! They just delivered more sweet and sour meatballs!"

Meanwhile, the bars stand virtually ignored, except for the occasional request for a ginger ale or sparkling water with lime. To fortify myself for the evening, I go to the bar and ask for a bourbon. Pleased to have business, the lonely bartender pours my drink and watches me while I make quick work of it and ask for another. From my quiet haven, I observe the stampede at the banquet tables. It's funny, how

Jews and liquor don't usually mix. Here are scores of waiters rushing about with trays of food, and three bartenders with practically nothing to do. Were it not for water and seltzer, you'd need only one.

After my second bourbon the bartender tells me that he has a really excellent Italian kosher wine, which he suggests as a chaser. "Thanks," I reply, "but I've pretty much reached my limit. Besides which, I get nervous about drinking wine."

"Why wine?" he asks.

"Listen," I explain, "you know what happens to a Jewish boy when he's eight days old, don't you?"

"Yeah," he replies. "You mean the circumcision, don't you, the bris, right?"

"Right," I answer him. "Well, my theory is that we don't drink a lot of wine because immediately after the circumcision the mohel, the guy who does the cutting, shoves a bit of paper towel soaked in wine into the kid's mouth. Understand? We associate the taste of wine with a memorable sharp pain, that's my theory."

"Ouch," he replies.

"Well, that's probably why I enjoy bourbon so much. I may be back for more later."

An elderly couple clinging to each other in the midst of the bedlam wanders into my path. I can't help but smile as I examine the lady, who must be well into her eighties, but scrawny and tough, with gray hair pulled into a neat bun. She is a little stooped over and very determined-looking, and in all reminds me very much of my two grandmas. Her husband seems more frail; he's using a cane and holding on to his wife's shoulder. "Don't worry, Leo, we'll find it," she reassures him. "Just hold on to me, so you won't get lost."

They look like they may need the bathroom or an exit, so I inquire, "Can I help?"

The old lady looks up at me with gratitude. "Oh, how kind you are," she says. "And tall, maybe you could look over the heads of these people and help us find the table with chopped liver. Mr. Jacobs here, my Leo, loves his chopped liver. They wouldn't have an affair like this without it, but all we can find is raw fish—imagine serving raw fish and getting away with it. Are people crazy? When they could have chopped liver and stuffed derma and gefilte fish. The world's gone mad."

I remember the huge sculpture of chopped liver being demolished at a nearby table, and lead her and Mr. Jacobs in that direction. He must be in his nineties, and he eats liver; hasn't he ever heard of cholesterol?

The chopped liver sculpture, though reduced in size, is still recognizable. Unfortunately, at least forty other people are milling about in an attempt to reach the same goal as the Jacobses. All of them are taller and most are wider than Leo and his wife, so I cannot abandon them. I take each one by the hand, and plunging into the crowd, I mutter, "Excuse us, pardon us," in our push toward the table.

Most of the chopped liver fanciers actually move aside, although I get a good number of scowls. We're almost there, but stationed between us and the liver stands an impressively sturdy woman in her forties with whom I would not choose to pick a fight under any circumstances. Her massive black gown studded with sequins advertises the breadth of her thick, powerful shoulders as she puffs herself up with outrage and impales me with a question. "Is there a fire?" she asks, imperious, "or are you simply being rude?"

"It's not for me," I explain weakly, "it's for them. I'm just trying to help."

"Well, in case you haven't noticed, there's a line here for chopped liver. And the line starts here." She begins to shovel the liver onto her plate. "You will have to wait."

But salvation arises in the person of Mrs. Jacobs, who inquires of the large lady, "Aren't you the Aarons girl? Aren't you Minna Aarons's second daughter, the one who married the eye doctor? I was at your wedding, you were such a beautiful bride. Remember, Leo, it was on Eastern Parkway in that nice hall."

"Oh, my God, Mrs. Jacobs," bellows the Aarons girl. "I didn't recognize you here, out of context. And Mr. Jacobs! You both look so well! You're getting younger. How do you do it?"

"I think chopped liver is their elixir of youth," I suggest with what I hope is an ingratiating smile.

"Liver! I almost forgot," exclaims the now friendly roadblock. "Here, give me your plates. Let me serve you — what a pleasure to see you both."

My mission accomplished, I begin to back away when I feel someone tapping me on the shoulder. It's Norman Ackerman, my accountant. "What are you doing here?" he asks. "I've never seen you at one of these before, and I've been coming for years."

"I'm here as a guest of Violet Finkel, one of the honorees," I explain.

He looks around, then whispers to me, "Finkel, huh? Very nice lady. Also very comfortable if you know what I mean; very, very, comfortable. Money leaking from every pore. And so charitable." He leers at me, he pokes me with a finger, "So what's up between you two?" he asks.

"We're new friends," I answer evasively. "We just met."

"Like goes to like, money goes to money, that's what I've always said, and it's really true. She's comfortable with a capital C."

"I'm not interested in her money, Norman," I explain, in the hope of nipping a rumor in the bud. "I don't care about her finances. She's just a friend." I doubt this will shut Norman up, but it's worth the try.

"Well, if you ever do want to know more, I can get the information for you. I'm friendly with her accountant's partner, I can help." He smirks at me. "Well done," he adds, "good hunting." Mercifully, he turns to go, and calling out a "good to see you," he's swallowed up by the crowd.

It's past time to look for Violet. In the dim light hundreds of women dressed in the obligatory black gown and bedecked with flashing jewelry compete for my attention. Two-thirds are blondes. I am near surrender when I hear that decidedly not dulcet tone, the distinctive brass, that unmistakable voice.

"Hooray, my hero! You look beautiful, though your tux looks a little tight in the crotch. Careful when you sit down, we don't want you turning soprano." Violet looks splendid. Her admirable breasts bear the weight of a blinding diamond and South Sea pearl necklace, with one huge pearl dangling provocatively between them. Her massive diamond earrings are outshone only by the tiara perched on her carefully arranged hair. Diamonds glitter on her wrists and fingers, and she is bathed in perfume. "So," she says, spreading her arms and asking for my approval, "do you like?"

"You are magnificent," I say, and I mean it. At that moment I have to admit wishing that she and I could slip out of the enormous banquet hall and find ourselves in a more intimate space—like my apartment.

Adopting the gala-speak exchange of honorees and guests at functions like these, Violet proceeds, "I don't know why they forced me, begged me, twisted my arm, to accept this honor. This is so embarrassing for me. It's not like I built the Taj Mahal—I only gave them half a million. Whatever, I thank you for being my escort on such short notice. I really didn't want to go through this alone. You are a real life saver."

I register the significant size of her donation. "Come on, Violet," I reply, "it's my pleasure, and I'm sure you more than deserve this honor. There is absolutely nowhere I'd rather be than here with you tonight. Thanks for inviting me." We air-kiss, and I breathe in the scent of her, which is sexy and sinewy. But then I step aside, as scores of other guests gather around Violet to offer their congratulations and thanks.

During a short pause, Violet hands me the Gift Journal and mutters her annoyance that there is a co-honoree. "Believe me, I wouldn't have agreed if I had known. I don't even know who the man is. I suspect he lives somewhere in Brooklyn. He must have given them a fortune." In the journal, I learn that Violet is receiving the Founders Award and a certain Solomon Fleischandler, the Master Builder Award. A sleek publication, professionally produced, with pictures of the charity's beneficiaries, the journal lists the donors under the various levels of giving: $5,000 makes you a Friend; $10,000, a Guardian; $25,000, a Pillar; and $50,000, a Golden Pillar. Only Fleischandler falls into the Master Builder category at $100,000, and finally there is Violet's Founder status at $500,000. Now that is impressive.

But it's also disheartening. For I'm simply not in her league. Would she be turned off if she knew that the largest charitable donation I ever made was the $25,000 I gave to Ellen's favorite charity, the Breast Cancer Task Force, when she died?

The lights blink off and on. The waiters no longer appear with fresh offerings. We are escorted to our seats. The tables are decorated in blue and white, each with a floral extravaganza that rises up three feet from its base and makes conversation across the table almost impossible. The more important tables, for the honorees, speakers, and dignitaries, are circled by those for the other guests. Tonight, I find that I'm important.

After the first course, an elaborate chopped salad with edible flowers, there is a massive rush from table to table as many of the guests—Violet among them—reposition themselves to visit with friends at other tables. When Violet leaves to speak to someone, a man whom I vaguely recognize sits down next to me. I don't recall his name or exactly how I know him. He is about my age, but with very little hair, and he has dispensed with a cummerbund, so his paunch spreads freely over the top of his tuxedo pants.

"Splendid evening," he says. "Great to see you, Dan."

"Yes," I reply lamely. But who the hell is *he*?

"How've you been?" he inquires. "So sorry about Ellen. I presume that you got my condolence note."

"Yes, thanks," I reply and, desperate for a clue I ask, "and how's your family?"

"Well, I'm sure you heard about Clara. That's life, I guess. What can one do?" he asks rhetorically.

"You're right," I agree. "We do the best we can." Only I've never heard a thing about Clara; I don't know a Clara.

"Absolutely," he agrees. "Well, at least we are here and can still help others, still give to charity, still make a difference. Thank God for that. So, stay well and give my regards at home. We should only see each other on happy occasions."

"Amen to that," I reply. "Glad to see you looking so well," I call after him. God alone knows who he is.

At least I remember the face of the next visitor to claim Violet's chair. It's Ellen's old high school classmate, Sonia something; I haven't seen her in years.

"Dan, Dan," she says, "what a lovely surprise. You look well, so fit. I often think of our Ellen and have meant to call you, but you know how life is. So what a treat to see you tonight—and at such an important table, next to such a famous lady. My table is terrible, near the door. Hard to see a thing, but I was so thrilled to see you sitting here, in a place of honor. You deserve it, believe me."

What do you say when you are praised for being in the right seat at a gala? "I hadn't noticed," I say awkwardly. "I guess they put me here because I'm Mrs. Finkel's guest, no other reason."

"Still in the same apartment?" she asks, seemingly out of the blue. "You know, the very same line on the third floor just went for three-point-eight million. I know because I'm a real estate broker now, and my friend Hilda had an exclusive on the apartment. Have you ever thought of selling, making a fresh start?" she asks.

"No," I answer quickly, now irked by Sonia something's ill-mannered line of questioning. "I've no reason to move. Besides, it's a real estate bubble. Where would I move to?"

"Well, if you ever are tempted, do remember that I would love to help, for old time's sake." She opens her little rabbit-shaped crystal evening bag and extracts her card. "Call me anytime," she says. "I specialize in Fifth and Park, top of the line, the best," she assures me.

At last, Violet returns. I stand and introduce her to Sonia, whose married name I can't remember. "Sonia, Violet Finkel," I say distractedly.

Sonia supplies her surname. "Hemmer, Sonia Hemmer," she says. "I'm a real estate broker, Mrs. Finkel, and I am particularly thrilled to meet you. You have one of the most extraordinary apartments in New York. I'm honored," she gushes.

"Well, it's not for sale, honey, so relax," says Violet as she takes my arm and leads me away. "Good-bye, nice to meet you, Mrs. Hummer," she adds.

"Hemmer," corrects Sonia.

"Bye, Sonia," I say as I am forcibly marched away by Violet, and I am thankful to be in her care.

Seconds later, we are accosted by a voluble woman whose enormous ruby chandelier earrings swing back and forth as she embraces Violet and kisses her on both cheeks. "Nobody ever deserved an honor more," she says, but blinking lights save us from another bout of gala-speak and return us to our tables.

Now the real food is served. The choices are roast beef, veal, and salmon, each described elaborately—and incomprehensibly to most of us—on the menu in French. The exhausted waiters shrug at requests for translation. To them, it's beef, veal, or fish, what do you want? The Fleischandlers want fish.

He is well into his eighties, a short man with a shrewd face, tired-looking, but exceedingly proud of the honor being bestowed on him, if utterly uncomfortable in his tuxedo. She is probably in her seventies—"Rachel, but call me Ruchi"—eschews jewels, except for her wedding ring, and exudes kindness. The Fleischandlers are called up for their award, he being introduced as a notable mogul and philanthropist. Violet chafes. "If he's a mogul, what am I?"

"A moguless," I reply.

"No way, that sounds like less than a mogul. Maybe a mogulmore."

"I have it: you're a mogulette." She agrees, and we shake hands on it.

At the podium, Mr. Fleischandler recalls his experiences in Europe during the Holocaust and relates how Ruchi and he survived, how they swore that with any fortune they gained they would help other people, and how grateful he and Ruchi are now to be able to make this gift to help new immigrants in Israel, especially the children. "There is no immigration without tears," he tells us, and the room becomes silent, but for the sound of Ruchi's muted weeping. He tells us how proud they are of their three children and sixteen grandchildren, all of whom are present tonight and each of whom is asked to stand up and be introduced. Ruchi is now crying in earnest, and she is not alone. Even Violet seems touched. She turns to me and whispers, "What a bitch I was to say that about them earlier; they deserve their award a lot more than I do." I agree but refrain from comment.

Once the Fleischandlers, silver award in hand, make their way back to our table, Violet is called to the podium. She rises quickly and walks self-confidently. Honored as a woman of valor who has set new standards of charity and loving-kindness for our community, she receives her award, a golden hued replica of The Temple Mount. Moved, she thanks everyone. Her voice laced with feeling, her speech eloquent, she praises the Fleischandlers and says that awards should be given not to the donors but to the professionals in Israel who do all the hard work day by day. "They are the true men and women of valor," she concludes.

I'm quite taken by her remarks, and as she returns I embrace her warmly. "You were wonderful," I say, and mean it. She glances at me, to see if I'm joking—and I'm not. Then she simply smiles and nods.

Is it simply the gala magic getting to me, or am I falling for Violet Finkel? Whatever the origin of my present state of calm, I don't really care. I am feeling happy.

After the coffee and dessert have been served, Violet seems suddenly weary. "Next year, maybe I'll give them double on condition that I don't have to attend and I am allowed to be absent guilt-free," she whispers, her mood suddenly solemn.

"Let's go," I suggest, ready to see what else lies ahead of us.

We rise and begin to gather our things, but more people want to congratulate, embrace, kiss, and compliment the now-wilting Violet. Noticing that even her golden hair has begun to droop, protectively I place my arm around her. "If one more person steps on my foot, I'll clock him," she says, and she may mean it.

Time to go, finally. And so we begin the lengthy social process known widely as the "Jewish Good-bye," which takes us a good thirty minutes. By the time we reach Violet's car, it is almost eleven o'clock. Her driver, wide awake this time, scampers around and ushers us into the car. "Did you enjoy your evening, madam?"

"Yeah, yeah," Violet replies. "But get me home, my feet are killing me."

I sit back in the smooth leather seat and close my eyes. I reach for Violet's hand but can't seem to find it. When I open my eyes, I see that she is looking out the window, and it's clear she's focused on something other than what I am thinking about.

Ten minutes later, we arrive at her building. "Would you like to come up?" she asks.

Both excited and nervous, I can merely nod in assent.

Violet's apartment, extraordinary in its size and grandeur, is mono-chromatic in varying shades of gold. Shiny gold fabrics are every-where, carved gold moldings adorn the ceilings, gold hardware is found on every door. Her decorator was clearly going for the Midas look. The entrance gallery leads to a reception room that opens to a living room on one side and a gigantic dining room on the other. In between is the library, which is about half the size of my whole apart-ment, and all the books have gold imprints on their bindings. The furniture is antique, probably from a French palace; anyway, so old you're afraid to sit down. Major art hangs on the walls. Irv must have left Violet all his estate, and he must have been drowning in money.

Amidst this golden splendor, Violet brings me a Diet Coke and excuses herself. "I've got to get out of this damned dress," she says. "Twelve thousand dollars, and the sequins are falling off—I'm shedding like a canary. Boy, will they hear from me tomorrow."

She returns a few minutes later in a loose silk robe, and I notice that there can be little underneath. We begin to rehash the evening, but I am distracted. I keep thinking of what lies beneath her robe. I wonder if I should make a move and why I feel so nervous. Then, I take her hand. I search her eyes with what I hope is a particularly passionate and expectant look, and I feel old faithful stir below.

"Are you nuts?" she says. "I know what's on your mind and you can forget it. Second date, masturbate, we used to say. You want more, you call me. It's late now, the driver is waiting for you downstairs. Go directly home like a good boy." She gives me a little kiss on my cheek. "Call me, and thanks again." I am dismissed.

I walk the ten blocks home. I need the fresh air, I need to cogitate. Isn't that what an old codger like me is supposed to do? Think, review, infer, consider. I shake my head as if I could shake away the humiliation of Violet's dismissal. How did I get myself in that position? Am I ready to date again? Do I really want a relationship? For months, I know I've been asking myself these questions, yet I don't feel any closer to the answers. I'm suddenly envious of all my married friends. When did I become so needy? There's no denying the empty hole Ellen's death left in my heart, in my life, but it's just not like me to feel wanting. So I won't be the richest guy in the cemetery; I'll still have had the best wife, the best son, the best everything. What is that old Talmudic saying, Who is rich? He who is happy with his lot. That used to be me. Used to be I didn't *need* anything.

Once at home, I open the door to Ellen's closet. I look in the full-length mirror on the back of the door. Let's be clinical. Before me stands an older man, not so bad for sixty. Hair gray, though I use a shampoo that brightens it. My attractive blue eyes; some say they're striking. A paunch, but no fat anywhere else. Good wide shoulders, great smile. Impressive-looking when I'm properly dressed, enough so that I still get little glances from women passing by. I'm not invisible yet, although I could certainly use a haircut and could lose twenty pounds. So when women flip over me, as they sometimes seem to do, why not give them a fling. I mean, I'm okay. Eric had to get some of his good looks from me. He's got Ellen's dark brown eyes, and her smile—with that dimple she had, same place on his cheek as on hers. But the rest he got from me. Sure, he's a few inches taller than I am and firmer, fitter, but then I don't exercise every day like he does; still, you can see that he's my son. Same shoulders, same long legs, same aquiline nose, same ears, and thick dark brown hair like mine used to be. He even dresses like me, conservative, never trendy. Expensive clothes but muted and worn until they are mellow with use, until the colors fade and the pants get baggy. So if he's as handsome as everyone says he is, I must be too. One big difference, though: There is no happiness on my face. I've got to get back to life; that's the best birthday present I can give myself—that and a pack of condoms. Yes. Get ready, ladies, here I come, limping but eager. It's time for me to take a chance. I want to be happy again. Of course, I also want to be six-foot-three, forty years old, and the heir to an enormous fortune. I probably have a better shot at all that than at being happy again. But I'll truly be damned if I don't give it a try.

4.

I am dressing for yet another dinner party. Adjusting my tie, I see in the frown of my concentration something of Eric as I stand at the mirror. Concern clouds my eyes as my mind turns again to his engagement. Although he and Carol have not yet set a date, I assume plans are being made—with or without me. Eric and I have not yet spoken since that horrible evening a week ago, and I haven't yet been able to call him and make amends. For where would I start? How can I possibly say I'm sorry when I am nowhere near accepting the idea that he wants to marry a non-Jewish girl? I doubt he has any idea how deeply hurt I am. So I'm dressing up and going out.

Going to a party feels like the last thing I should be doing, but I refuse to sit home and mope. If nothing else, an evening out will be therapeutic. So I taxi over to the upper Park Avenue building and arrive just in time for the cocktail conversation and for Susan Kleiness. She's tonight's designated female: a plain woman in her forties, short dark hair, and, dare I say it, fat. Fat is a sin in New York, and this lady is a real sinner. She has squeezed herself into a black dress and wears no jewelry, not even a ring; she might as well be in mourning, although she has smeared on some very red lipstick, I suppose as a concession to the occasion. At dinner she is seated across from me with my friend Judy, the hostess, between us. Yes, she is definitely my date.

Watching people eat is often not a pretty sight, but I have to admit that Susan eats nicely, in nibbles so delicate that, I'm certain, she must go home and eat like a horse to maintain her considerable weight. The dinner table conversation meanwhile begins to hum. Judy, defending Hillary Clinton against all comers, has launched into a spirited and soundly reasoned defense of Hillary's motives as senator of New York. With interest and in awe, her husband Sam listens to what he must have heard many times. They make a great pair, Judy admires herself and Sam agrees. A perfect marriage. I smile to myself, as I imagine sharing that thought with Ellen.

The conversation widens to include Madeleine Albright in the discussion. Judy has strong views on Albright. "I dislike her," she says. "Of course she must have known she was Jewish. Her grandparents were killed in the camps, after all. A person who hides her identity cannot be trusted."

"I always thought she was Jewish," says Susan, "because she wears jewelry so well. No one but a Jewish woman or a French woman wears jewelry that way, and, believe me, nobody ever accused her of being French." I look at Susan to determine whether this observation comes from a sense of humor or complete madness. She gives me a wink, and her plain features are transformed by her smile.

"You're Jewish. Where's all your jewelry?" I ask.

"At home," she says. "I'll wear it if they make me secretary of state." I laugh.

"What do you do?" I ask, ignoring the growing din about Albright, and learn that Susan is the president of a major apparel company listed on the stock exchange. I am impressed; it's rare for a woman as young as Susan to have attained so much business success.

By now, the whole table is offering opinions about Albright, and the political discussion grows more heated and mildly unpleasant. When it comes to an impasse and dinner finally ends, an exodus begins almost immediately. I dutifully ask to escort Susan home. She accepts cheerfully.

Despite the cold wintry air, we decide to walk the few blocks down Park Avenue to her apartment house. I offer my arm, which she takes, and she responds earnestly to my questions about her business. I pay close attention to her succinct and rather brilliant analysis of her company, as all business stories are interesting to me. We stop in front of her building to finish our conversation. "It's cold," she says, "Why don't you come up for coffee?"

"I'd love to," I say, surprising myself. I feel a certain part of myself beginning to relax, or maybe thaw.

Her apartment is large and impressive but it seems unfinished: no art, no frills. I follow Susan into the kitchen while she prepares the coffee. "Decaf," she says, as she turns and smiles, a coffee mug in each hand. We sit at the little kitchen table; her breasts are full, heavy and I am very much aware of them.

"You seem sad to me tonight," she says.

"Do I?" I respond. "I'm just a little down."

"Why?" she asks.

The question is simple, but the answer's complicated and long. Still I try—for her sake and my own. "You know I'm a widower. My wife's been dead now for two years, and I think I'm entering a new phase of my life. That's the good part. What's really got to me is my son: he's getting married."

"And that's a bad thing?"

"In this case, yes. Well, maybe not all bad—but the woman is not Jewish, and I'm having a hard time with it. That's all."

"Life is strange. We never know what's going to get us," she says, reflecting. "Take me. No family, never married, nothing but my business, which I love, and I'm piling up money but with neither the time nor inclination to spend it. Sometimes I get sad, I dream of a different life; but, most of the time, I have to admit I like my life. It's all in how you look at it."

"That makes sense, it really does. And I'm sure something good will come of this, only I'm just not sure what that good will be."

"Listen, you can cry on my shoulder anytime; I always like company. Now, would you like something to nibble on with the coffee? I've got the world's best cookies: chocolate, macadamia, peanut butter." Her eyes sparkle. "Or, wonder of wonders, an oatmeal and sweet raisin to die for. Or, one or two of each." I hesitate, thinking of my DDS condition.

"A cookie is good for you at night, it helps you sleep. Of course, I like them in the morning too; they make you want to get up," Susan adds.

"What about the afternoon?" I inquire, relieved that the conversation has shifted from feelings to cookies.

"You never heard of afternoon tea?" she asks, and we both laugh. "I love my cookies, it's not my fault they're fattening."

"Stop with the fattening, you're a great-looking woman," I say, wondering how we got on this subject but feeling that it is time for a compliment.

"Thank you, kind sir." She delicately chews on a morsel of chocolate cookie, then carefully and thoughtfully licks a few crumbs off her fingers, in a manner that I find attractive, erotic, and even slightly arousing. It strikes me with great clarity that two years without sex has actually started making me crazy. I figure I better get out of here. "It's late," I say, as I get up from the kitchen chair. "Old guys like me need their beauty sleep."

"You're not old, Dan," she disagrees, "and you certainly don't need a beauty sleep. You are quite beautiful as is."

Now I've been called many things, but never beautiful—not even by my mother, she should rest in peace. "Susan, if you think I'm that good-looking, make an appointment with your optician. You need glasses." Smiling, I turn toward the door.

"Don't run away," she says. "Cookies get me going. Here I am, turning into a seething volcano before your very eyes, and you are scurrying home. Scaredy cat." Can people get drunk on cookies?

She gets up and walks toward me. "May I have a good-bye kiss?" she asks sweetly, licking a cookie crumb off her lower lip.

Not unwillingly, I comply. She presses close to me; our lips meet and her breasts brush against me. I catch the sweet, pleasant scent of her perfume and when we break the kiss there is a more serious cast to her eyes. She is no longer joking.

So the moment has come, in this most unlikely manner and with this most unlikely woman. In a kitchen. I can stay, or I can leave right now, except I really have no desire to go home again to the empty apartment. A little nervous, I take her in my arms.

"This is most unusual for me," she says as I hold her. "I want you to know that. Do you believe me?"

I do, and I say so. "Come," she says, and she leads me by the hand to her bedroom. "Stay the night. If anything happens, good; if not, that's okay too." She goes into the bathroom and I undress. I look at myself in the mirror, and I look old to myself, out of shape, not what I used to be, my DDS quite apparent. I wonder how beautiful she'll find me now, or I, her. I turn off all the lamps but one.

I've not yet climbed into bed, when the bathroom door opens. She is wearing a modest but pretty nightgown. Embarrassed, her eyes not looking into mine, and a bit wary, she hesitates. Her body is plump and attractive. You might call it luscious. I approach her and hug her close; she smells sweet and clean, and my desire for her grows. Together we pull down the covers and get into bed. For a little while we hold each other, then she removes her gown but waits for me to take the initiative, and I do. I am in a hurry now. I don't know how long I can last, and I am urgent with her, but she responds passionately and matches my heat with abandon, and we are both breathing hard, heavily, near gasping, when I hear a sound . . . A fart. (Was it me?) Then another, louder. (It wasn't me.) My mind is riveted by it even as my body completes its round. Afterward, we are lying there, still breathing hard; I look at her quizzically.

"It was me," she says. "It's never happened before; must have been the coffee. I apologize. Please, excuse me." I try hard not to laugh. I lose my widower's virginity and she congratulates me with a fart. She begins to laugh, at first hesitantly, but soon we are both roaring with laughter. I tell her that women are not supposed to fart, and remember how surprised I was in my early twenties to discover that they actually do. After a silent minute or two she says, "You may find it difficult to believe, but this was unusual for me. I mean the sex, not the other thing. Both are actually unusual for me," she corrects herself, "particularly since we've only known each other for a few hours."

"A few hours, and it all ends with a fart. Sounds like life in general."

"Life is just a gas," she says, and we both groan as I get up to wash and dress.

After I dress I sit down on the bed next to Susan. She hasn't stirred, and I am concerned that she is embarrassed about our encounter. I take her hand, I lightly stroke it.

"Remember that program on TV, *Can You Top This?*" I ask her. "Well, you said this was an unusual event for you, but I can top it. This was the first time I've been with a woman since my wife died— the first time I've allowed myself to relax enough, feel comfortable enough with someone, to be able to. And I'm really grateful to you because you're warm and intelligent and kind and you made me feel safe with you. No kidding around, thanks."

I can see that she is a little startled. Her eyes examine mine, and she determines that I'm sincere. Her face softens, she gives my hand a squeeze. "Thanks for telling me that, Dan, I appreciate it." She sits up and kisses my cheek: it's the kiss of a friend, a little peck on the cheek. She adds, "If you want to see me again, please feel free to call."

Susan slips into a robe and accompanies me to the front door. We kiss, and I wish her goodnight. As I wait for the elevator I am pretty sure that I will not call Susan again, but I am sure glad she and tonight happened. It's good to be back in the saddle again, so to speak.

5.

The next morning at the office, I am taken aback when my secretary Tina tells me that Carol Hoffman is on the line. Immediately, I feel ashamed: I still haven't spoken with Eric since our disastrous dinner almost eight days ago.

"Dan? It's Carol," she says hesitantly. "Carol Hoffman."

"Yes, yes. Of course. How are you, Carol?"

"I know it's short notice, but I was wondering if you would like to have lunch. Just the two of us."

"That would be lovely," I hear myself say, but I am wondering why Eric didn't call, why didn't he call and invite me to lunch, father-son. And does she know Eric and I haven't spoken?

We make a date, but I insist on being the host. We agree to meet at my club's dining room, a quiet place at lunch, where we will be able to talk. I want to make amends for my behavior, though I don't know just what I want to say—or how I want to say it. In one way, I am relieved to be facing Carol instead of Eric, yet in another way, I realize that I am no more than postponing the inevitable: Eric and I will have to confront this issue head on.

Carol arrives a little late, flushed and very pleasant-looking. "Sorry," she says, "I got stuck on a conference call. I hope you haven't been waiting too long." We exchange pleasantries and order our meal.

"As a lawyer," she then begins, "I try to think things through unemotionally, but I must admit I have been having trouble understanding why you are so dismayed by what Eric and I are planning to do. We really want to expose our future children to both religious traditions—Christian and Jewish—and let them decide for themselves, once they are old enough, what religious path to follow. Could you help me understand?"

"Did Eric send you, or was this your idea?"

"My idea. Eric is angry. He says his mom would have been much more understanding. He thinks you don't even believe in a personal God. You've got to know that I've been begging him to call you, but he hasn't, so I figured that I would speak to you instead." Her words come in a worried, impassioned rush, and I can see that she is trying hard to connect.

I take a deep breath and try to keep my voice measured, for I, too, am trying to think my way through this unemotionally. "I don't know how to begin, Carol, but one thing I will tell you, Eric is wrong. His mother would have been unhappy about this. Marrying a non-Jewish person is a rejection of us, of who we are. It's also the end of a five-thousand-year-old story, for my part in that story will end with my grandchildren. For me, for Eric, it will be over. As to God, we brought God into our home. Ellen always lit the Sabbath candles, we had wonderful Seders. We talked about morality. We prayed.

When Eric was little, my mother taught him a prayer to say before going to sleep and one to say upon awakening—does he still do that, when he wakes up?"

"I don't know," she says. "Not out loud."

"I say it every morning, automatically, and I figured Eric still might. It's not much maybe, but I just can't take it in that he would think I am not a believer—difficult as it is, believing, after the Holocaust and all the holocausts and all the inequities and injustices in this world. Listen, how can I explain to you what I hardly understand myself? But one thing I know, I don't want Eric to be the last Jew in our family. There are only thirteen million of us left in the world, and every evil force singles us out for attack. Still, we have survived five thousand years. I don't want to see my only son leave the parade. It has nothing to do with you personally, and I'm sure that if you and Eric get married, I will grow to love you. But that doesn't change the way I feel; it can't. And Eric is full of it when he tells you he doesn't understand my reaction. He knows."

We sit quietly, she picking at her food, I sipping my water. "Look Carol," I say quietly, "you asked me, I'm telling you the way I feel. If Eric wants to talk, he knows how. If not, then I'm not sure what more I can do."

Carol looks up at me and says, "I'm also proud of my religion and of my family. I also have memories to be proud of . . . I'm going to do something, something I've been meaning to do, and now I'm going to do it. I've bought a couple of books on Jewish history and about the religion, and I'm going to read them and I'm going to learn how to make you feel that I am not your worst nightmare. We'll talk again, you and I. Okay?"

I nod yes. "Thank you," I say.

"I'd like to know more and understand more, and I will. Until then, please be patient with me." Moved, I take her right hand in mine and raise it to my lips. The gesture, unusual for me, perfectly expresses my feelings. I can see that she, too, is touched, and we share a different kind of silence, a pleasant one, the tension gone, the emotion spent.

After a little while, she glances at her watch: She has to rush to a closing downtown. I sign the bill, and as I put her into a taxi, she begs me to call Eric. "He's waiting for your call," she says. "Literally, every time the phone rings, he jumps. Please, promise me you'll call him." So I promise.

With every intention of calling Eric, I get back to the office and I'm about to, when Charlotte Kayer phones me. I am anxious to talk to her, to anyone familiar, to put off the call I promised to make, and Charlotte does have dramatic news. She and Dave are splitting up.

"What happened," I ask, dismayed if not entirely surprised, given the rumors that have been floating around our circle of friends.

"Right after your party, Dave told me he met someone. A man."

"A man?" I ask in shock.

"Yes. An airline steward."

"How are you? Is there anything I can do?"

"I'm coping. I still don't quite believe it," Charlotte says steadily. "I've had to increase my sessions with Dr. Abrahams, my analyst, of course. But I'm convinced that this is a passing phase in Dave's life, and I intend to outwait it."

"What about the kids? Have you told Debra and Sam?"

"No. I need to give everything more time. Besides, they are away at school. For now, Dave is still at home but sleeping in the guest room."

She seems calm, even serene. I know I have trouble with feelings, but where are hers, I wonder.

"The reason I am calling is to see if you are free tonight. We have four tickets for the opera, and Dave is planning to bring Tim. I couldn't think of anyone else other than you that I'd feel comfortable bringing."

"Are you sure you even want to go?"

"I'll be damned if Dave's latest escapade interrupts my life!" she says forcefully.

Without a second's hesitation I accept her invitation. I ponder Charlotte's disclosure of the new sexual dalliances of my friend Dave. Who would ever have thought? But then again, who'd ever believe my own little erotic excursion the other night with Susan Kleiness.

That evening my ticket is waiting for me at the Met box office when I rush in a few minutes before eight. I have barely enough time to say hello to Charlotte and Dave, to meet his friend Tim, and to note that Charlotte, who is beautiful on ordinary days, has outdone herself tonight. Her dark hair shimmers and she's highlighted the soft curves of her admirable, trim body with a clinging dress and a low décolletage. Dave looks different, too, sharply dressed in an expensive sporty getup instead of his usual rumpled suit. But Tim is the real surprise; a strong, athletic-looking man in his forties, dark hair, a wide and open smile, a firm handshake. Whatever I expected, Tim wasn't it.

As the opera begins, Tim, I notice, rests his hand lightly on Dave's knee, a gesture at once possessive and absent-minded, as if they were a married couple. I try not to look at them and feel protective of Charlotte. Uncomfortable myself, I'm sure that no matter what she says, she must be completely ill at ease.

Soon, though, I surrender to Puccini's *Turandot,* and by intermission, I feel more relaxed. Dave goes to get a drink, Charlotte heads for the ladies' room, and Tim and I are left with each other. We have been talking about the performance when, abruptly, he asks me, "What's doing with you and Charlotte?"

"Charlotte is still Dave's wife," I answer a bit too peevishly. "She and I are very old friends. What's doing between you and Dave?"

He smiles at my rejoinder. "A lot more than what seems to be happening between you and Charlotte."

"Well," I say, "different, anyway."

"Do you think we are going to be friends?" he asks, smiling, and again extends his hand to shake mine. I take his hand and hold it briefly.

"I'm not Dave's keeper. Although, as his friend for a long time, I am surprised."

"You would be surprised by a lot of your friends," he says ironically, just as Charlotte returns.

"I hate it that I have to use the ladies' room and you guys almost never have to go. Women's plumbing is so unfair. It's why you men dominate everything; you take over while we're in the bathroom."

"A politically incorrect theory," comments Tim.

"A completely madcap theory," I add.

"Not according to Dr. Abrahams," says Charlotte, citing her guru. "He says that genetics create destiny, and I think a woman's need to sit down to pee has been underestimated as a factor in history." As Dave rejoins us, she accosts him. "Dave, did you have to use the men's room? . . . No? See?" Charlotte seals the argument to her own satisfaction.

"Enough with the toilets," says Dave, "the lights are dimming." We all resume our seats and allow the opera to weave its spell. Still entranced by the magical last act, we walk outside together in a relatively congenial mood, the awkwardness of the situation not yet asserting itself.

"Dan, always great to see you," says Dave, shaking my hand and giving me a warm pat on the back. I can see in his eyes his gratitude. "We're going to walk home," he continues. "I trust you two will be okay?"

"Yes, yes, of course," I assure him, taking Charlotte's arm in mine. Dave hugs Charlotte, who hangs back just slightly.

Then, as Charlotte and I look for a taxi, she says, "Thank you for that."

"How are you holding up?"

"Okay, I guess."

"As your old friend, may I be straightforward with you, Charlotte?"

She responds by raising her eyebrows.

I continue. "Dave is having a relationship with this guy, and you invite him to the opera? I am not just curious; I am also a bit concerned about what's going on with two old friends."

"Well, Dave has been talking to me about his interest in men for some time. In the beginning I was shocked, but Dr. A says that Dave has no choice in the matter, not really, and I've come to feel less betrayed than if Dave had left me for another woman. It's easier for me to take this way, and Dave and I still care for each other. Dr. A feels that I'm acting in a mature way."

Minutes later, at her building, she invites me up in such an unconvincing way that I plead an early morning meeting.

When I get home I fiddle with the answering machine, which I finally have learned to operate. I get a few words from Della, who still has not figured it out—she picks up, speaks, and then hangs up—but nothing from Eric. I know I should call him, as I promised Carol; I just don't feel quite up to it yet. Maybe tomorrow.

There is a message from Violet. I glance at my watch: it's too late to call. She'd asked that I call her, but obviously she couldn't wait, and I figure that's good. I smile as I head for my bathroom, and I'm still half-smiling when I get into bed. Violet's a handful, but I could do with a little of that joie de vivre.

6.

The next morning, when I get to the office, Violet has already called. I call right back, before taking off my jacket. She sounds excited, happy. "Listen, I've just been invited to accept an honorary doctoral degree at the Meiron University in Safed. I'm so excited. Me, a doctor! You've got to come with me. I'll pay for everything. It'll be fun; maybe we'll stop in Europe on the way home. Say yes."

What is it with this woman? Always in a rush, always demanding something. Is this joie de vivre, or is it simply self-absorbed imperiousness! "Violet, wait a minute. Take a breath. Where is Safed?"

"In northern Israel, in the upper Galilee. Don't you remember? It's where the Kabbalah was written. It's an ancient city built on a hill, but poor, with an artists' colony and old, mystical synagogues. The great Rabbi, what's his name—Ari—lived there. It's now home to lots of new immigrants, all of them poor. When I learned the city had started a little college I was so moved that I built them a campus. There's a wonderful mountainside hotel there, too; we'll have a great time. And nobody will ask you for money, I already gave it. Dr. Violet, that's me. But I can't go alone. Also, you'll have a chance to meet my daughter Maria from my first marriage to that Italian bum. So are you going to come?"

"When is it?" I ask, stalling.

"In three weeks. Say yes. When was the last time you were in Israel?"

"A few years ago, but the terrorism makes me a little scared now," I say, only I'm thinking of my last trip to Israel with Ellen, right after she was diagnosed.

"You think you're safer in New York? Six million people live in Israel, so be brave and join them for a week. Besides which, once you're there you don't ever feel scared. And I'm paying—how can you refuse!" As usual with Violet, it is barely a request.

I remind her that we hardly know each other, that traveling together tests the best of relationships. "It'll make us or break us," she says. "Remember, Israel is the land of miracles."

"Listen, I need to think about this. But if I go, I pay my own way."

"Whatever, but remember, first class is six or seven grand, so maybe you'll think twice. Please join me. I'll wait for your yes."

Maybe this trip is what I need. The Western Wall, the sunset over Jerusalem. Images of that last trip to the Holy Land pierce me. Ellen insisted that we go for the week before her treatment was to begin. I worried that the long trip would drain her energy, but she was determined. We shared several memorable moments on that trip, but the most poignant for me was at the tomb of the matriarch, Rachel. The small, stuffy space was crowded with praying women, some of them weeping and imploring, while others of them wound red threads around the tomb. These red *bendels* they then cut up and wore on their wrists, and thus sought the intercession of the matriarch.

I stood at the entrance of the tomb; I remember I felt somewhat put off by the scene. It struck me as superstitious. Then one of the women spoke quietly to Ellen, and with kindness and solemnity she tied one of the *bendels* around Ellen's wrist. Ellen was moved to tears.

The thread didn't save her, of course, but it did help her. It made the difficult months ahead somehow easier for her. She never took off the red *bendel* until the very end. She would sometimes hold it as though she gained strength from it. Yet she spoke of the matriarch only once: "Rachel died young," she said to me as we sat in the car after leaving the tomb that day. "But she is still remembered thousands of years later." I said nothing. I just hugged her.

I don't know about thousands of years, but as long as Eric and I are alive, Ellen is not forgotten.

Memories of that last visit to Israel sharpen the pain of Ellen's absence. Yet if I return to that place of miracles with Violet, might I not start to face down my fears and learn how to live again? My reluctance begins to yield to resolve.

7.

D r. Bert Boze is my contraindicator: If he buys, I sell. He's almost perfectly wrong—another two or three clients like him and I would be able to publish a contrarian newsletter. His calls are always "urgent," so I return this one immediately.

"I'm taking this in the operating room," he says, his voice excited, alternating between a whisper and a shout. "I'm working on this guy's pelvis, so I have to make it quick. The guy is the CEO of a big public company, and when they put him under he starts talking, you know, the usual blithering nonsense, but then he takes hold of my hand and tells me that his company's buying another public company next week. But the damned anesthetic takes over and he's out for the count before I can get the name of the other company. This guy is loaded; everything he touches turns to gold. When I have the name, I'll call you from my cell phone—I don't want to give you the company name and the order at the same time, who knows who is listening. Oh, shit, they're sawing—wait a minute." There's a loud burst of noise that sounds like a lawn mower, then he's back. "So I'll just call you and say the name of the company to be acquired, nothing more. Then you go and buy a hundred thousand dollars' worth of the stock, okay? I knew eventually I would hit the jackpot!"

"Dr. Boze," I say, "I can't execute an order that you don't explicitly give me; it isn't proper. Also, the guy is under sedation, he may be dreaming. This just isn't smart." I try to be patient.

"All right, I'll go to a regular phone, I'll give you the order. Forget what I said, scratch it, I was just teasing you. Listen, I've got to fix the guy's ass here, let me get busy." He hangs up. Woe to the company being acquired; with Boze buying in, hundreds of millions are bound to be lost. I pray the poor patient never utters a word.

Two hours later, Dr. Boze is on the phone again. This time more subdued, even a little depressed. He complains, "The chintzy bastard wouldn't talk. Over and over he repeats 'Putzel, Putzel' and occasionally he says 'Mommy.' Imagine—at his age. I looked, there's no Putzel on any exchange; must be someone's stupid name. My big chance down the drain."

I console him as best I can, cover some shorts, and try not to give in to a welling sense of boredom with my job. If only I were able to retire . . . If only, if only. My father always warned me against "if onlys." "Stick to reality," he said, "that's the only thing reliable." Sometimes, though, it's hard to find motivation in the reliables.

"Timothy Wells calling," says the secretary on the intercom.

"Who is that?" I ask her, and she finds out.

"Dave Kayer's friend." I take the call.

"Hi, Dan, I'm wondering if I can enlist your help."

"With what, exactly?" I ask, curious.

"I want to give Dave a surprise birthday party. He's going to be sixty, and I want to do something special."

"I just celebrated my sixtieth," I say.

"Yes, I know. Dave told me. I thought it might be fun to turn the tables on him. What do you think?"

"To tell you the truth, Tim, it's tough for me to talk in the office. I'm a broker and it's busy. Maybe we'll talk in the evening." Feeling a bit uncomfortable, I want to stall for time. "Why don't you call me tonight at home?"

I turn my attention to the market and watch the tape halfheartedly. Work has become boring, routine: forty years of discipline may get me out of my apartment every morning, but I no longer experience the thrill of the chase. My mind drifts to Eric, whom I still have not called. It's only getting harder, the more time I let go by. So I pick up the phone and dial his cell. I'm put right into voice mail. "It's your father," I say. "We need to talk. Please call me." I hope he hears the love in my voice.

At three-forty precisely I make my daily call to Shimmy Levine, my most consistent, dependable client. For more than ten years now Shimmy has spent the last twenty minutes of each market day with me, buying his onesies and twosies, sometimes threesies, and lovingly building his collection of stocks. Every penny Shimmy has or makes or borrows on margin goes into his purchases, the positions growing "like plants," he says, "like pretty plants." When his wife died some years ago, possibly from boredom, he buried her in the morning so we'd not miss our daily call. As we went through the roster of stocks, his voice remained perfectly normal and his focus on his stocks never once wavered. When I'm away, my assistant makes the call; Shimmy doesn't care, he's been doing his own thing for so long now all he wants are a voice on the other end of the line and order executions—no "Internet, shminternet" for him.

Three times in the past ten years, I have had occasion to visit Shimmy in his little Riverdale apartment. Mesmerized by the market tape, he sits on an old frayed couch, and he wears a T-shirt and socks—winter, summer and in between, there's no change in wardrobe. He keeps a blanket at hand to cover his privates if a woman happens to be present—his daughter, the cleaning woman, or an elderly aunt who sometimes visits. Otherwise, he makes no concession to any visitor on any day when the market is open. He reputedly skipped his daughter's graduation and his son's, as both fell on business days. But not without success. Under his watchful eye, his portfolio equity has grown steadily from the pittance he inherited from his tailor father to over four million dollars, although at times his margin debt almost bankrupted him. Yet even in the face of such risk, Shimmy never blinks, his voice never falters; and he remains a cool cucumber.

"Where's Albertson's?" he begins. We continue through the alphabet, buying a few hundred here and there of this or that. We finish at four o'clock and he hangs up, no good-bye, no further comment.

I walk home slowly. A fine mist fills the air; it might rain. Everybody around me seems to be rushing as I plod on, my spirits low. How many more days, I wonder, will I be doing this. How many more dollars: I count the day's commissions—there never seem to be enough, not when I consider the three hundred grand that I loaned Eric a couple of years ago to launch his two businesses. I don't regret it, of course, but it would be nice to see a return. I don't know how else I'd be able to help him again, should he need it.

The apartment is fragrant with Della's cooking; the comforting smells displace my worries. In the kitchen, I'm cheered by the familiar sight of her: her heavy dark face moist with the kitchen warmth, her hands holding a breaded cauliflower hot from the oven. There is sunshine in her kind face.

"There you are," she says. "Salad is on the table; you wash up and get your wine. I don't know one bottle from another." I do what I'm told—everybody obeys Della. I can feel my neck and back beginning to relax as Della serves me dinner. She reminds me not to eat too much, to remember what the doctor said.

"No dessert?" I ask jokingly.

"That isn't funny. There's no dessert tonight or any other night, either, and you know it. Not unless you want some applesauce."

She brings me my small ration of applesauce, then pauses. I can see that she has something to say. I wait. "Tea?" she asks. I nod my assent.

She places the tea on the table, and then, standing over me, she asks, "What's wrong? I know something's wrong—you don't look right. Aren't you feeling well?"

"I'm all right," I reply, hesitant, not sure whether I should tell her about Eric and Carol yet.

"Drink your tea," she says, "it'll perk you up. You sure don't look good lately. Have you gone to the doctor?"

"I don't need a doctor, Della, I need a new life—a twenty-five-year-old body instead of this one, and no children. That's what I need."

"Well, you should be grateful that you're still kicking at your age, and kicking high. And why are you so unhappy about children. What did Eric do now?"

"Nothing much, he just introduced me to a very nice non-Jewish girl whom he wants to marry. Other than that, everything is fine."

Della's eyes fill up. She's not Jewish herself, but she's so much a part of the family that I know she understands my pain.

"I've got to sit down," she says. She plunks herself down; she looks a bit dazed, as if in shock. "That's not right," she says. "The Lord didn't intend to have these mixed-up marriages. These children think, they get big, they can do whatever they want to do, but they'll have to answer for it; yes, sir, they'll have to face a mighty judge. There's still a God in Heaven." And she shakes her head. "Ellen would have stopped it," she adds. "She would have found a way."

She has taken the words right out of my heart. Ellen would have gotten through to Eric somehow, I'm sure.

Della and I sit in absolute silence for a few minutes. Her eyes are closed, as if in prayer.

"You told him how you feel? You didn't talk sweetie-sweetie now, did you?"

"No, I was perfectly honest. But he hasn't called me back."

"Children," she says, "it's a different generation. What are we gonna do?" Again, we are silent, and take comfort in the presence of each other.

Ellen used to tease me about my overprotective attitude toward her and Eric. "Do you think we fall apart when you're not around?" she'd say. And it was true: I worried, I hovered. And why not? Eric was a premature baby—he weighed only three pounds eight ounces at birth—and it was touch-and-go for both him and Ellen, but they made it. And we rejoiced in Eric, in his achievements, all the more so because Ellen could bear no more children. We went through so much with him, for him, and now . . . Why? What in the world is life all about, anyway?

The telephone jars me out of my thoughts. I get it in the kitchen on the third ring.

"I've been out, did you call me?" It's Violet. "Listen, I know I'm rushing you, but I've got to say yes or no to the people in Safed and I'm telling you again, I just can't go without you. So are you going to rescue this lady in distress or not? Are you going to be my knight, audacious and brave, or a milquetoast, meek and weak? In plain English, have you got the balls, yes or no? It's not like I'm asking you to trek through Central Asian steppes. We're talking about Israel here—good people, safe water, passable food, and everyone is related to you. Come on, *toujours de l'audace?*"

The sheer brazenness of her voice jolts me from my torpor. This woman is throwing herself at me: She's beautiful, she's rich, she's available—so what am I, nuts? I should be afraid of some eighteen-year-old lunatic terrorist? I could get hit by a car right here.

"I'm standing here in front of the mirror. I've just undressed and, yes, I do have the balls," I assure her. "And you have a traveling companion."

"Yippee," she screeches, "I knew you wouldn't fail me. Safed is a very romantic place—one of the reasons those Kabbalists had lots of kids. The thin mountain air will turn you on, and who knows where that will lead! I'm ordering the tickets, leave everything to me." And she's gone, like lightning.

Romance? Thin mountain air? I like the sound of what she's suggesting. I hardly know her but what the hell—the worst that happens is I have a good time. Who knows, maybe I'm on my way to becoming a rich woman's husband—no more worries, no more clients, no more ups and downs. My father always said that love is good, but love with noodles is better, and Violet seems to have lots of noodles. I smile into the phone before putting it down.

I feel good about my decision, and when I tell Della that I'm going to Israel in a few weeks, she agrees. "It'll be good for you," she says. "You'll enjoy it. Maybe you can bring me back more of that holy Jordan water, like last time."

My promise that I will is punctuated by another ring of the telephone. This time it's Tim, calling to discuss his ideas for Dave's party. Unable to put him off again, I ask, "What exactly did you have in mind, Tim?"

"Well, I was thinking about hosting the party at my apartment in Chelsea, but I'm not sure it's big enough for your crowd. So I would really appreciate it if you could come take a look and let me know what you think."

Come to his apartment? What is this guy after, anyway, I wonder. "Is that really necessary?" I ask.

"That I have another motive, I admit: I think you and I should get to know each other. You're one of Dave's closest friends, and it's important to me—and to Dave—that his relationship with you, and others, stay as normal as possible"

"I can assure you, Dave will always remain my friend." I am almost defiant, as I do not appreciate this guy meddling in my friendships. Still, he seems to be sincere enough.

"Would you mind just coming over for tea or a glass of wine?" he asks simply, and relenting, I agree. We make a plan for the coming Saturday.

It's raining that Saturday afternoon, and I have a tough time getting a cab. I'm only a little late when I finally reach Tim's building, an unimpressive walkup in the upscale part of Chelsea: socially correct, but crumbling. He's on the first floor and has a small garden in back.

"If it doesn't rain, of course, we could always have the party out here," Tim says, pointing to the garden. Then he ushers me into the very sleek, minimalist living room, one of its walls exposed brick. A bottle of wine is waiting with some cheese and crackers, and we sit down and have a drink. He is dressed in a self-conscious way, a careful evocation of how a man at ease should look, his jeans spotless and tight, a bright red T-shirt one size too small, to accentuate the lines and planes of his well-toned body.

"So how did you and Dave meet?" It's my icebreaker.

"On a flight to Rome. Dave was a first-class passenger and I was a steward. It was lust at first sight."

"What do you mean, lust?" I ask. "Dave was fifty-eight or fifty-nine, and you're around forty."

"I'm attracted to older men, always have been," he says. "When I was fifteen, I was chasing guys in their fifties."

"You need Charlotte's Dr. Abrahams," I say jokingly.

"I've already had him," he replies.

"If it's older you like, I guess I better watch out."

"Just don't bend over," Tim warns me jokingly, but I promise myself I won't.

The conversation swerves to Charlotte. "She's in love with Dr. A," Tim says. "No love left for anyone else."

"Why are you so concerned about Charlotte?" I ask, a bit rankled by his assumed expertise on the state of Charlotte's mind and heart.

"I'm concerned because Dave's concerned. He loves her, you know—and he is suspicious of Dr. A."

The rain stops, and we go outside to look at the yard, which would be difficult to tent but not impossible. It could accommodate another dozen people. We decide that's the way to go and set the date just before my trip.

"Do we tell Charlotte? Can she keep the secret?" asks Tim.

"Absolutely," I say.

Back inside, I retrieve my umbrella from Tim's bathtub and prepare to leave. But what he had said about Charlotte still rankles me. "Were you serious when you said that Charlotte loves her psychiatrist?" I ask him.

"You know how attached people can get to their shrinks. Charlotte is addicted, has been for years. I don't think it's love exactly, but it sure is dependence. That was certainly one of the reasons Dave took a hike. Nice to realize that every time you say boo instead of baa it's being reported in detail to Dr. A. Must have been fun, huh?"

"I better watch my every move," I say, half believing it.

"All is no doubt being faithfully shared with the good doctor," he assures me, "I, for one, would be tempted to give Charlotte something memorable to talk about."

"Thanks for the suggestion," I say as I open the door to leave. "If you need any more help with the party, just let me know." Tim accompanies me to the door of his building where we shake hands while he thanks me for coming. I step into the street and hail a taxi. I get in, and after I give the driver my address, I am surprised to see that Tim is still standing there, in the doorway, watching as the taxi roars to a start and pulls away.

8.

I t's Saturday evening when I return home from Tim's apartment. With no plans—no dinner party, no birthday party, no designated female—I am looking forward to an easy chair and a new detective novel. But when I play my messages, I hear Eric's voice, strained and urgent. "Dad, I need to talk to you. Call me as soon as you get home."

I call him, and he picks up immediately. "What's going on?" I ask, worried, adrenaline already pumping through me.

"Can I come over now? I need to talk to you."

"Of course." A tiny voice in the back of my head wonders if maybe he and Carol have called it quits.

Ten minutes later, the doorbell rings and there he is. His face puffy and pale, his demeanor peculiar, he is agitated, unusually ill at ease. We go into the living room. Sitting in his chair, he looks at me in a dazed way. "Come on," I say, concerned, "what is it?"

"Dad, I don't know where to begin. You know that I've been having problems with my two companies, but I haven't really let you know just how bad things have gotten."

"Oh?" I say, both alarmed and angered that he hasn't let me in on this turn of events. It's unlike him.

"In one, I have a great product with too little money to reach fruition, and in the other I've pissed away a lot of money on PR and research, and I still can't get my product to perform. You know we've gone through a lot of cash and that our burn rate continues. And today my lead investor turned me down; he's adamant, he won't infuse any further cash into either company. I've got a small bank line in one of them and absolutely not more than ninety days cash in the other. I'm dead. All my money is tied up in these two companies, and I don't know what I'm going to do. It's like one of those Greek tragedies—I can see the damned wall and I can't avoid hitting it. You're about to lose three hundred grand, and I'm down the tubes almost two million, everything I ever made. Because I put every penny back into the game, and it's over." He leans forward, head in hands, bereft. I am silent until he sits back in the chair, exhausted.

"Have you told Carol?" I ask.

He seems baffled by the question. Searching my face, he replies, "No, just you."

"Good," I say. "Maybe we can work something out. Maybe I can help fund you for a little while, buy you a little time." While I am sincere in my offer to help, there is a real limit to what I can do.

"No, I won't take more money from you, it wouldn't be fair," Eric objects, his self-recrimination beginning to overwhelm him. " My God, what have I done? What happened to me? What's Carol going to think? She doesn't have a clue; I've never talked about any of my business problems with her. I won't have a pot to pee in, not a dollar left. So much for the big man with the prime apartment and expensive German car. It's back to the subway for me, and a studio on Avenue B."

I try to calm him down. "Come on, don't get carried away. You'll be able to keep your apartment and your Nazimobile. You'll get a job—you're still one of the top technological executives in New York, you won't be selling apples. At thirty you're not going to be on your ass for long. So, before we assume failure, let's go over the details of each company; maybe you're overreacting. Three months ago, you were full of hope, let me hear it out."

And for the next few hours I listen to all the details, learn about all his mistakes, most of them rooted in the promise of easy money to be made in the high-tech industry and in the expectation that more funding would always be available.

As I sit there, sharing his pain, I appreciate that he turned to me first, that the son came to the father for counsel and comfort. I tell him to sleep here tonight and suggest that tomorrow I'll join him at his office so we can maybe figure something out, the two of us, together. Like the little kid he once was, he obeys me, and goes back in his old room; within minutes, only half undressed, he falls fast asleep. I sit next to his bed and wish that I could comfort him with prayer the way my Grandma Bella did me. She'd talk to God as though He were always at hand. Most of her prayers were in Yiddish, but occasionally, when her request was succinct, she'd speak it in English. "Watch over him," she would say when I went off to school. Or if I was sick, she would complain, "You should be ashamed for such a fever." I thought it was funny then, but in the last few years I find myself wishing I had her confident, visceral faith.

Weary, I go to my bathroom and splash some water over my face. That's when I smell it: Ellen's perfume, that particular fragrance of hers as though she is right here by my side. I look around; the fragrance lingers on for a moment or two. Then I get into bed. I am somehow comforted.

The next three days are exhausting. I try to help Eric make hard decisions concerning his companies. We meet with the lawyers, and the banks. We bargain, we plead; we stop short of begging. I am proud of my son's fortitude under such pressure, but I can't help feeling a bit dejected—if only I was in a financial position to help him more generously. Of course, Eric hasn't asked for my help; he insists that he wants to resolve the problems on his own terms. But if only . . .

One company will go bust for sure; the other will get a reprieve for at least a few months. I help Eric slash the burn rate on paper. I strategize with him, but he does the actual firing and the slashing and the cajoling, and he grows in my eyes as he declines in his own. I don't ask him about my other concern; I don't ask him about Carol and their wedding plans.

At the end of a tumultuous week, Eric and I walk out of his lawyer's office and head uptown. He turns to me and says, "Thanks, Dad. I couldn't have done it without you."

"I wish I could have done more," I say quietly.

"You've done more than enough, really. I may still go down, Dad, but at least we gave it our best."

"Of course we did. And remember, you're a lot more than a balance sheet. You may have gone a little nutty in the last few years, but you're still loaded with talent and drive."

"Dad, I want you to know that you will see your three hundred K again. If not more. I promise."

"Don't even think about it, Eric. It's the least I could have done—I wish I could do more now."

"You've done plenty. More than any son could expect. And by the way, I finally said something to Carol."

"How did she take it?"

"She loves me more than ever," he says, smiling.

I try to be happy for my son. I pat him on the back, and we say our good-byes.

I go home longing for my bed, but Della is waiting with supper. Dutifully I sit and eat. I tell her some of what's been happening with Eric, and with genuine sympathy she says, "I'll pray for him. We have a mighty God." I also tell her, and I will tell nobody else, about Ellen's perfume, how certain I was of its scent in the bathroom the night before. A little embarrassed, I wait for her reaction. She does not disbelieve me. She says the Lord gave me a sign, and I should be grateful. "Thank Him," she says, "don't forget to thank Him. He is a God to be praised."

9.

T im is alarmed. Over sixty people have accepted the invitation to Dave's surprise party—largely because Charlotte went crazy and invited the whole world, he tells me. "Now what'll we do?" he asks.

"About what?"

"Well, space. Is there any chance we could have the party at your apartment?"

The idea of hosting a party makes me cringe, especially as I'm leaving for Israel in just a few days. "My housekeeper Della is in her eighties," I explain in a lame attempt to bow out. "She can't do hard work. I would have to hire waiters."

"No need," Tim assures me. "My friends and I will take care of everything, including a thorough cleanup." Whatever my objections or excuses, Tim has ready answers, and while I'd like to kick myself for doing it, I agree.

What started out as a quiet Sunday gets noisier, with another frantic request—this one from Violet, or her daughter Maria. Or Maria's neighbor in Jerusalem, rather. It seems that Luba, the neighbor, has a sister who emigrated from Russia to New York with her son about the same time Luba and her family went to Israel. The sister, Tatiana Andrevsky, has a small parcel that they want to be delivered to Luba, it contains their mother's necklace, which they are afraid to entrust to the mail as it is so precious to them both. Evidently it is essential to Luba that she wear the necklace at her son's forthcoming bar mitzvah.

Violet, of course, has already agreed to bring the necklace; however, since she is now calling me from a spa in Arizona, she needs me to make the arrangements with this Tatiana. More than a little annoyed, I remind Violet that security is tight at El-Al at JFK and they always ask whether anyone has given you anything to take on the flight. "So you'll lie a little," she says. "It's not a grenade, it's a necklace. It'll be all right." I don't say no, and I wonder what it is about this woman that makes me cave into her demands without the barest fight. Do I actually want to be handled, manipulated, bossed, like those pitiable men whose wives—strong women, brazen women, often rich women—seem always to run the show? Even as I try to imagine how relationships like that work, I realize I do find true comfort in Violet.

The next week goes by quickly. Eric and I talk every day, but he is now entrenched in following through on the deals we have made with the banks, as well as sorting out the personnel issues. I'd like for him to ask me to be there by his side, but he doesn't. Who needs whom? I wonder.

So I don't too much mind being distracted by Tim's constant interruptions in my life. With the surprise party approaching, Tim is a frequent visitor, arriving with rented chairs one day, china and cutlery the next. A week in Israel with Violet may feel like a rest cure.

When I call Dave and invite him to dinner on Saturday night so the two of us can celebrate his birthday together, I get a funny feeling that someone has told him about the surprise, maybe Charlotte, because he doesn't in any way hesitate to accept. We plan to meet at my apartment for drinks beforehand.

By 7:30 P.M. on Saturday night sixty of Dave's closest friends are packed into my apartment, drinking, sweating, and bumping into each other. At around 8:00 P.M. we are silenced by a call from the doorman. In walks Dave to a heart-stopping roar of Surprise! The rest of the night is a symphony of chatter, a succession of vivacious encounters with people talking to me, hugging me, thanking me, and asking where's the bathroom.

Charlotte is at her best, superbly dolled up and working hard at being charming. No detectable sign of unhappiness crosses her face or shadows her eye as Dave's friends and family for the first time meet Tim. At least twice, I see her standing arm-in-arm with Tim, her smile vibrant with good humor. Some of Dave's friends offer verbal roasts, but not Charlotte. She toasts him warmly, calling Dave her husband, partner, and friend, and in no way acknowledges their separation. She virtually beams when Tim toasts Dave and Dave responds by giving him an ardent hug.

It's only when she and I are standing together in the back hall that she looks suddenly weary and sad, and I realize just how painful this evening really is for her and, no matter how beautiful, just how fragile is her façade. I take her hand and squeeze it. She responds with gratitude. "After you return from Israel," she says, "I'd like to have dinner with you, just the two of us. You've always been a good friend, Dan, and I want us to stay close."

"Are you going to be okay?" I ask.

"Why shouldn't I be okay?" she replies sarcastically. "After all, everybody tells me how well I look. The fact that my husband prefers a man in his forties to me shouldn't matter so very much. We're in New York, anything goes, right? What's a little infidelity among sophisticated people?" She pauses, looks up at me a little teary-eyed. "Sorry," she says, "I'm taking it out on you, and you've been so kind."

"It's okay," I say, hugging her warmly. "Would you like to use the powder room?" I ask gently.

She nods meekly and makes her way down the hall.

When I reenter the dining room, Dave, with his arm around Tim, has just blown out the candles on his cake to the cheers of the crowd. "Wow," says Tim, and as he begins to cut the cake, "what a great blow job."

It's almost midnight when people begin to say their good-byes. Charlotte is among the first to leave. She kisses me on the lips as she thanks me, sadness now evident in her beautiful eyes. Her perfect posture can't quite conceal her vulnerability. I feel protective of her as she walks solemnly out the door.

Then all but Dave and Tim have left. Tim sends Dave on ahead, explaining that he's promised to help me restore my apartment to order. Tim sets to the cleanup; at his insistence, I sit down on the living room sofa and relax. Although it is now past two in the morning, he works diligently.

When the apartment is close enough to its pre-party state, I suggest, "Tim, why don't you go home. It's so late. Della will deal with whatever is left on Monday."

Instead he sits down next to me on the couch and thanks me for my part in the event. "You're lucky to have a home like this," he adds, "a place you can enjoy and entertain in. I'm jealous. I'll probably never have a proper home."

"Why not?" I ask him.

"I'll never settle down with my perfect man," he says. "I don't have it in me. I've been flitting around from one guy to another since I've been fifteen. I'm now forty-three. What do you think my chances are?"

"People change," I say wearily; it's late, and I'm not in the mood for a life story, though it looks like I'm in for one nonetheless.

"Not likely," he says. "I am addicted to the new. Yes, it's exciting, but why can't I just be happy, settle down, build a life with someone?" He pauses, looks sideways at me. "Sorry," he says, "you are listening to a drunk. I am boring you with my shit. That's your punishment for being so generous with your home and your time."

Only now he has me interested. I take my chance: "So how does Dave fit into all this?"

A look of clarity passes over his face. "I don't know," he answers warily. "It's been almost six months, a long time for me. I can't say."

Maybe Charlotte's right to wait it out. It's not unlikely this guy will toss Dave back, and his adventure into the land of homoeroticism will pass, like the proverbial phase. "Why are you so interested in whether Dave and I will work out?" Tim inquires. "As a friend of Dave or have you some other agenda?" He leans forward. I can smell the alcohol on his breath; his eyes focus intently on me.

"I asked as Dave's friend, that's all." Then I add, "It's time for you to go home. It's late; we're both tired."

He doesn't move. "Is that what you really want, for me to go?" he asks. "Haven't you ever wondered what it would be like to be with another man?"

"Tim, it's not my thing."

"Nobody will ever know, it can stay just between us. Why don't you give it a try?"

"Go home before we both embarrass ourselves," I say as I stand up. "I'm not interested. I have a tough enough time dealing with women, I'm not looking for any additional complications."

Tim doesn't move, but his eyes do. Suggestively they wander down my body, then back up to my face.

"Enough," I say forcefully. "Get up—please, and go. I'm tired and I'm beginning to lose patience."

His expression reverts to polite indifference. The moment has passed. "Sure," he says, "sorry. A moment of nuttiness: I should not have presumed on your good nature like this. Please, forgive me. I'm really sorry."

"It's okay," I say. "I take it as a compliment."

"Still friends?" he asks as we walk to the front door.

"Absolutely," I assure him. I open the door to let him out and shake his extended hand.

"*Chacun à son goût*," he says.

"I got a C in French," I tell him, "and that was about forty years ago."

"Each to his own taste," he translates, then salutes me briskly and proceeds down the hall to the elevator. He's whistling softly to himself. He doesn't look back at all.

10.

I am having sex with Violet. She is playful, relaxed, and the house phone is ringing. It rings again, insistently. I am startled awake: Violet relaxed and playful? Only in my dreams. My head begins to clear, and I realize the doorman is still buzzing. I shuffle to the intercom. "Yes, yes? What is it?"

"It's Mrs. Andrevsky."

I had forgotten all about the Russian lady. I grab last night's pants, now rumpled, from the chair and pull on a T-shirt.

I open the door. Mrs. Andrevsky is dressed head-to-toe in black, her coat, scarf, gloves, handbag, stockings, shoes. Her thick, glossy black hair is pinned up in a seemingly artless way, and her dark eyes are intelligent, shining. Tartar eyes, Mongol eyes, big and deep.

I don't think I gasp out loud as I gaze at her, but if you can issue such a thing as an internal gasp, then that's what I do. Suddenly very self-conscious, I stand before her barefoot and unshaven.

Thank God she speaks first so I can collect myself. "Good morning." Her soft, silky voice bears a major Russian accent. "I am Tatiana Andrevsky. I am so sorry to disturb you. I must have awakened you, so please, please forgive me, but you did say ten o'clock, did you not?" Pronounced though her accent is, she enunciates every word clearly. Charmingly.

I find my own voice. "Please come in. And please excuse my appearance. Late night, long party. Let me have your coat."

She allows me to take her coat. It strikes me as being much too flimsy a coat for the cold weather; surely, she must have a heavier one, coming from Russia.

As she walks into my living room, I admire her generous hips and behind, swaying slightly from side to side. I'm half mesmerized by her poise, her grace, but I'm not wearing a lick of deodorant, while God alone knows about my breath.

"Please," I say, "Mrs. Andrevsky, please make yourself comfortable while I get my slippers. I'll only be a minute."

"Of course," she purrs. "Take your time, please. There is so much to admire in your beautiful home." And she flashes those Mongol eyes at me: I imagine a fierce Asian invader ravishing her great-great grandmother to bequeath her those eyes.

I rush into my bathroom. I gargle with Listerine, wet my hair down, slap on some deodorant, and where the hell did Della hide my cologne? I find it behind my shaving cream, I spray it on liberally. I pull on a clean shirt and step into my slippers, then rejoin Black Beauty in the living room.

She is standing at my piano, her lovely hands lightly stroking its well-preserved surface. "A Bechstein," she explains, "an old Bechstein. My parents had one very much like it in our home in Kiev. We only had two rooms, but they bought it and played it together whenever possible;

luckily, the other two families sharing the apartment liked music. My sister Luba has it now in Jerusalem. For me, seeing a Bechstein is like seeing an old friend."

"Do you play?" I ask as she turns toward me, and I drown in those eyes again.

"Not very well," she replies. "But my son, Niki, is a remarkable pianist, a natural like his father. That's why we came to New York really, to see that his talent is properly developed. We were tempted to go with my sister Luba to Israel, but this is the classical music capital of the world. So here I brought my son. He spends hours practicing every day, hours, although he is only nine years old. He's like a force of nature; out comes the music like water dancing from a fountain." Her face brightens as she talks of her son, and pleasure shimmers softly in her dark eyes; she seems suddenly vulnerable. I glance down at her legs, don't tell me these are great too. But they are, my God, is there no flaw in this woman. She must have been Miss Russia. And I look like hell; not that she would even notice—me, a man old enough to be her father, the old guy who's doing her a favor.

"Let me give you the necklace. You are so kind to help us." She puts her large black handbag on the top of the piano. With some impatience she fishes around for it, then exclaims with unhappiness when she cannot find it. "It's in a little box. I know I put it in. But the bag is so full." I tell her to take her time, but she pushes about the contents of her bag only more frantically. "Have I lost it?" she asks herself. "Dear God, let me not have lost it."

Strangely moved by her distress, I reach out and touch her arm. "I've got no plans today, just to pack for next week's trip. I'm in no rush, so take your time, relax." She does, and I remember how many times I would watch Ellen doing the same thing—desperately searching for something in one of her huge handbags, growing increasingly more annoyed and charming me even in her annoyance, thrashing about still more and finally blaming me if she could not find whatever she was looking for. What I wouldn't give now for one more such encounter, blame and all.

Ah, triumph, as she finds the box entangled in a plastic rain hat. She hands me the box, noting that her sister's name and number are on it but that Luba will call me at my hotel in Jerusalem and arrange to pick up the jewelry. "Thank you so much. This is such a big mitzvah, a good deed, that you should bring this so that Luba can wear my mother's necklace at her son's bar mitzvah. I thank you from my heart."

I take the box from her and put it down on the piano. "I'll take good care of it," I promise her.

"It's all that we have left of our mother," she says, not sadly or even sentimentally; she is simply stating a fact.

"Your parents are gone?" I ask.

"Yes, my husband also. Niki and I have only my sister and her family, no one else." More fact; her voice remains neutral in tone.

"I'm doing you a favor with the necklace," I say to her, and surprise myself with my boldness. "Now you do me one and have a cup of coffee with me. I haven't had my breakfast yet."

"With pleasure," she says. She follows me into the kitchen. "How big, how pretty, the little table and the stone floor. It's a castle you live in, and everything so neat. You are quite a surprise, Mr. Gelder."

"Dan, call me Dan. May I call you Tatiana?"

"Of course," she says. "Now point me to the coffee." I enjoy watching her move about as she prepares the coffee, and I confess that I find those firm, round hips devastating. With the coffee and some cookies on a tray, she joins me at the table. A slightly awkward but also vaguely heady silence descends on us. We are, after all, strangers.

I clear my throat to break the silence. "You mentioned that your husband is gone, Tatiana," I say. "How is he gone? Divorced?"

"No," she replies and her expression suddenly turns sad, "he was killed in Chechnya. He was a career officer; it's how he made his living, and it's how he died. He came from a poor Russian family, so he never was able to afford the training to make music his profession; but he was very talented. Niki has difficulty remembering him."

"I'm sorry, I didn't mean to pry."

"There is nothing to be sorry about. You are all kindness; I find it a pleasure to speak with you," she says as she rivets her wild, dark eyes on mine. And she may see kindness there, she might see a nice, comfortable sort of old guy, but I'm betting that she can't see what he's thinking, how he'd like to jump her and throw her down on that stone floor she likes so much and bury his head in that glorious hair of hers. Better be careful of sweet old guys like me—we're full of surprises.

"So," I say, swallowing my desire, "it must be tough for your boy. New country, new language, and all that piano practicing. How is he doing?"

Her face tightens, reddens with conviction; I've touched her. "He's strong," she says, "my Niki is strong like his father. With any-thing, he can cope. My boy already is near a man. I bring him here so he can have his big chance. He wanted to go to Israel with Luba and his cousins, but he chose to be brave and come to New York where he can try with his music to make a big career. He'll be okay. There is a synagogue two blocks from our apartment, and the rabbi lets Niki practice on the piano in their reception room six days a week. I took the nerve to ask, and the rabbi said yes."

I can't imagine any man saying no to Tatiana, even a rabbi, and I make an offer of my own. "Well, if there is ever any problem with that, he can always practice here, on my piano."

"Thank you, you are so kind," she replies, her lips now moist from the coffee, her face a little flushed, and I want her, right now, right here. The intensity of my lust surprises me. First, I wake up dreaming I'm having sex with Violet, and now I'm sitting in my kitchen ready to pounce on a beautiful, utterly unsuspecting, Russian woman I've known for maybe twenty-seven minutes.

I try to contain myself. "Where do you live, Tatiana?"

"On Second Avenue, at Eighty-ninth Street, over a greengrocer. I have a room in an apartment rented by another family from Kiev, where I come from. Nice people. The building is old, a walk-up, but very clean, very safe."

She bites into her second cookie. A crumb tumbles down onto her ample breasts; trembles on the sheeny fabric of her black blouse. Lucky crumb. She catches me staring, and looks down, sees the crumb, plucks it up with her fingertip, puts it delicately on her saucer. She acknowledges the moment with a fleeting but knowing smile. What she doesn't know is the urging in my groin, that readiness, and how damn near I am to touching her.

"More coffee?" she asks, and I say no, because if she doesn't go now, I'm going to make an absolute ass of myself.

She gets up and takes our dishes to the sink, quickly rinses them off, and piles them neatly on the counter. We walk together to the front hall; I help her on with her coat. "Thank you again," she says. "I can never thank you enough."

Oh yes, you can, I think, but I say, "It's my pleasure," as I open the door for her. "Bon voyage," she says as she steps into the elevator, and I keep my eyes on her until its doors slide closed.

Perfect: I have just been flummoxed by a penniless Russian refugee and single mother devoted to forwarding the career of a nine-year-old prodigy. It's true, what they say: when the penis stands up the brain leaves the room. Well, at least I'm still alive. Not my finest hour perhaps, but I'm still kicking—though only God knows why.

11.

I t's the morning of my departure for Israel. Packing for the trip is
easy. All I really need is one suit for Violet's university ceremony, some sportswear for the rest of the stay, a pair of good walking
shoes for the cobblestone streets of Safed and Jerusalem, and a hat
for protection against the sun. I put Tatiana's parcel in my hand luggage, and I'm all set to go.

I get a thank-you call from Dave and one from Charlotte. I decide
to call Eric and touch base before leaving.

"So you'll be all right?" I ask him.

"Yes, Dad. I'll be all right. Besides, I know where to find you."
Indulgence colors the tone of his voice.

"How are the bank negotiations going?" I don't want to let go just
yet, but as Eric summarizes the various situations, I find myself listening less to him than the small voice inside me that's wondering
how things are going with Carol.

"Well, I best be off," I close without asking, but add, "Give my regards to Carol."

"Of course, Dad. And don't worry," Eric says firmly.

I determine to take his advice. It's time for me to have some fun.

The security at the airport is rigorous. Before entering the terminal, we are asked about the nature of our relationship, which I describe as "friends," and our bags are scrutinized. Some stalwart-looking young men with earphone pieces are meanwhile watching everyone. Among the mostly Jewish people, American and Israeli, waiting to enter the building, I notice a contingent of mostly black and Hispanic church members—on a guided tour, no doubt— looking around like visitors to Mars. The Jews are noisy, with three or four family members for each passenger; they kiss, they remind, they hug, they part, and the travelers pass through security and head toward the plane.

Having traveled coach to Israel several times before, I am truly grateful that Violet's prodigal ways placed us in first class. I shall not miss the thirty or forty old ladies who will spend the entire ten-hour El-Al flight walking slowly up and down the coach section (they're doing their laps) and stopping for a chat with anyone whose face looks half friendly. There will be prayer groups, too, that will gather at least once during the flight. So will endless lines at the bathrooms in coach, although El-Al has more bathrooms per customer than any other airline.

The flight begins nicely. I hold Violet's hand in mine, as we make small talk. A natural intimacy begins to grow between us. Whether this stems merely from the fact that we're traveling companions or from some other, deeper affection, it feels familiar, comfortable.

Only half awake, with Violet close but quiet beside me, I wonder what will be the course of our relationship: whether it might lead to marriage, and if I even want it to. Certainly, it is not easy to find the right person. She would have to be trustworthy, someone who would take care of me should I fall ill, someone for whom I'd happily do the same. And yet, can I indeed afford marriage at this stage in my life? There would be financial expectations, and though my brokerage business is solid, I still couldn't afford to buy an apartment like the one I now own at today's crazy prices. The floor below me sold for almost four million dollars six months ago, a seven-room apartment; it's nuts. I, too, could sell, but where would I move to? The Bronx? Much as I'd hate to leave my wonderful Park Avenue building, Ellen still so inhabits our apartment that if I were to marry again, it would be hard to bring a new wife there to live with me. The truth is, I'm tired of working. Day in and day out, month in and month out, the same clients, the same emotions, up and down with the market—I've had enough. Maybe I should consider marrying someone like Violet, someone who could free me from my routine. A rich woman. Like something's wrong with rich? Rich is good. Rich means that your children are nice to you. Rich means that you are treated well. There's that old Yiddish saying that when you're rich you're handsome, you're charming, and you sing well, too. And my Grandma Bella used to say it's not that being rich is so good, it's that being poor is so terrible— and she certainly knew about being poor. Everybody beats around the bush on this issue, but look at all those annoying personal ads in the magazines: Everybody is looking for "comfortable" or "established' or "professional," but what they mean is money. They claim they like Tuscan villas, rainy walks in Paris, scuba diving in Fiji. How do they afford all those trips? With money, that's how. Maybe I'm looking for a merger as much as a marriage; maybe Violet and I could broker a partnership like that. She obviously is attracted to me, and I to her, although underneath that formidable exterior lurks, I suspect, an even more formidable interior. One thing, with Violet I would not die from boredom. On that thought, I slip into sleep.

When I wake up, it is almost five in the morning New York time. The plane is quiet except for the whisperings of the stewardesses with the two stewards. Here and there someone is reading. The pleasant buzz of the airplane relaxes me. Violet is fast asleep, mouth open, and I decide to use the bathroom. Near the end of the aisle, between me and the bathroom, stands a cluster of men. I excuse myself.

"Could you join us for just a few minutes for the morning prayers?" one of them asks. "We need a tenth man, it would be a big mitzvah for you."

"I don't have things I need," I say. "No skullcap, no phylacteries."

"It's okay, I have an extra skullcap, and if you just stand here, we can then do all the prayers. Please."

So I comply. The men don their prayer shawls and begin to pray in rapid-fire fashion largely by heart. Swaying back and forth and occasionally from side to side, they pray with devout concentration. At first I feel awkward, but soon their earnest devotion envelops me, and I consider that I am flying through the air en route to Jerusalem in this circle of men faithfully praying as our ancestors have for thousands of years. The traditional words are lost to me—there are only a few that I still remember—but I stand there, slightly abashed by the emotion welling inside me, and I pray for my son and for myself and for Israel. And I feel spiritually invigorated. Maybe it's the altitude.

I finish with the bathroom in time enough to beat the rush. An hour and a half before we land, some twenty or thirty ladies head for the toilets. In appearance all askew—many have slept in unflattering gym outfits and slippers—they chat amiably while they wait their turn. One by one they enter the unspacious compartments, and one by one they emerge transformed. Have they got a beautician in there? Their hair and faces redone, their clothing changed for the family reception committees already no doubt forming at Ben Gurion, they turn every aisle into a fashion runway.

They take charge, too, when we deplane. I resign myself to my fate at the baggage carousel, where I am surrounded by several women ready to tackle their bags solo, their cardiac-prone husbands having been instructed to sit on the sidelines. Their luggage tends to be large and heavy, and when sighted each piece is greeted with cries of pleasure and a sense of urgency. My own bag arrives promptly; but while I'm waiting for Violet's three mammoth lavender and gold cases to appear, I become a baggage handler for four commanding ladies whose thanks come with specific directions as to handling and placement.

Sweating but exhilarated, with Violet's bags in tow, I find our waiting driver, and we head for Safed high in the mountains of Galilee. The landscape recalls for me prior trips to Israel, trips with Ellen, as do the soldiers we pass on the road: young Jewish men, tough and strong; some women, too. They make me feel proud, and I feel absurdly close to them all, as if we were truly all one family. As if I had come home. Violet soon brings me back to the more immediate reality, however. First the air conditioning is too low, then it's too cold. Then she cannot find her glasses, or the phone number of the director of the university. And can't we travel any faster? By the time we reach Safed, her complaints have reduced me to silence and the hardened Israeli driver to exasperation. He cannot follow instructions if she does not make them clear, he protests.

Over the next two days, though, the Violet-centered celebrations, change her whole affect. She is moved to tears when she receives her doctoral certificate, and when the students begin a spirited hora dance around her, she joins in with tremendous enthusiasm and a happiness and excitement that match the gusto of the young dancers. Afterward she seems strangely calm, her manner gentle and friendly, and her instructions, though still incessant, are issued with a touch of sweetness, more like requests than commands. In between the ceremonies, we walk the old, colorful lanes of Safed, and rediscover at almost every turn the mountain views that have inspired mystics and artists for centuries. We stroll hand in hand, and we revel in the clarity of the air, the sunlight sparkling on the distant Sea of Galilee, the Golan Heights to the east, and in every other direction the hills of Galilee vibrant, covered with wildflowers and trees. On one of our walks, we get a little lost. We find ourselves in an alley too narrow for cars and lined with houses, some of them painted bright colors, and most of them smothered in flowering vines. We stumble upon a small square dominated by a relatively large building that Violet thinks is the Synagogue of the Ari, the great Kabbalist. We try the door. It swings open, and we enter a prayer room, obviously hundreds of years old, with an elaborately carved podium at its center, and even more striking, an exquisite ark holding the Torah scrolls. The place is empty except for an old man who had been dozing in a corner. Awakened by our entry, he calls out, "Shalom!" We both return his greeting.

Violet asks him if he speaks English, and he replies, "English? Of course. Also French and Hungarian and Yiddish and Hebrew. At your service," he adds in accented English.

"Is this the Ari Synagogue?" I ask.

"Yes, it is," he replies before launching into a canned speech about the building, the rabbi, dates, details, miracles. Looking around the exotic but shabby room, I notice that little pieces of paper have been rolled up and stuck into the crevices of the podium. When the old man pauses for breath I ask him about them.

"Prayers," he tells me. "Many people believe that if they put their prayers into this place, the great merit of the Ari will help lift them up to the attention of God."

"I could use some heavy lifting for mine," says Violet, "but I need a pen and paper." She opens her handbag, takes out a fifty-dollar bill, and asks where she can leave a contribution for the upkeep of the synagogue.

The old man, already pleasant, becomes downright charming. He hastens to bring us paper and a pen, then offers us a charity box, into which we each drop our contributions. We take turns writing out our prayers. Feeling a little self-conscious and silly, I write just "Dan and Violet." I am about to approach the podium when Violet stops me. "I'll show you mine if you'll show me yours," she says.

"In a synagogue?" I ask. "You can't wait till we get back to the hotel?"

"The prayers, Bozo, just the prayers and nothing but the prayers."

"I've got nothing to hide." Giving her mine, I take hers, which reads "Violet and Dan." Our eyes now meet in mutual surprise tinged with a hint of promise. The old man takes our two prayers and twirls them together into one compact note, which he inserts with a practiced hand into a crack. "May your prayers be fulfilled for good," he says, then adds, "Amen and Amen."

The old man escorts us a few steps beyond the synagogue and points our way back to the hotel. In a sort of reverie, filled with anticipation, I walk with Violet arm in arm. Maybe it's the atmosphere of this town, its mixture of sanctity and poverty, the many art galleries, the vivid scenery, I don't know, but I am floating on air. Only good things can happen here, I think.

* * *

That evening, our last night in Safed, Violet knocks on my door. She has changed into a silk bathrobe, and her hair is loose and free. She looks young and a little coy. There can be only one reason for her visit. So I take her in my arms and hold her tightly to me, while I try to figure out how to get her to the bed with some degree of grace. She stirs in my embrace then, and tears are brimming in her eyes, which gleam too with determination. And it is she who leads me to the bed, she who opens the silk robe, and for all her formidability, her body, assuredly beautiful, is surprisingly delicate. Very soon, perhaps too soon, I have satisfied myself and, I hope, Violet as well. She offers no clues. She does not speak, she barely moves. The tears are gone, though. I search her eyes, and she looks at me a little mischievously, then smiles as she asks me whether I have ever slept with a doctor before. "A couple of nurses, but no doctors," I admit. "So, tell me, Doc, what's your diagnosis?"

"The patient will live," she replies enigmatically, and as I hold her hand in the few minutes before sleep, for the first time in a long while, I feel well, in body and soul complete.

The next day, we are driven to Jerusalem. As we ascend through the steep Judean hills—the trees etched against the sky, the boulders aglint in the sun—my heart is pounding with anticipation. And then there it is: the big curve in the road as you pass Motza, and then, high on its hills, Jerusalem. Next to me Violet sits absolutely still and silent. I wonder if she is as profoundly moved as I am. But I say nothing in my awe.

I surrender to the city, to the beautiful children, the young soldiers, the ultra-Orthodox in their black garb, the old people slowly climbing up and down the hilly streets. I have never lived here, but it somehow feels like home. I remember viewing the Old City with Ellen from the top of Mount Scopus—the gold Dome of the Rock, the Tower of David, the magic of the ancient streets—all of it wondrous.

In the lobby of the King David Hotel, at the windows looking out on the Old City walls, I miss Ellen painfully now. The last time I stood here, I was with her. She was wearing a sun hat; I remember the way it half hid her face, the way it made her seem a little mysterious. She was so very lovely. As soon as we've checked in at the King David, I tell Violet that I want to go straight to the Wall, even before we unpack. Violet smiles indulgently at my excitement, but the first thing she wants to do is wash up, so I go ahead alone, and in minutes I'm taxiing through the Jaffa Gate and heading for the Western Wall.

It is late afternoon, and the city, bathed in the light of the declining sun, takes on a golden hue. In the plaza, I stand facing the Wall. Many of the people are praying in groups, while others walk solemnly about. Some stand or lean against the Wall. Women gather in one area, men in another. There is no privacy, yet you can be alone in your thoughts. I find a space of my own. To my right a young soldier, gun strapped to his back, is praying with his eyes closed. To my left a Japanese tourist stands silently, facing the stones, and I wonder what he might be thinking of this, the last remnant of our ancient Temple—or does he see nothing more than a retaining wall? I surrender to the sanctity of the place. I put both my hands palm down against the Wall. The stones are cool and craggy, filled with rolled-up papers in many colors and prayers in many languages stuck into the cracks. I say Ellen's name. Then Eric's. I say, "I'm here," and then I repeat, "I'm here." I keep my hands pressed on the Wall. "I'm here, I'm back. . . . Please help us. Please help." I cannot move, the din of many voices surrounds me, but I only really hear my own. "Please," I become silent and I am near tears. I swallow the sob in my throat, I blink back my tears. I don't know how long I stand there, as if spellbound, at the Wall, before heading toward the Dung Gate and a taxi back.

The moment I see her, Violet breaks the spell. Dissatisfied with our two rooms and outraged by the management—where was the complimentary fresh fruit she'd come to expect on her arrival (they'd not forgotten the flowers)—she has had us moved into adjoining rooms, the doors now unlocked and opened, and she points triumphantly to the just-delivered bowls of fruit and nuts. She announces that she's going to take her shower now and more than suggests that I should take mine, because her daughter Maria will be here in an hour. But first I should unpack. I find that I do not resent Violet's instructions. On the contrary, I welcome them. They simplify matters; they relieve me of authority and responsibility.

So I dutifully proceed to shower. Afterward, as I'm reaching for a towel, Violet steps into my bathroom. Still damp from her own shower, she approaches me with confidence and slips out of her robe. A remarkably energetic romp, with her seated on the marble sink top and me standing, leaning toward her, puts us both in the greatest of good spirits. In a rather elevated state we dress and head downstairs to see Maria.

For whom I am utterly unprepared. Maria is beautiful, yes—I expected that—but she is also soft-spoken, serene, plainly dressed. She greets her glittering, meticulously coifed mother; Maria's glossy black hair and delicate features heighten the contrast to Violet's blonde, sculptured beauty. Beside Maria stands a young man wearing a skullcap; Orthodox; this is Aaron from Toronto. Introduced to each other by their respective rabbis, Maria and Aaron are obviously enamored of each other, but they are also

34. Barney Frank, "So Call It a Victory Dividend," *New York Times*, May 1, 1991, p. A-25.

35. E. J. Dionne, "Gulf Crisis Rekindles Democrats' Old Debate but with New Focus," *Washington Post*, January 3, 1991, p. A-16.

36. "Confrontation in the Gulf, Day 2: Lawmakers Debate War and More Time for Sanctions," *New York Times*, January 12, 1991, p. 6.

37. George Bush and Brent Scowcroft, *A World Transformed* (New York: Knopf, 1998), pp. 389, 445; "A Sampling from the Debate on Capitol Hill," *New York Times*, January 11, 1991, p. A-8.

Chapter 2: "I'm Running Out of Demons"

1. See editorial, "Don't Shoot Down Iraqi Aircraft," *New York Times*, February 19, 1992, p. A-20; Andrew Rosenthal, "Stressing Foreign Policy Could Cut Both Ways," *New York Times*, February 16, 1992, section 4, p. 2; Michael Kramer, "The Cost of Removing Saddam Hussein," *Time*, October 24, 1994, p. 39; Philip Shenon, "U.S. Quietly Intensifies Attacks on Iraq, Destroying Radar Sites," May 5, 1999, p. A-6.

2. Marshall interview, May 22, 2009; Michael Kelly, "Clinton Defends Position on Iraqi War," *New York Times*, July 31, 1992, p. A-13.

3. Thomas L. Friedman, "Clinton Asserts Bush Is Too Eager to Befriend the World's Dictators," *New York Times*, October 2, 1992, p. A-1.

4. Jim Wolffe, "Powell: I'm Running Out of Demons," *Army Times*, April 5, 1991.

5. Elaine Sciolino, "Christopher Sees a Place for Force," *New York Times*, January 14, 1993, p. A-11.

6. Daniel Williams and John M. Goshko, "Reduced U.S. World Role Outlined but Soon Altered; High-Level Disavowals Follow Official's Talk," *Washington Post*, May 26, 1993, p. A-1.

7. Susan Bennett, "Clinton's Allies Push Him to Act Against 'Ethnic Cleansing,'" *Houston Chronicle*, April 21, 1993, p. A-15.

8. Colin Powell, *My American Journey* (New York: Ballantine Books, 2005), p. 561.

9. Taylor Branch, *The Clinton Tapes* (New York: Simon & Schuster, 2009), p. 187.

10. Derek Chollet and James Goldgeier, *America Between the Wars* (New York: PublicAffairs, 2008), pp. 65–70.

11. Ibid., pp. 147–48.

12. Ibid., p. 102.

13. David Halberstam, *War in a Time of Peace* (New York: Scribner, 2001), p. 352.

14. Ibid., p. 421.

15. Andrew J. Bacevich, *American Empire* (Cambridge: Harvard University Press, 2002), pp. 154–55.

16. Halberstam, *War in a Time of Peace*, pp. 423–25.

17. Bill Clinton press conference with Jiang Zemin, January 28, 1997.

18. "Clinton Criticizes Bush Decision to Renew China's Most Favored Nation Status," press release, June 3, 1992.

19. Interview with Nancy Pelosi, May 21, 1996, quoted in James Mann, *About Face: A History of America's Curious Relationship with China, from Nixon to Clinton* (New York: Knopf, 1999), p. 308.

20. Memo to Interested Parties from Greg Craig, March 11, 2008.

Chapter 3: Democrats in Exile

1. Jeffrey Goldberg, "The CIA and the Pentagon Take Another Look at Al Qaeda and Iraq," *The New Yorker*, February 10, 2003, p. 40.
2. See Michael Isikoff and David Corn, *Hubris* (New York: Crown, 2006), pp. 125–26.
3. Richard C. Holbrooke, "Give Diplomacy More Time," *Washington Post*, September 7, 2002, p. A-17; Richard C. Holbrooke, "It Didn't Have to Be This Way," *Washington Post*, February 23, 2003, p. B-7.
4. Samuel R. Berger, "Foreign Policy for a Democratic President," *Foreign Affairs* 83:3 (May/June 2004), p. 47.
5. Dan Balz, "Bush Assails Kerry on Iraq Remarks," *Washington Post*, August 11, 2004, p. A-4.
6. Interview with John Podesta, February 4, 2010; Bill Keller, "The Sunshine Warrior," *New York Times Magazine*, September 22, 2002, p. 48.
7. According to Podesta, the principal donors helping to launch CAP were Herbert Sandler, George Soros and Peter Lewis, along with their families.
8. Podesta interview.
9. Lawrence J. Korb, "Trim Fat from Pentagon Budget to Help Pay for Katrina Relief," *Baltimore Sun*, October 13, 2005, p. A-15; Caroline P. Wadhams and Lawrence J. Korb, "The Forgotten Front," report by Center for American Progress, November 6, 2007.
10. Lawrence J. Korb and Brian Katulis, "Strategic Redeployment," report by Center for American Progress, September 29, 2005.
11. Kurt M. Campbell and Michael E. O'Hanlon, *Hard Power* (New York: Basic Books, 2006), pp. 7–8.
12. Podesta interview; interview with Lawrence J. Korb, December 1, 2009.

Chapter 4: The Trout Fishers

1. Interview with Morton Abramowitz, December 21, 2009.
2. "Statement on Postwar Iraq," issued by Project for a New American Century, March 17, 2003; interview with James Steinberg, November 13, 2009.
3. Bill Keller, "The I-Can't-Believe-I'm-a-Hawk Club," *New York Times*, February 8, 2003, p. A-17; Bill Keller, "My Unfinished 9/11 Business," *New York Times Magazine*, September 11, 2011, p. 34, http://www.dlc.org/documents/Progressive_Internationalism_1003.pdf.
4. "Progressive Internationalism: A Democratic National Security Strategy," October 30, 2003, pp. 3–4, http://www.dlc.org/documents/Progressive_Internationalism_1003.pdf.
5. Ibid., p. 5.
6. www.trumanproject.org/about/mission/values.
7. Nancy Pelosi, "Power and Principle," David A. Morse Lecture to Council on Foreign Relations, March 7, 2003; Steinberg interview, November 13, 2009.
8. Remarks by Al Gore to MoveOn PAC, May 26, 2004.
9. Ceci Connolly, "U.S. Combat Death Rate Lowest Ever," *Washington Post*, December 9, 2004, p. A-24.
10. Interview with Kenneth Pollack, March 2, 2010.
11. Peter Baker and Shailagh Murray, "Democrats Split over Position on Iraq War," *Washington Post*, August 22, 2005, p. A-1.

careful not to touch each other; indeed, they are determinedly
unerotic with each other.

At dinner, Violet seems reserved, even wary, in her speech, as she
is trying hard to be considerate of her daughter's sensibilities, and I
see yet another Violet, this one quite likable, almost vulnerable. The
conversation flows easily. Violet and I are invited to Friday night
dinner tomorrow at Maria's apartment, and the evening ends pleasantly. The minute Aaron and Maria leave I ask Violet what in the
world she was talking about in describing Maria so negatively. She
gives me a sardonic look. Without reserve, she says, "Stick around.
I'm sure you'll find out."

Friday is a peculiar day in Jerusalem. The Jews are preparing for the
Sabbath that evening, and the Arabs are already observing theirs. By
noon, the city quiets down. Men carry flowers home. Children, off
from school, are playing in the streets. The atmosphere is serene,
and, escorted by one of Violet's beneficiaries, we have a great day. I
begin to understand, too, something about Violet and all her charitable activities: how they make her feel something like Queen for a
Day. As the benefactress of blind children, or of immigrants hit by
terrorism, or of schools and hospitals, she garners warmth, gratitude,
praise; and it is bewitching. For hours we are cosseted by the gratitude of Violet's loyal subjects. It is late afternoon when we return to
the hotel.

We have tea on the verandah overlooking the Old City, and there
amidst the busy tables, but divorced from the bustle, Violet allows
me a glimpse of still another side of her. For all the goodwill of the
day, all the praise, has humbled her. She seems shaken, but quiet,
almost at peace. I ask how she is feeling.

"Fine," she says, "happy."

I probe. I ask about her past; I want to understand her better, want to get closer to her soul. "Talk to me."

"In a way this is my real life, what I live for," she says, almost eager now to open herself up to me. "I'm a Brooklyn girl, Avenue J. My father was unable to cope with the world, and my mother was a tough, overworked woman who raised us kids by herself. I started college, but my brother had to go to medical school. So guess who had to quit and go to work? I ended up a secretary, what else, and got married young, had Maria, and two years later I'm divorced. My second job, I worked for a big, funny-looking guy named Irv Finkel—the Handkerchief King everybody called him. For two years I worked for him, and he never once touched me, but that didn't stop the love from growing between him and me. He was the most generous man I have ever known, a real sucker for every sad tale. You can't imagine, no one will ever know what good that man did, how much he gave. I fell in love with him, with his goodness. It was never the money. I'd not take a man away from his wife, from his kids, for his money. It was hard for him to leave his kids, but we had no choice: we loved each other so much, either we got married or we would never see each other again—it was that simple. For almost twenty years I had him, and from him I learned how to deal in the world, in business, in charity, but what I learned most of all was what Irv always used to say: that the only thing you can never lose is what you give away. It's true. Because no one can take your good deeds away; they can take everything else, but not them. So when Irv died—some damned doctors killing him with their screw-ups—I carried on for him. I know what people think. I know why they kiss my ass—let them; it feels good—but I'm doing it for Irv, I'm carrying out his wishes as best I can. Every kid, every poor soul, I help, it's for him, so he'll be pleased with me. I want you to know that I still love Irv, and I will until I die. What we did, you and I, on this trip, it's the first time in years. I was scared, but I want to thank you because you were a gentleman, which is why I chose you. I'm still a little scared." She stops then, and she avoids my eyes.

I am surprised by her humility, taken aback by her show of vulnerability. "You know, Violet, I'm pretty new to all this, too. It's only been two years since Ellen died, and I'm still trying to get used to just the idea of me out on dates. But you make it easy. You are so real, so larger than life . . ." I'm afraid to say more.

But then there seems to be no need for any more words: Violet's eyes meet mine, and she clasps my hand. The dusk gathers. The mountain air grows cool, fragrant.

There are virtually no Jewish taxis on Friday night, and we are not going to risk using an Arab one, so we have to walk. In the streets, Orthodox men are heading to synagogue. Everywhere windows shimmer with lit Sabbath candles. Violet takes my arm, and we walk happily close to one another.

"Here we are." She stops in front of an old three-story stone building. "Remember, don't shake hands or kiss the women; save that for later, if you're a good boy, with me." Very much together, we climb the two flights. "Did you bring a skullcap?" she whispers, and I triumphantly pull one out of my pocket, bought that day.

The apartment, modest in size, is devoid of decoration but clean and filled to overflowing with flowers. "Mom," whispers Maria, "thanks for the flowers, but I can't imagine what you spent. I had to put some in the kitchen and in the bathroom, and we've now got a jungle on the balcony."

"There's no such thing as too many flowers," replies Violet, and compliments Maria on her appearance. Maria has dressed up a bit, maybe for her mother, maybe for the Sabbath.

Aaron is already there, together with a group of young people, all of them fresh-faced and neatly dressed. At the table, Violet and I join the others in their observances: the blessing over the wine, the ritual washing of hands, the blessing over the bread, and, after the meal, the prayers sung to traditional tunes, some of which I remember vaguely. The food is simple and good; the young people are voluble and argumentative on the topics of politics, terrorism, and religion, but they joke with one another, too. That there is no physical contact between these spirited young men and women, not even the most casual touch, adds a certain tension to the atmosphere. The young people leave by nine-thirty, but Aaron asks us to stay.

The minute the four of us are alone, Maria joins Aaron at his side, and it is clear that an announcement is in the offing. Violet is immediately poker-faced, and I wish I had not been caught in this uncomfortable family moment. Maria blurts it out: She and Aaron want to get married, and they want Violet's approval. Aaron is going to spend a few more years studying at the Yeshiva, Maria tells us, and then they hope to return to New York or Toronto. Aaron provides some details about his family in Toronto, and Maria says she has already met his parents, months ago, and that Violet will no doubt love them. Violet says nothing.

She sits very still once Maria and Aaron have finished, and the silence hangs heavy. The candlelight flickers. One overhead bulb, its light dim, hums. The room is cast in shadows, and the young couple nervously waits for Violet to speak.

"Can we talk alone?" Violet asks Maria. Both Aaron and I quickly rise to leave the room, but Maria insists on our staying. "It would be better if we were alone," Violet insists, and I open the glass door to a little iron-railed balcony. I step out into the cool air; Aaron joins me. Round one to Violet. In the Sabbath silence of Jerusalem, however, Aaron and I cannot help but hear every word in the room behind us.

"Maria, this is your life, and there are limits to a parent's ability to guide her child," Violet begins, "but I have to ask you why you think this ultra-Orthodoxy will last with you. You are, after all, the same daughter of mine who three years ago took the name of Lakshme and spent your days meditating with a guru in Nepal—which, I might add, was a real improvement over your relationship before with that wonderful forty-year-old married man who hung out regularly at Gamblers Anonymous. Do you realize how hard and demanding such a life will be with Aaron? You are likely to produce a bevy of kids, and when you discover your next spiritual adventure, what are you going to do with them? Don't expect me to pick up the pieces. How do you know this romance of yours with Orthodoxy is not a passing fling? Here in Jerusalem it may feel all hunky-dory, but back in New York you may find it to be very different."

Aaron's face, cast in shadow by the half-light from the door, registers no surprise. He probably has heard a similar argument with a Canadian accent. He is a handsome kid, sure of himself, and he's been around enough to have chosen Orthodoxy with some mindfulness. Neither he nor Maria seems a sap, so why shouldn't they take a chance with each other and their faith? And I wonder, then, how I would feel if Eric had chosen the Orthodox path. Would I be as upset by such a decision as Violet is now? No. I doubt it.

Maria replies, her voice firm, the voice of a true believer. "Look, Mom, I'm grateful for everything you have done for me, so please don't be hurt by what I need to say. Why do you think I've bounced around from one thing to another? You and Irv were wonderful to me, you really were, but I've always needed something more, some way of grappling with life, and you offered me none of that. You did not bring spirituality into our home. You embraced charity, but do you honestly think that in giving to charity I can find religion, a faith? At least I'm trying to lift myself up. Would you rather I had married some nice member of the stock exchange and lunched daily with ladies? Tell me the truth, would you?"

"Yes, I would. I would like you to find some balance, but you insist on going to extremes, like that obsessive father of yours. Maybe it's genetic. Your father can't seem to help himself—always running from one business to another, from one woman to another—and as a result, he's never arrived anywhere. How are you different? You think now that the Orthodox life is preferable to an apartment on Park Avenue, a couple of kids, and a smart husband. You'd rather turn off the lights on Saturday and go to synagogue, keep your hair covered, cook and clean for a house full of children? Let me tell you, most people would choose Park Avenue. And what if this Aaron of yours changes his mind? Suppose he goes back to his previous life and leaves you holding the bag, what then? You are both new to this. Here in Jerusalem you're surrounded by all this holiness, history, tradition. It sucks you in. And you're going to wear shapeless long dresses and long sleeves and look like a nice modest girl from Crown Heights? Remember Madison Avenue."

"Mom, I'm at peace with this decision," Maria says calmly. "It's been a year and a half. I feel like I've come back to where I always should have been. I feel like Grandma would be proud of me."

"Grandma!" Violet exclaims. "She worked herself to death, to an early death, from the aggravation of raising us kids as well as a husband who never grew up. You think she wouldn't have traded it all for lots of money and fun? She wasn't so naive as you imagine. She was stuck, that's all, and I'm trying to save you from a similar fate."

"I appreciate it, Mom, but if you can't see how happy I am, how happy Aaron and I are, then you just don't want to. Aren't you at least pleased that I've returned to Judaism as a way of life?"

"I just want you to be sure. Can't you give it more time?"

"You know we're not allowed to touch each other, Aaron and I," Maria reminds her. "How long can we bear that? The natural thing is to get married. Trust me, please. I'm twenty-eight. I've wandered, I've strayed, but now I'm home. Please don't ruin this for me. Please be happy for me."

A long silence. Then a chilling sound. Through the glass door Aaron and I see Violet, her head bowed in both hands, sobbing. Maria does not move; she does not touch her mother. After a minute or two the sobs stop. Violet pulls herself erect, with a strange formality, and like any departing dinner guest, she thanks Maria for dinner.

When she comes to the terrace door, her face is steely, composed. We step back into the apartment, and with neither the tension nor the issue resolved, we all say our good nights. Aaron leaves with us, but goes his own way a few blocks further on.

Violet takes my hand. Hers is cold—maybe it is the mountain air, maybe not—but holding it firmly, I try to warm her with my empathy.

Back at the hotel, I go to my room, but leave the door ajar. The many faces of Violet that I've witnessed during this trip pass through my mind: Violet humble, angry, grateful, vulnerable, sexy, scared. Violet brazen, pushy, and bossy, too. But she is also genuinely kind. And such an indomitable spirit . . . I may be falling for her. Sometime in the very middle of the night I am briefly awakened when Violet joins me in my bed. She needs to be held, she says; in my arms she falls asleep.

* * *

On Saturday afternoon, Tatiana's sister Luba and her husband, Gregor, stop by to pick up the necklace. Soft-spoken people, pale and European-looking, they have clearly not yet acclimated to Israel. Luba, a pretty woman, but faded, weary-looking, has none of Tatiana's fiery beauty. We have coffee in the lobby, and they seem to relish the luxurious surroundings. I enjoy their company and the photographs they show me of their two boys as well as other family snapshots, which they've brought for Tatiana, if I'd be so kind as to carry them. And in my mind's eye, I see her again: alluring, mysterious, dressed in black, standing at the piano; or in the kitchen, and a cookie crumb settles on her breast, and I want her, and what am I, nuts? I think I'm falling in love with Violet, and here I am, harboring lustful thoughts about Tatiana.

A few hours later, after the Sabbath has ended, Violet receives a call from Maria. "Damn!" Violet reports. "I wanted to spend tomorrow in Tel Aviv shopping, but Maria is begging me to meet her rabbi, and he can only see me at three in the afternoon. It ruins the whole day. We leave Israel tomorrow night, and when am I going to pack? Plus I have to wear a dress with long sleeves and a high neck, and preferably not too fitted—according to Maria. And isn't that me to a tee. First, they make me a doctor, and then I'm turned into a nun." I let Violet rant on. I've got her modus operandi down by now.

The next morning, Violet and I are relaxing at the hotel pool when an anxious Maria appears. She has come to help her mother dress for the audience with the Kanczuga Rebbe. They join me later for lunch, and Violet is indeed a changed woman—her hair covered by a scarf, her clothes dark and demure, but the look she gives me pugnacious, like she's daring me to say, or even to think, one smartass word. Unable to resist, I rise and welcome Mother Teresa to the table. "Don't press it, buddy," she replies. "They may have rewrapped the package, but it's the same old bundle inside. Now sit down, and eat like a good boy, we've got to move our collective asses to get to the Rebbe on time." And we do.

When we reach the Rebbe's home, a modest, unadorned building made of the local stone, we're ushered into his study, where books march up the walls and heavy red velvet drapes keep out most of the light. In the center of the room, behind a small desk, sits a very old bearded man, wearing a black skullcap and a striped silk caftan; two attendants in black hats and black suits stand to either side of him. The Rebbe is halfway through a glass of tea when we enter, but he receives us with a sweet smile and waves the three of us in. The Rebbe's heavily accented English requires all my concentration. "Sit, please, welcome to you all." Then in rapid-fire Yiddish, one of the attendants explains the reason for our visit. A long silence follows. The Rebbe is absolutely still. The two attendants wait, motionless. Violet, Maria, and I sit in silence under the Rebbe's gaze.

Then: "A story," the Rebbe says. "Once there was a great king who ruled over a city. He was a just king, but his judgments were very severe and he was much feared. A man lived in that city, and he had three friends: the first he spent most of his time with; the second he was very fond of; the third was an old friend whom he hardly ever saw anymore—in wealth and position he had grown beyond that old friend. One day, the man was called to judgment by the king. He was terrified. He called upon his first favorite friend and asked that he accompany him to the judgment. His first friend said no, he would not even accompany him to the door—somebody shouldn't see them together. Disappointed, the man turned to his second friend, who said that he would walk with him as far as the king's palace, but not farther, for he was too scared. Feeling he had been betrayed by his friends, the man walked through the streets in despair. There he bumped into his half-forgotten third old friend. Why did he look so scared, the third friend asked him, and when the reason was told the friend volunteered to go right up to the royal throne and plead to the king for his mercy. So, my dears, what is the meaning of this story? The man with three friends is about to die and must face the judgment of God. The first friend is money and power, and when you die they will desert you and not even go to the door with you. The second friend is family. They will escort you, but only as far as your grave. The third friend represents your mitzvot, your good deeds. They will accompany you to God's kingdom and before God's throne and they will plead for you."

The Rebbe now focuses his gaze solely on Violet. "I tell you this because, Mrs. Finkel, you have been described to me as a person of many good deeds, and in one hundred and twenty years they will surely accompany you and protect you. But in this world, more is required of us than just good deeds. We must all serve God, each in his or her own way, yet within the framework of tradition. It can be difficult to find the way back to tradition. Maybe God is already rewarding you here in this world by helping your daughter Miriam, as we call her, to find her way to her faith. I myself had a hand in introducing her to Aaron, and I ask you to rejoice with her and to thank God that she will, but only with your permission, enter under the wedding canopy according to the laws of Moses and of Israel. Many parents must live through much sadder events."

Slowly, the rabbi's eyes move to me. He does not speak but looks at me with such sympathy that I think that in some inexplicable way he must know my concerns about Eric. Tears come to my eyes in the face of his unsolicited fellow feeling. My lips are dry, I cannot move.

He then turns to the women, "Mazel tov," he says to them, and again, "Mazel tov. It should be in a good hour, and the children should build a truly Jewish home."

The Rebbe seems suddenly to withdraw into himself, his gaze now averted. He looks exhausted, as old as his many years. His hand quivers slightly on the desktop. After a minute or two, an attendant kindly ushers Maria and me out.

After maybe ten more minutes, Violet rejoins us outside in the harsh sunlight. The busy street is filled with the Rebbe's neighbors, loud, gesticulating, very much of this world, while we are still wrapped in the spiritual warmth of what we've each experienced. Without a word we walk back to the King David. Before Violet and I go up to our rooms to pack, she tells Maria to set the date and she will be back with bells on. Maria can have the reception here at the hotel, Violet tells her: anything Maria wants.

In the elevator, I remind Violet that she is still wearing that scarf tightly wrapped around her head. I suggest that she take it off, as it must be hot.

She looks at me, but I feel I somehow have no presence. Then, touching the scarf absentmindedly, she says, "No, not yet, later."

Even though we spend the next fifteen hours in each other's company, all the way to Ben Gurion, then all the way home to JFK, and even though we are comfortable with each other, I sense a change in Violet. A distance has intruded between us; those ten minutes she spent alone with the Rebbe have drawn her not away from me, maybe, but more into herself. I shan't probe just yet. She'll need more than ten minutes to figure it all out.

12.

With great relief I walk into my apartment. I breathe in its familiar scent. My eyes rest on the walls, the furniture, and I sit down on the front hall bench. Once I feel a bit more composed, I listen to the answering machine. Charlotte welcomes me home and asks me to call. Ditto Eric. I'll take my time. I'm not yet ready for full reentry. But then the phone rings and I pick it up.

"Hi. It's Violet," she says, her voice tired, like mine.

"Hi. How are you? You sound tired."

"I'm fine," she says, then pauses. "Listen, I want to thank you for going on the trip with me. I know I can be a little rough around the edges, but you were a real gentleman, and I appreciate it."

I wait for the jab of a punch line, which, uncharacteristically for Violet, doesn't come. "My pleasure," I say. "I enjoyed every minute of it."

"Sleep well," she says and hangs up. So polite, so proper: What happened to that intimacy we enjoyed and developed in Israel? I wonder, and in my gut I realize that Violet has backed up, if not away. I feel strangely, surprisingly bereft.

In a somber mood I return Charlotte's call. We chitchat briefly about my trip, and she invites me over to her home for dinner on Saturday night, just the two of us. "That sounds delightful," I say emphatically, without convincing myself, distracted and dismayed as I am by Violet's sudden change in attitude toward me.

I then call Eric.

"Hey, Dad. How was your trip?"

"Great, great," I say. "How are you? How is everything going?"

"Things are moving ahead. I finished the layoffs, and all the bank deals are negotiated. Now we just have to wait and see how the new software develops. I am optimistic, but you never know. There isn't much time."

I'm actually more than curious about the status of his relationship with Carol. I decide to take an indirect approach. "You should take Carol to Israel—that would be a special trip for the two of you."

"Maybe in a few months," he says offhandedly, "but I can't leave now. I'm still trying to save my ass. Besides, I'm not really in the mood for a vacation."

"I see." I'm disappointed in his response, because I can't help but believe that if he went, he would share my excitement about Israel, and begin to feel more strongly about his Judaism. "I would love to see you."

"Me, too. I'm just so busy right now. Let me have Carol call you. I let her make all our plans." He chuckles.

I don't think this is the least bit funny; but I laugh with him: that my son can't figure me into his schedule on his own, though, I find nothing to chuckle about. "Well, I better run," I say.

"Yeah, Dad. Talk to you soon."

I know he's busy, I know he's working under tremendous stress to keep his one remaining company going, I know he has a fiancée now; and I know he loves me, too . . . I just wish the boy would show it every once in awhile.

Brushing aside paternal anxiety, or trying to, I call Tatiana, who should be home from work by now, and is.

"Mission accomplished," I say, straining for joviality. "I have some photos for you."

"How wonderful!" she says excitedly.

"But there is a price you have to pay for those pictures."

She is silent, perhaps confused.

"Will you have dinner with me?" I try my best to sound casual, but as her pause grows longer my confidence wanes.

"Yes," she says, finally, "I would be happy to." And by then I feel every day of sixty and deflated.

Nevertheless, I make a date for Sunday night. I will pick her up at seven.

The next few days are tough. Feeling guilty because I've been out of touch with my clients, I am determined to get back to business. My assistant gives me my messages, a stack of them, all of them apparently "urgent." The first call I return is to Dr. Boze. He's in surgery, as usual.

So I continue: I dispense advice, console the losers, celebrate with the winners, and at the same time I relive the trip to Israel and ponder the change in Violet's attitude toward me. I wince at the thought of losing her now, after we've actually begun to understand each other, not to mention become lovers. More of my mind is in Jerusalem than in New York, and I review again last Friday night, how together we felt as we walked through the quiet streets to Maria's apartment. I'm not ready to let that feeling go—that warmth, that intimacy—not without a fight.

My secretary informs me that Dr. Boze is on the line, from the O.R. Background noise, an alarming sound, like grinding, makes it difficult to hear him. "They're sawing through the bone," he yells into the phone. "Where's General Electric?"

I tell him. He doesn't hear me. More grinding; then a pause. I repeat the figure.

"Really? Down? And I was so sure of that one—Put the damn clamp on, will you," he shouts, not at me, presumably, and then he's back. "Any reason you know why I shouldn't buy some more?" he yells.

"No special reason, no news," I respond.

"Okay, I'm in a bullish mood—Wait, not that one—the femur, for Christ's sake! Stop eating and concentrate! . . . Dan, you still there? Buy five hundred shares for me, what the hell."

I execute his order. Then, before anything else distracts me, I sell two unrelated trading positions out of my own account. It's the Boze effect: He buys, I sell.

Shortly after that transaction, I receive a call from a Ben Levine, Shimmy's son. "Mr. Gelder, I have some sad news. Dad fell over dead on his couch while watching the tape." Actually Ben doesn't sound all that sad. "Nobody knew until lunchtime, when the maid brought him a sandwich."

Shimmy was only fifty-four. "What a tragedy," I say. "My condolences to you and your sister. Your father was my daily phone companion for many years. I'll miss him greatly." Then I add the obvious, "At least he died doing what he most enjoyed, watching the tape."

So the next morning I drive to Riverdale. At the funeral chapel, I find myself in a small circle of people, none of whom I know. A young woman in her late twenties and a younger man in his early twenties sit as mourners—Ben and his sister, I assume. I introduce myself to Ben, who introduces me to his sister, Rita "Le-vine," as she informs me, "not Le-veen." "I'm still a Le-veen, but my sister got fancy," Ben says as his sister gives him a baleful look. With a hint of a British accent in her speech, she asks me to visit her and Ben at home the next day—to discuss some business matters with me, she says.

Once the funeral begins, the rabbi struggles with the fact that he obviously didn't know Shimmy well, if at all, although he had officiated at Shimmy's wife's funeral some years before, as he reminds us, twice. Using the old Talmudic adage that you may judge a tree by its fruits, he then praises Rita and Ben, and, by indirection, Shimmy. In the middle of the rambling eulogy, a cell phone rings near me, and I have to suppress a smile. I could half expect Shimmy to be calling to ask, "Where's Albertson's?"

After the funeral I scoot back to the office, where my day ends with a pang, no Shimmy: I look up Albertson's price for old time's sake.

When I enter Shimmy's apartment the next afternoon, I expect to find the usual signs of a mourner's house for the week following a death. But no black drapery covers the mirrors, no mourners sit shoeless on boxes. Nor is the stock tape on the television screen, and, of course, Shimmy is not plopped down in front of it, although his blanket still lies folded on the couch.

Rita greets me pleasantly, her speech very clipped and formal. "Thanks for coming so promptly, Mr. Gelder. Ben and I are eager to sort out Daddy's stocks, which he so carefully collected over the years—his babies, his plants, he would call them, and indeed they received all his loving care."

"Yes," I say almost wistfully. "Shimmy accumulated them like any great collector. With love and care, he created his portfolio, nurtured his holdings, built each position slowly, saved and scrimped—but you must know all this."

Rita smiles wanly, then calls to her brother. "Ben, darling, do come in and join Mr. Gelder and me. Hurry, sweet."

Rita is sounding more British by the minute, so much so I find it difficult to believe she is Shimmy Levine's daughter. Still, she bears a marked family resemblance to Ben, I note, when he strolls in.

"Tea, anyone?" she asks, and when I decline, she launches into her explanation of the need for my visit. "Daddy loved his stocks, we know, but Ben and I feel that we must be practical: We have to dismantle his life's work in order to preserve our capital. Ben has just finished college, and I find my work as an assistant editor simply too trying, especially financially. I know it must seem tacky, but we've been in touch with the lawyer, and as soon as we are legally able, we would like you to sell. In short, we want cash."

"Certainly," I reply, somewhat taken aback. "I actually brought a list of Shimmy's holdings for you to review at your leisure." I hand each one a copy.

"Oh, Daddy's favorites," exclaims Rita as she runs down the list. "How often I heard him talk of them with such feeling, such passion. Life is so cruel—but they must be all sold as soon as possible."

"Well, we've got to handle them with care," I explain. "Shimmy accumulated large positions in stocks that sometimes do not trade actively, so there are considerations." I feel myself getting unreasonably angry.

"Dad was a good guy, but he was goofy about that stuff. We just want the cash," says Ben.

"You're sure about this, are you? You've thought through the long-term ramifications?" I keep thinking of Shimmy's years of hard work.

"Look," says Ben, "I loved my father, but he spent most of the last ten or fifteen years sitting here balls-naked watching the tape. We had the fastest funeral in history for Mom because it was an active market day. He missed both our graduations, and he refused to visit a doctor unless he could be seen before the market opened or after it closed, which is why he never had a stress test and never knew he had a heart condition and died. Well, there's no trading wherever he is now, and we've got all these stocks, so let's sell them and have some fun."

"You're right, I know you're right," says Rita, her voice now laced with emotion. "Well done, Ben, well done; but it hurts to sell his beloved Albertson's, his dear Renal Care, that Headway he so adored, and his darling Seven Seas. They were his passion, every share of them, Syms, and Publicard, and don't forget Ariba. Or his absolute paramour, General Electric."

Although Rita seems to be very familiar with Shimmy's holdings, she doesn't sound the least bit remorseful. "Our attorney, Gaston Schlussel of the firm of Ganz, Schlussel & O'Reilly, will be calling you when all the paperwork is ready," says Rita. "Please call me at that time, and together we'll do the deed with sadness and determination. Oh, the grief of it all." She punctuates this crescendo of emotion with a pause of the merest second, then adding, "Please send me your commission schedule — bulk sales deserve bulk rates, don't you agree? And now let me show you out."

Rita escorts me from Shimmy's apartment down the long hall to the "lift," as she insists on calling it. "Ta, ta," she says as the elevator door closes.

Standing in the elevator, shaking my head, I feel overwhelmed by weariness. There's an old Jewish saying, "Better a live dog than a dead lion," and as I ponder it and the behavior of Shimmy's daughter and son, it strikes me that with my commissions on the sale of Shimmy's portfolio, which will be good—not great, but good—at least I will be in a better position to help Eric. Fathers, sons.

By the time Saturday evening arrives, I'm more in the mood for a good book and some TV than dinner with Charlotte. Except that she's cooking, so I've got to show up. Somebody once said, I think it was Bob Hope, that ninety percent of everything is just showing up.

Charlotte's apartment—the one she has shared with Dave for over twenty-five years— an old prewar on Park Avenue, is beautiful, if decorated down to the last little detail by some lunatic, with everything matching and nothing out of place—except maybe for Dave, after twenty-five years. Charlotte looks especially pretty tonight, her dark hair piled up and pinned in back, her eyes warm and shining. The dinner is splendid, and when we are ready for our coffee, she surprises me. "Dr. A is really encouraging me to create new relationships," she says. "He feels that I am ready."

She certainly looks ready for something. Her eyes seem to brood over some unrevealed plan, her left hand drums nervously on the dining room table, her usually lovely smile looks eager, intense. "Dessert?" she asks, and gets up to get it.

Not for the first time I admire her trim figure, especially alluring in the cling of her silk pants and blouse as she moves about. Maybe it is the wine, but a certain electricity seems to charge the air. My admiration of Charlotte once, years ago, prompted Ellen to enumerate for me some of Charlotte's various plastic surgeries—an accounting that immediately cooled my ardor. By then she had had her thighs reduced, her breasts enlarged (what lovely breasts), and her belly tightened (and I wonder does the belly-button shift in such cases, to one side or the other). I hope her nose is the original; I've always liked Charlotte's nose. It flares as she places, warm from the oven, a homemade cherry pie on the table. I am filled with antici-pation, but not for the pie. When a woman in Manhattan makes a homemade anything, she is yours for the plucking.

Her face flushed, her blouse opened at the top, she fans herself with one hand. "It's warm in the kitchen," she says. "Dr. A says that it is important for me to bake; it's one of my creative outlets. I hope you like cherry." I do, indeed, and she cuts a large piece for me, but before passing it to me, licks a bit of cherry syrup from her finger. She cuts a very small piece for herself, which she delicately samples cherry by cherry, after she seats herself closely next to me.

"Dr. A says that most of the sadness I have been feeling lately stems from a lack of simple sybaritic pleasure," Charlotte says, "because suddenly I have no one to hold, to be physically close to. I'm a normal woman, after all, and I need—enjoy—the company of a man. Like tonight, a man to cook for, a man to bake for, a man to talk to." She pats my hand gently as I savor the last of my pie. "More?" she asks solicitously.

"No," I say, pointing to my paunch.

"But that's nothing at all," she says. "You've got the body of a man twenty years younger; it's extraordinary. Dr. A says that a man who keeps his manly figure is usually self-absorbed, but in your case that's certainly not true. You're so giving, so kind."

At that moment it's clear. Tonight, probably in the next few minutes, I am going to do a mitzvah and make Charlotte very happy—and me, too. There is the nagging fact that I may be betraying Dave—he is one of my oldest friends—but, hell, he's out there fooling around, so why shouldn't Charlotte? Why should poor Charlotte be denied her needs. Besides, she looks so damned sexy tonight.

"What does Dr. A think of sex between two old friends?" I ask, my reservations fading rapidly.

"Dr. A thinks that any two consenting adults should do whatever they like," she replies with great solemnity, while looking me straight in the eye.

"You have my consent and you're the only other adult in the vicinity," I say, "and just about the most beautiful woman I know." Which is true. Without another word, Charlotte takes my hand and leads me to her bedroom.

Charlotte's decorator really hit a frenzied pitch in the bedroom, and I sincerely hope I do too. But the setting is so august: green silk walls, yellow silk sheets, and the remarkable antique carved wooden canopied bed, like something carted off from the palace at Versailles. And in the midst of all this splendor—and in the presence of a collection of framed family photographs: Dave, the kids, a big black-and-white of Dave's mother, whom I knew—we undress. I don't know if I can really do this.

"Dr. A says that one should always have the lights on during sex in order to maximize the experience," she says, touching me gently with her lovely hands. I begin to respond, and we move toward the bed. "He believes in vigorous foreplay," she assures me as we lie down.

Yes, I can indeed do this.

Charlotte has propped herself against several pillows. Her expression passionate, her position suggestive, she reaches out for me. We kiss; then, slowly but with clear intent, she lowers my head to her breasts before guiding me further down. So, it's my mouth she's after: I attempt to assume the requisite position, and immediately both my right shoulder and my lower back complain. To myself, I lament the passing of the old meat-and-potatoes way—what is it anyway, these days, with oral sex—and do my best. Hurry up, I'm thinking, the pain now excruciating, hurry up, Charlotte.

On cue, Charlotte responds. Her legs flailing wildly, she exclaims, "Oh, oh, oh, oh. Yes, yes, oh, Dr. A, Dr. A, oh, Dr. A." Noisily she consummates her passion.

And I go limp. Dr. A! Void of desire, if not of pain, I consider that I've been listening to Charlotte talk about the great Dr. A all night, and now he's as good as in the bedroom with us. Well, three's a crowd, and not only that, Dave's mother is staring right at me.

I slide off to the side. "Charlotte," I say quietly. "I don't think I can go on." I choose my words carefully, as I want her to believe I'm the one with the problem.

"What happened? Are you okay?" cries Charlotte in concern.

"It's just not going to work tonight. I'm sorry. It's too soon for me, I'm not ready for this yet."

Charlotte, apologetic and slightly remorseful, watches me dress, then accompanies me to the door. For my part, I try not to hobble or stoop like an old man, although my back is killing me.

I walk home feeling peculiar, foolish, and age-inappropriate. Sixty is a bit too old to be playing at being Charlotte's sex toy. Charlotte, Susan Kleiness, Violet, Tatiana: What the hell do I think I am, an adolescent running on hormones? "You should grow like an onion with your head in the ground," my grandma used to scold me when I'd been bad. Maybe I have. I've certainly learned that if you peel an onion, it makes you cry.

13.

O n Sunday evening, out of breath, I stand at Tatiana's door, where I try to collect myself after climbing the long stairs of the walk-up. And why: Is this a date? I have still not heard from Violet since the day of our return from Israel, and I continue to worry over her sudden loss of interest in me. And yet here I am pursuing another woman. I ring Tatiana's doorbell.

A stout Russian lady, probably the co-tenant, greets me. Her gold teeth flashing, her figure sturdy, her manner welcoming, she guides me to the living room, where I am introduced to a solemn little boy. Wide-eyed, he gives me a very formal hello, and tells me his mother is just a few minutes delayed. His dark brown eyes seem to assess my every move. At a loss for conversation with a nine-year-old I do not know, I show him the photos of his aunt's family, and he confesses that he had wanted to go to Israel with them but that his mother insisted they come to New York so he could become a pianist. "Here is the capital of music in the world," he informs me, then looks again at the pictures of his young cousins and runs his fingers over the images.

An awkward silence is broken by Tatiana. Apologizing, and looking wondrous, her dress as black as her lustrous dark hair, she wears no jewelry except for a wedding ring, yet I doubt that anyone could fail to notice her in any room, in any glamorous city on the planet. A little flushed, a little diffident, she smiles—and I know I am in trouble. I know that I had better make the evening short, keep it light, leave her early, and forget we ever met before it's too late. The shabby living room of the shared apartment, the worn rugs, the solemn little boy with the mop of blonde hair, they're all wrong for me.

"Would you like to see your photos from Luba?" I hand her the packet and she shuffles through the photos quickly, voraciously.

I watch her. She can't be more than forty, forty-two. Technically, I'm old enough to be her father and Niki's grandfather, and no doubt she thinks of me in that light, so we will have a pleasant evening—and then call it quits. After a short but seemingly emotional exchange in Russian between mother and son, Niki looks unhappy but shakes my hand very formally and allows me to escort his mother to the front door. As we go down the stairs, Tatiana apologizes for her son's behavior.

"Niki can be very possessive. He hates to be left alone, even though the very nice co-tenants are at home. But he must learn," she says, but she looks like she would rather cancel our dinner and run right back up the stairs to him.

"I understand. I have a son, too," I say, trying both to ignore my misgivings and to sound supportive; nor do I particularly want to be reminded of Eric right now, either of his circumstances or our difficulties.

We are both quiet, or preoccupied, as we walk to the restaurant, but once we are seated and have ordered dinner, Tatiana becomes animated when she begins describing her new job to me. Excited, earnest, she speaks of her work for a charitable federation where, as a caseworker for Russian speakers, she must daily grapple with the problems that new immigrants encounter on their arrival here. But I find it hard to absorb her words. Her physical beauty distracts me, dizzies me: her moist lips, the way she tosses her hair away from her face, those haunting eyes of hers. Her dress reveals some of her cleavage, and the soft curves of her breasts look so smooth . . . I find myself aroused. As the words tumble from her impassioned mouth, I contemplate the variety of ways that I would like to stop them, silence her, and please myself all in one fell swoop.

When our knees touch, neither of us withdraws. "He's just four-teen," she is saying about one of her new cases, "still a little boy, and he refuses to go to school. His teeth are so misaligned he looks almost like a rabbit, and that's what they call him, the kids, Rabbit. Back in Kazakhstan it was more bearable. There many lived with such deformities because there was nothing to be done, no one had the money. But not here. For two thousand dollars his teeth can be corrected. Only where do I get him the money to pay for a cosmetic procedure when other people are actually going hungry? Yet he's afraid to leave the apartment, he's ashamed to walk in the street. I promised to find for him the money, and Thursday and Friday I spent banging my head against the bureaucratic walls of every agency that might help. To no avail. No money; not from the city, not from charity. Not for a boy with rabbit teeth. Who has money for such frills? His name is Rafael, he will be handsome when his teeth are fixed."

Tears are running down her face, but she doesn't brush them away. "I know that this is not life-and-death, but it is to him. And you should see his mother's eyes when he cries. I really thought I myself would burst into tears when I was with them. There are so many tragedies that one cannot possibly fix, certainly not with just two thousand dollars, but here's a case one could, and I feel so useless. Sorry," she adds, "I'll get used to it, that's what all the other case-workers tell me. It gets easier, they say."

Embarrassed, now she looks straight at me. "Oh my goodness," she says, "I did not mean to trouble you with all this. I talk so much, please forgive me. Tell me about your trip, about Israel. How did Luba seem to you? Is she happy, do you think?"

"Just a minute." I reach inside my jacket pocket for my card case, where I always keep two checks. "I'm going to solve Rafael's problem first. Then we'll talk."

"Oh, no, no, no. I was not asking for your money. What a fool I am! You must not think that, I will not accept your money. It is not your problem. No!" she exclaims and presses her hand down on mine. "Put back the check," she pleads. "I am a fool. I could kick myself."

"I'm writing the check," I say. "You don't understand, this moves me. When Eric was little we had big problems with his teeth; major work had to be done. I want to help, so please let me do this."

Tatiana doesn't reply. She looks down at her plate solemnly. Only when the waiter brings our salads, do her eyes meet mine, and her chest is heaving with emotion. I didn't do this properly; I botched it: I wanted to make her happy, but instead I've caused her distress.

"Look," I say, "I know you didn't mean for me to do this but I'm really happy you told me. I need all the mitzvot, I can get—and this is a double one. I make the boy happy, and I make you happy. There's no way that you are going to change my mind, so tell me how to write the check."

She cries again, and I find her facial expression difficult to read. Then, taking my left hand in both of hers, she lifts it to her mouth and kisses it. When I pull my hand away to hold down the check, I can still feel the warm aftermath. She tells me the full name of the charity.

I hand her the check. "If you kiss my hand for this good deed, what do I get for a lifesaving one? What can I expect?" I smile at her quizzically.

"You'll always get exactly what you deserve," she replies, her eyes now teasing me.

"I'd be in big trouble if I got what I deserved in this world," I tell her.

"You would never regret anything that I would reward you with, that I promise you." Her eyes sparkle with bright mischief. "No man has ever filed a complaint against me, not in the Ukraine and not here. Nor do I expect any complaints in the future." And she's outright flirting with me—not that I can take it too seriously. The old guy writes a check, she gives him a little thrill.

By the time we get to our coffee, I have managed to calm myself down a bit; the thrill has submitted to reason. Without question this woman is beautiful, and she seems to be a kind and decent woman, and God knows I'd like to take her to my bed, but what the hell do I think I'm doing? I'm old enough to be her father: What could attract her to me besides my check-writing ability. And isn't that ironic!

When Tatiana goes off to the ladies' room, I make my decision. We're going to skip this evolving calamity; I'm going to nip it in the bud. We'll walk to her home together, I'll give her a little kiss on the cheek, maybe we'll share a warm embrace, and then I send her up those unending stairs alone. I'm not climbing Mount Everest again, that's for sure. No, it's time to say bye-bye and good luck.

As we stroll toward her place she gets me talking about Ellen, about our life together, about Eric. It spills out of me. In some corner of my mind a small voice is telling me to shut up, she cannot possibly care, yet when I look at her I see concern, interest, sympathy, and I speak what's in my heart. I tell her even about my unhappiness over Eric and Carol.

"I married out," she says, "so did Luba, and yet all our children will probably turn out to be Jews. You never know what will happen. You do not know what is best."

Her words, perfectly ordinary and predictable though they are, nonetheless help me. She takes my arm, and we walk the last several blocks in comfortable silence. We say good night at the foot of the stairs, as I had decided. Is she thinking the same thing as she thanks me formally and hesitates a moment before she turns to go up the stairs? But then she turns again, and looking me squarely in the eyes, she says, "Thank you. I had a wonderful evening. Truly wonderful." Quickly then, she goes up the stairs.

All the way home I recall how wonderful it was, and how comfortably it ended, with my arm linked in hers. But not only the evening ended. I am just too old for her.

Violet still hasn't called. Our time together in Israel begins to feel more like a dream than a memory, and I continue to wonder just what happened in those ten minutes she spent alone with the Kanczuga Rebbe. It was right after she met privately with him that Violet's demeanor seemed so dramatically changed. Until then, we had been having fun; I was beginning to really like her, and I had evidently performed satisfactorily in bed. I had thought we'd continue, but . . . I decide that I'll call her. I am not ready to tiptoe off into the mist just yet.

"Oh hi, Dan," Violet says, as if we'd just spoken yesterday.

In fact, she seems pleased to hear from me, so rather than plunging into any kind of confrontation, I say instead, "Would you like to have dinner tonight? I know it's last minute—"

"I would love to," she says, cutting me off—and that sounds like the old Violet.

She chooses the restaurant, and the minute I walk in the place I hate it. Although Violet has not yet arrived, the maitre d' seats me. The food is fake fancy. The menu offers not grilled salmon, but rather *saumon en fin jus de vin balsamique* with seared arugula and honey-glazed carrots with sesame-coated *champignons*. The geographical origin of each item is proudly announced—mushrooms from Poland or orange slices from Honduras—and I am not thrilled. God knows what fertilizer they use in the Polish marshes, but I know for sure what's used in Honduras! And the prices: thirty-two dollars for sea bass, my favorite, with the Dover sole going at some astronomical "market price" yet to be revealed.

Violet arrives twenty minutes late. She looks wonderful as she crosses the restaurant. Her blonde hair is piled intricately up and fastened with a diamond clip worth probably half the current price of my apartment, and her dress is cut low enough to flaunt those breasts of hers. What does she do to make them bounce and jiggle that way? I had been there, I know the reality, but the illusion she creates is still surprisingly exciting. Before she reaches our table, she has been embraced at least four times by parties of diners and has exchanged with them little screams of greetings. She plops herself down opposite me and smiles radiantly. Her gaiety is contagious, and her rapid-fire conversation engaging, yet I can tell without question that our relationship has changed.

She prattles on—Maria, the trip, a new contribution she is contemplating to the Kanczuga Rebbe's yeshiva—and I sit there, the lame duck, for it is abundantly clear that I am history. And I'm somehow sure it's the fault of the Rebbe, who will probably be rewarded with a new building for his trouble. Meanwhile, I'm out two hundred and fifty bucks, or more, for dinner.

"I remember my Grandma Bella saying to me that not everybody with a beard is a rabbi, goats have beards too," I say jovially.

But Violet is horrified. "And just what are you implying by that?" she asks indignantly. "The truth is, with one glance the Rebbe had your number."

I don't say a word.

We're eating our main course when I finally ask her point-blank where we stand.

"We do not stand at all," she replies, "after all, we hardly know each other. What is it, maybe six weeks?"

When you are dead, you are dead. Still, I try again. "I seem to remember a certain intimacy between us, Violet, and I am not referring to the physical. We enjoyed a certain closeness, an emotional warmth, a growing understanding of each other. But after the Rebbe you seemed to change. I would like to know why. I think I am entitled to know why."

Violet's expression changes, she loosens up a little. "I can't tell you and then let you pay for dinner," she says. "It's too damned expensive here. I'll only tell you if you will let me pay."

"You are not paying. Stop with the paying, and just tell me the truth."

At that particularly inopportune moment, our waiter appears. There's no stopping his soliloquy on dessert: Crème brûlée laced with Hawaiian macadamia sauce on a nest of Washington State cherries or chocolate surprise with Chilean apricot sauce lightly sautéed with buttermilk or California pear tart with homemade walnut ice cream and wild raspberries from Provence. Violet ponders the alternatives and then chooses the tart and a cappuccino; I ponder my fate and order tea. I get more choices: "Earl Grey, Moroccan Mint, or Chinese Surprise?" the waiter asks. He vaguely disapproves of my choice of the mint but finally prances away.

"It was the Rebbe," Violet says and locks her eyes on mine. "In a few sentences he stripped away all my pretenses and bared the truth. He's a saint, he changed my life. I'm going to build him a wonderful new study hall and refurnish that little home of his, but it won't begin to pay the debt I owe him. He made me see myself with new eyes, Dan. The only good I do is cheerfully hand out Irv's money. I'm like a charity conveyor belt; the money pops up, and I hand it out. That is not a life; or if it is, it's an empty one, and I'm tired of it. I'm thinking of getting rid of my chauffeur, and I am putting away most of my jewelry in the safe. I want to spend more time with Maria, studying in Jerusalem. I have gained perspective. I feel free, wonderfully free." She takes my hand and pats it lightly, her eight-carat emerald ring cool against my fingers. "You're a wonderful man, Dan. You deserve someone who can focus entirely on you. I cannot offer that. There is a new Violet in the making, and I have to feel free to grow in any direction that I find I need. I am seriously thinking of reverting to the name I was given at birth: Vivian, it means life, the equivalent of Chaya in Hebrew. Which do you like more? I thought Vivian sounded too Brooklyn, so I became Violet. A ridiculous choice. False, false, false. You can call me Chaya from now on."

There are many things I would now like to call her, but I restrain myself. And I will wait. I know a passing phase when I see one. In a couple of months, she could be calling herself Petunia and wearing a diamond nose ring—and who knows what Maria will have decided to become; a Marigold perhaps. The apple doesn't fall far from the tree.

"The Rebbe told me a story," Violet continues, "a true story. It opened my eyes, opened my heart. There was a great holy man in Poland, his name was Reb Zusya, and people revered him not only for his learning but also for his kindness. When he was quite old and it became evident that he was dying, his disciples gathered around him. They were astonished to discover that this holiest of men was truly afraid of the judgment that he believed he would face in the next world. 'There is a Judge and there is a judgment,' Reb Zusya said, 'and I fear it.'

"'How can that be, rabbi?' asked one of his closest disciples. 'You are like Moses, our greatest teacher; what can you have to fear?'

"Reb Zusya replied, 'I'm not going to be asked whether I was as good as Moses, I'm going to be asked whether I was as good as Zusya could possibly be, and so I tremble.'

"I remember sitting in silence in that little room when the Rebbe finished the story. He did not say another word. I sat there, and wept. I don't even know who I really am anymore, and I have to find out, so I can become the best I can be. I can't do that, Dan, with you."

"Why not?" I ask, "why not with me?"

"Because you are too self-absorbed. You don't have innately generous impulses. You don't want to be a *Baal Tzedakah*, a Master of Charity, like Irv was, like I want to be. You measure everything in dollars. I don't know how much soul you have, but I think you must rebuild your spirit, Dan. Me too. That's why I'm going to study the Bible and the Talmud. What's your Hebrew name?"

"Daniel, the son of Yechiel."

"Okay," she says. "I'll add you to my prayers, Daniel, son of Yechiel." Then, she takes a bite of her tart. "Oh," she says, "you could just die from this, it is so good."

We fight over the bill, and I let her pay. To hell with her, she can deduct it from her contribution to the Rebbe. We part on friendly terms. Then I take my self-absorbed uncharitable little soul to a nearby half-empty Irish bar and have two bourbons.

14.

The telephone wakes me up the next morning. It's Charlotte. "I have an odd request, Dan," she says, her voice warm and cozy. I'm almost afraid to ask: "And that is?"

"You know how important to me you are, Dan, how meaningfully you have figured in my life—in fact, you're the only man I have ever been with other than Dave—and, well, I told Dr. A all about our evening, blow by blow. So he thinks it might be a good idea for him to meet you, to help him determine why you were the one I chose. He feels it would be useful in my therapy."

"Well, do you think that's really necessary?" I say, haltingly. I'm not at all comfortable with the idea although I have some curiosity about the guy, as it was his name Charlotte called out at her consummate moment.

"It would really mean a lot to me," Charlotte persists.

"Okay, then," I agree. What the hell?

* * *

Two days later a matronly receptionist ushers me into the office of Dr. A, a handsome man in his fifties, with an elegant mustache and black hair oiled back, shiny, he is dressed like a duke and exudes self-confidence. The room is carefully decorated but spare: soft and inviting chairs, a large leather couch, softly lit lamps, and boxes of tissues everywhere. I admire the exceptional Persian rug on the polished wooden floor.

"What a remarkable and unselfish act on your part to join me today," says Dr. A as he beckons me into a chair. When he sits down next to me, his searching eyes and powerful cologne compete for my attention. I turn down his offer of water or coffee and try my best to match the intensity of his gaze. He is testing me in some way, and I am beginning to dislike him profoundly.

"I know this is highly irregular," he says, "but both Charlotte and I want very much to understand what motivated her to make you the only man other than her husband with whom she chose to be intimate. I feel this may help me help her to resume some semblance of a normal life. Perhaps you would tell me a little about yourself."

Jealous, I think; he is jealous. It's that transference thing; he is crazy about her, and he wants to get a look at the lucky guy who bagged her, I think. So I recite the simplest biographical facts about myself, and he gives every appearance of being fascinated with my tale. I am meanwhile imagining how he and Charlotte have no doubt been dancing in circles around each other for months, both of them wanting, longing, to jump on each other. No wonder Charlotte screamed out his name, and I suddenly have this dark, irresistible urge to tell him, and I don't really try too hard to suppress it, and then I'm saying, "At the climactic moment, she shouted out your name—"

I don't finish the sentence. His eyes widened, his face very red, Dr. A is suffering from a sneezing fit: once, twice, three times, and again; pause, then another one. He swabs his face with his handkerchief, gets up and goes to the window, holds onto the windowsill, sneezes at least five or six more times. I stopped saying "God bless you" after number three, and now we're both waiting to see whether he has finished. "Sorry," he says. "I cannot imagine what . . . what . . ." Again, a powerful sneeze, and this time a little blood trickles out of one nostril. "Shit," he says, "these damned allergies are ruining my life." They are also ruining his shirt collar; more blood comes dripping out. I begin to wonder whether Dr. A's attack might be more than coincidental—maybe he is allergic to my climbing Mount Charlotte.

He sits down with his head arched backward, handkerchief pressed to his nose. I cannot resist, I want to see what happens—that Rebbe was right about me, this is not nice—but if my experience with Charlotte prostrates him like this, how, I can't help wondering, will this nut job react to my encounter with Tim? It could prompt even more unattractive symptoms; better perhaps to leave him alone.

"Maybe it's the aftershave you are using," he says accusingly while he himself is reeking of cologne.

Though annoyed, I put a muzzle on it and suggest that maybe I should go. "No, no," he says. "Just give me a minute. I'll move away from you."

That does it. "Well, there is one other thing I probably should tell," I begin with devilish delight. "It's just a side issue, and I don't know that it has anything really to do with Charlotte. But her husband's lover—Tim—tried to seduce me. I guess that wouldn't pertain to Charlotte."

He straightens his head; his eyes hard and hot, his finger pointing at me, he rants, "Charlotte, Tim. What about Dave? Why leave out Dave? What are you doing? Stalking them? You won't be satisfied till you sleep with each of them? Are you lying now in ambush for Dave?" His nosebleed resumes in earnest. "Get the nurse," he says, "get the damned nurse in here. This blood is ruining my tie. My Ricci tie!"

The nurse handles him coolly, expertly. This is obviously not the first time for them, but for me it is definitely the last. Feeling guilty but exhilarated, I walk quietly out of Dr. A's office. If Dave ever should try to jump me, this guy will pop his lid: They will have to carry him out. I wonder at the absurdity of my own behavior, and at the intensity of my dislike for Dr. A. I probably need a psychiatrist of my own, a Dr. B. I should be ashamed of myself. But I am still giggling when I get home.

15.

That evening, I am reading in my favorite chair, when the phone rings. It is Carol, her voice lilting and anxious to please.

"Hi, Dan. Am I interrupting?"

"No, no. How are you, Carol?"

"Great. I've been busy reading all these Jewish books, and I find them fascinating—such history. I'm actually driving Eric crazy with my enthusiasm," she says, laughing.

"I see." A neutral response; for I don't care to discuss Eric's enthusiasm—or his lack thereof—with Carol.

"We've started thinking about our wedding, and I was wondering if you might be able to help me find a rabbi. I thought it would be nice if a rabbi officiated, as well as a minister. What do you think?"

I think she would not want to know what I think, but I say, "Of course. I can call Rabbi Granite; he presided over Ellen's funeral. I have had only occasional contact over the years, but I am sure I can book an appointment for the three of us. How soon do you want this to happen?"

"As soon as possible. Can you do it early next week?"

"Let me see what the rabbi's availability is like—I will get back to you."

"Great. You can call me at Eric's."

"I see."

When I hang up, I call Rabbi Granite's office. Lucky for Carol, he is available on Monday morning.

The rabbi receives us in his book-lined office. He is a formal man trying to be friendly. Obviously, this is not the first time he has dealt with a pending interfaith marriage, and his eyes are sympathetic when he glances at me, shrewd as he assesses the young people. He listens to Carol and Eric without interruption, and when he fully understands the situation he speaks in an authoritative voice.

"First of all, I want to wish you all the best, and I hope, Carol, that you will continue to learn about our religion. I invite you to call upon me and upon our synagogue with any questions you might have. You must understand, however, that I am unable to perform your marriage ceremony, because, as a rabbi associated with the Conservative movement, I do not officiate at interfaith ceremonies; nor, of course, would an Orthodox rabbi. Some Reform rabbis might, and there are a number of interfaith ministers who mix and match the various religious traditions. Whatever you choose, we hope you will begin to attend our services, you and Eric, and that you will join our congregational family."

"That's that?" asks Eric.

"Unless, of course, Carol would like to convert. But that takes time, and you would need to delay your marriage until she completes the process."

"How long?" asks Carol.

"That depends. But usually around a year."

Eric looks at Carol and says quickly, "We don't have that kind of time."

The rabbi gives me a sympathetic, almost conspiratorial, glance, but I keep my expression blank.

Eric and Carol look at each other, realizing they are being politely dismissed, and in a gesture of love and support Eric squeezes Carol's hand. "Well, thank you for your time, Rabbi," Eric says respectfully, extending his hand.

When we get outside in the street, Eric suggests we forget about contacting another real rabbi, and Carol comes up with an alternative proposal. "A friend of mine used an interfaith reverend named Kugelmass. I actually have his number and address with me. Should I call?" asks Carol, so well prepared that I wonder if the visit to the rabbi wasn't a mere gesture and now we'll pursue what she's really after.

"Yes, why don't we get Kugelmass to do it," Eric agrees. "I'll call and make the appointment now while we are all together. Maybe we'll get lucky."

And we do. An hour later, we are seated in the living room of Reverend Kugelmass's Upper West Side apartment. Religious artifacts of all sorts adorn the walls and on the tables. What appear to be metallic Hindu gods mingle with olive wood statues of Jesus bearing his cross while several menorahs share table space with a small Buddha and books of scriptures in several languages. A very pleasant Mrs. Kugelmass serves us tea. She tells us that her husband, the Reverend, as she calls him, will be with us momentarily, and we meanwhile learn that she too is an interfaith minister. Her background is Methodist—she and Carol can compare notes—but she willingly incorporates into a marriage ceremony whatever traditions wedding couples desire. "I love the Jewish custom of the groom smashing a glass with his foot at the end of the ceremony," she says, "and I always try to convince my couples to do that, no matter what backgrounds they have. It's just so wonderfully final, and everybody loves it."

On that note, Reverend Kugelmass enters. A tall man, smiling, his hair wrapped around his head in a disconcertingly unruffled way—either he's wearing a terrible hairpiece or attempting to cover a large bald spot—he is effusive. "Welcome, welcome," he says as he joins us. "Tell me all about your forthcoming wedding and how I can be of service."

Comfortable in this receptive atmosphere, Carol does most of the talking. I myself am riveted by his hair, which, I finally decide, is real and is indeed covering a bald spot—had he been a rabbi, a skullcap could have saved him a lot of trouble after every shower.

"What I love most about my work is that each couple calls for something very special, very individual," Kugelmass enthuses, "and I tailor the ceremony to their needs. We could begin with any sort of processional you want, but I would suggest you have a Jewish wedding canopy, a chuppah, for a nostalgic touch. We can intermingle traditional Methodist and Jewish prayers, and then, just to please my Letitia here"—and he pats Mrs. Kugelmass's shoulder—"Eric could break the glass. By the way, will we be indoors or outdoors?" Carol explains that the venue has not yet been chosen. "Well, if it is outdoors," Kugelmass says, "I would suggest doves."

"Doves?" I ask.

"Doves," he says. "They are so ecumenical, everybody loves a dove. Remember Noah's ark? Doves are symbols of peace, and they transcend all traditions. White ones would be particularly appropriate, maybe two dozen of them to be released the moment that Eric steps on the glass. No tent, though—they can get caught in the tent and hurt themselves. And it's only one thousand dollars for twenty-four doves, keeper and all. A small cost for such a dramatic moment."

Letitia Kugelmass agrees. "It's such a lovely way to say peace, peace to all, near and far. And it so heightens the spiritual experience of the ceremony. Most of the doves do return to the keeper's dovecote, by the way, so you don't have to worry about them flying all alone out in the wild. It is really quite spiritual."

"Do we get a discount for doves that return?" I ask. "The keeper can reuse them, after all."

Letitia gives me a sweetly disapproving look. "I feel so sorry for those that fly off," she says, "you just know they're going to be gobbled up by some predator. And no, there is no discount."

Kugelmass is now quite excited. "I cannot wait to help you plan this happy event, for I truly love each young couple who comes our way. Unfortunately, I do have to impose a small fee for my services, but, believe me, you will get our sincere and individual attention. There are so many details to be ironed out: yes or no to skullcaps, prayers in Hebrew or English, what kind of music. Letitia especially loves an ancient Confucian chant, which adds luster to any service, and I like bouncy Jewish music to accompany the doves as they are let loose. It makes for quite a finale."

Thoroughly enjoying his vision of the event, he absentmindedly tugs at his hair (clearly it must be his). "I simply can't wait. Just set the date and the venue, and I'm all yours," he says, spreading his arms in an airborne embrace.

Eric's face is unreadably blank. Carol seems to be entranced. I am ready to go, the thought of twenty-four doves shitting above the assembled guests is too much to bear. I'd pay a thousand dollars to make sure that no birds whatsoever flew overhead—have a hunter to shoot any of the damned things that came near.

We bid our warm good-byes to the Kugelmasses. Quiet, we wait for the elevator. It arrives; we quietly step inside. And Eric bends over, his face red, bursting with laughter.

"The fucking doves," he says, "and that guy's hair-mop. Oh God, oh God! I can see Aunt Esther running in horror from the birds. I can see dove dung splattering over the chopped liver. I can see the look of shock on everybody's face when the band breaks into an ancient Confucian chant." He has straightened up, but tears of hard laughter are streaming down his cheeks. "I thought I'd fucking burst in there. Oh God, did you notice Kugelmass's hair? He must use Crazy Glue."

"One of those doves got stuck in his hair, it'd carry him away," I add.

"Only to bring him back to the keeper," Eric reminds me. By the time we get to the lobby both of us are out of control. Carol, standing between us, is a little embarrassed.

"I thought he was sweet," she says, and sends both of us into fresh paroxysms of laughter. You can see she's thinking maybe this is some kind of Jewish joke, as she watches us both trying to catch our breath.

"Okay, I agree: no Kugelmass," says Carol, and we greet her decision with applause.

"That guy would marry you to a snake," Eric says. "Come on, Carol, you can't have been serious."

"All right," she concedes, "he's a little peculiar, but I thought they were a sweet couple. Still, if it's no Kugelmass, it's no Kugelmass."

On that note, I leave them. As I stroll home, I don't know whether to laugh or to cry: Maybe there is still time for Eric to change his mind. Then, smiling, I recall the two of us laughing together in the elevator. I'd not felt so close to Eric, so at one with him, in a long time. A good sign.

16.

S ince returning from Israel, I have turned down two dinner invitations from Evelyn and Bob, the couple who introduced me to Violet. I surmise that their persistence can only mean they're aware that Violet is not interested in me and they are trying to find her replacement. When Evelyn calls a third time, I realize I have run out of excuses.

"I promise—it's only your company that is wanted. There will be no potentially significant other invited, just three married couples and a woman named Myra Forshpise whose husband Billy is away on a business trip. I need another man at the table," Evelyn entreats, and I agree, but reluctantly.

I am not really in the mood for a dinner party. Rabbi Granite's decision not to marry Carol and Eric continues to bother me. I understand his position, of course, but that doesn't diminish the hurt. I'd like to feel that I was able to suggest to Eric that Carol consider converting, but worry that such a tactic would be too bold, too intrusive of me. Yet a part of me can't let go of the fantasy that Carol's newfound enthusiasm for Judaism might ultimately persuade her to convert. Is that asking too much?

I'm asking myself the same question as I arrive at Evelyn and Bob's. I feel distracted. My life has suddenly become a total mess: Violet has disappeared, and Eric may as well have disappeared — and I am faced with the onerous task of being sociable and polite. A quick glance around the living room tells me that I know everyone except the tall woman, probably in her middle fifties, with long black hair that's streaked with gray. Myra, presumably. Her strong face and prominent nose add to her decidedly regal air. Her long, thin fingers are bedecked with Native American rings, while bracelets, some of them turquoise and about the size of handcuffs, clatter around her wrists and over her hands. She is wearing no makeup, although clearly she doesn't need any. Her big dark eyes flash dramatically, and I am attracted to her.

Evelyn has told me that Myra travels extensively since she is actively involved as a volunteer in human rights work. That should provide me with enough ground to explore in conversation with Myra to get us through most of the bloody evening.

After we are seated, I turn to Myra, sitting silent and composed next to me, and say, "Myra, tell me how you started in your field," as I start in on the endive and avocado salad.

"All my life, since my teens, I have been driven by the need to involve myself in helping others," Myra answers with a surprising depth of feeling. "I was blessed to come across two organizations, both of which have commanded my attention and energies for years. One is the Friends of the Guyutera & Tagalu Indians, while the other attempts to make chums of Israelis and Palestinians. We take them on trips, we subsidize clubs for them. We try to help them rise above their narrow tribalizing and build human bridges." She pauses, as if to hold back tears over the futilities in the Middle East. "The Indians, though, are so charming, so unspoiled. They live near the Amazon and run about in little skirts of leaves. Of course, they're unhampered by any of our Judeo-Christian neuroses, so sex is simply natural, like death. Nobody makes a fuss about either. They are really quite admirable. We have brought two or three of them to New York, but they simply cannot bear being here. Then, too, their habit of urinating and defecating whenever they need to and wherever they happen to be makes a visit to the city difficult. I had one stay with me for several nights, until my maid threatened to quit; so I had to send him packing. The lack of bathroom training, it rather annoyed her."

I laugh appreciatively. Myra, however, is not laughing with me.

During the main course of veal and sautéed spinach, I try to sanitize the conversation. "I just got back from a trip to Israel, which I loved," I say casually.

"Oh, how could you go there?" she asks. "They are oppressing the poor Palestinians! I am so ashamed that I was born Jewish when I see Jews acting like everyone else, taking advantage of those benighted souls. I hope you at least went into the Palestinian towns, bought some of their olive wood products or their embroidery. They need the business. We are told that tourism is down sharply."

"It isn't safe to go into the Arab areas, they hate Americans. Tourism is down, but it's down because of their terrorism, and I, by the way, can live without embroidery. I'm really quite taken aback by your position —"

"I am a universalist. I hold to no particular religion. If anything, I follow the ways of Gandhi with a little Martin Luther King mixed in. One has to sympathize with the Palestinians; they do these nasty things you call terrorism because America and Israel humiliate them. We are not sensitive to their feelings. We should buy more of their products: If they made a decent living, they wouldn't be quite so willing to blow themselves up, would they? It's all our fault—which is why I have made efforts to befriend Palestinians studying here and to show them that I find much to admire in their culture."

Her diatribe spurs her appetite. She devours her dessert of chocolate mousse, then looks longingly at mine, untouched on my plate. I wonder if there is any truth in the old adage that women who eat with gusto have sex with gusto. Maybe she is telepathic, because at that very moment Myra asks me to escort her home. Her husband is away, and this way she would feel safer, she says, as she rests her hand on my arm, and for the first time this evening she looks at me flirtatiously. Despite the intensity of her diatribe and her ailing sense of humor, I am again finding Myra very appealing, as I did when I first saw her across the room. Perhaps it is the strength of her personality, all that regal presumption; or perhaps it is merely the challenge of putting such a forceful, dominant woman in her place. I'm not sure, but I am intrigued.

As we stroll up Park Avenue, Myra talks earnestly about the rights of women, and when we pass two bag people bedding down for the night in the doorway to a doctor's office, she speaks passionately on the rights of the homeless.

"And what about the rights of men?" I ask teasingly.

"They have the right to orgasm just as much as women."

"The right to orgasm?" I ask. "Old guys, too? Me, too?"

"Listen, my husband is away, but even if he were here, he and I have an understanding—neither of us wants to be bound by any artificial barrier to free expression. If you want to come up, we'll have sex." Then, without blinking, she asks, "By the way, are you big?"

"Big?" I repeat, not really knowing the answer. "Nobody has ever complained."

"Good," she says, "a woman has the right to be satisfied, and I cannot have an orgasm with a little penis. It's a pity, really, because it is so limiting, but I do need length."

"Well, I can't prove anything on Park Avenue," I say. So we go up to her apartment.

"Are you quite fresh," she asks, "or would you like to wash up?"

I choose to wash up. In the bathroom, I strip and take a good look at myself in the mirror: I would not call it long, but it's certainly not short. I open the door and, holding in my gut to the best of my ability, present myself for inspection. Myra looks me over, then continues to undress, so I suppose I have passed muster. She steps out of her clothes. Her body is long and lean, her hair tumbles over her naked shoulders. She lies down on the bed and beckons to me. She is alluring.

I am ready. I climb on top of her; I start kissing her, caressing her, exploring her, and she responds ferociously. She grabs my private parts, with a practiced hand slips a condom on my penis, flipping me over in the process. Pushing me down on my back, she straddles me. Her eyes closed, she begins to press down on me, and soon her vigorous ride is harrowing my lower back. The pain gets worse. I try to move her off me.

"Not yet," she gasps, "not yet."

"My back," I groan. "You're hurting my back. Get off, please, you're killing me."

"Just another minute. I'm almost there. Just hang in there, just a minute, I need it, I need it." She pounds away as I pull away, shrinking, the pain overtaking the pleasure.

"Sorry," I say. "It was a bad position, my back is killing me."

"We can assume another position."

"Not tonight. I've got to take care of that pain or I'll be in trouble."

"What about my orgasm?" she says. "You cannot leave me like this; it's wrong. Rest a little, and then we'll finish what you started."

"Look, I'm in pain. My only hope is to put no pressure on my back. Maybe it will ease up. I'm not finishing anything tonight."

"Extremely selfish of you," she says. "There are other means—you can satisfy me with your mouth, your hands. I have the right to an orgasm. How can you be so selfish? Lie still and use your hand, that won't hurt your back. Why should I suffer because you have a bad back?"

I can no longer argue. I surrender my left hand, which she takes in both of hers and uses to satisfy herself. As I lie there otherwise motionless, I wonder how Gandhi or Martin Luther King would have handled this situation and whether my refusal to actively participate constitutes passive resistance. It takes some while for her to realize her right to orgasm, and when she finally does, she collapses on top of me, sending pain down my back and legs, and I yell "Shit!" as she roars with pleasure.

Slowly, carefully, I extricate myself. I limp toward my clothes. In agony, I dress myself. Our eyes meet as I'm putting on my shoes.

"I don't suppose you would like to try again some time," Myra says.

"No, once mauled, I usually choose not to return to the scene of the assault. It's my right to life and limb that I am exercising," I say more than a bit angrily.

She laughs but I am not joking. The next time she wants a finger or two, she can use her own.

"I'll wait for you," she says confidently. "Next time wear your back brace."

"The fish waits while the master baits," I quote to her. "It's an old saying those Amazon Indians might appreciate, or maybe even the Palestinians. And by the way, if you ever come across a single Palestinian, or Amazonian, who sits up nights worrying about Jewish rights, let me know—I'd like to meet him." With that and a shred or two of dignity, I limp out of Myra's apartment. I've got loads of sympathy for her next victim, whoever he may be.

For three days, my back strapped up, I nurse my wounds. Relishing a slew of politically incorrect thoughts about Myra, I limp about my life. On the evening of the third day I unstrap and cautiously stroll over to a political fund-raiser for Democratic Congressman Rob Dodge at Evelyn and Bob's place. I'm planning to spend not more than an hour at this must-show event, but when I arrive among the fifty or sixty people milling about with drinks in hand, the congressman is about to speak. Though he represents a district in Ohio with few Jews and lots of farmland, he has national aspirations, espouses various liberal views, staunchly supports Israel, and constantly appears at New York functions.

As I circulate among many acquaintances I am shocked when I see Tim Wells standing with the congressman. We greet each other warmly, and Tim introduces me to Dodge with an air proprietary enough for me to realize that Tim is more than just a political devotee—that he and Dodge are here together. I manage to pry Tim loose and ask him in confidence, "What's happening? Where's Dave?"

"It's over with Dave. I'm on to new and exotic haunts."

"What, Dodge? That's exotic? Ohio is maybe more exotic than Idaho, but don't get carried away."

"No, no, not Dodge. You see that darkish young fellow with him, his aide? He's a Pawnee Indian with something rather marvelous like

Haitian or Creole mixed in. He drives me crazy, which is not a big trip for me. Look at those eyelashes. Look at those teeth when he smiles. I've become a Democrat after a lifetime as a Republican."

"How did Dave take it?"

"He's back with good old Charlotte. She waited like a lapdog, and when he snapped his fingers, bingo, back she came. She's probably never had any man other than Dave, and that alone is reason enough to sympathize with her. I hear that she introduced you to her Dr. A; she says that you insulted him in some way. Evidently, he had to have his nostrils cauterized after meeting you. Did you punch him?"

"Not at all. We had what seemed to me a very pleasant conversation, but he was apparently allergic to me—couldn't stop sneezing."

"What he needs is a night with my Pawnee. That would take his mind off his nose for sure."

"Was there ever anything between you and the good doctor?" I probe.

"Yes, but it was just a one-night stand." He regrets the response the minute he says it.

"Like we might have been," I say jovially.

"Yeah, but the good doctor took his pants off." We both laugh. "By the way, he has to dye that shoeshine black hair of his, because his pubes are gray. People should be more discerning with hair dye, don't you think? It brings one up quite short to discover such inconsistencies. Rather deceptive, I think."

A waitress offers us little smoked salmon canapés on a silver tray, and when I glance up I find myself eye to eye with Tatiana, in a black and white uniform, with a frivolous little white cloth tiara on her head. "Napkin?" she asks and I take one, I place the canapé on it, I look at her helplessly. She is out of context, and not just because I am standing here with a guy who tried to have sex with me. Do I introduce them? Do I greet her? She looks startled and lost. "Hello," I finally say. "Tim, this is my friend Tatiana . . . I suppose you are working here tonight," I blurt out stupidly.

She blushes. "Yes, I frequently take such extra work. Please forgive me, but I must move on. Nice to see you, Dan; nice to meet you, Tim."

She leaves silence in her wake until Tim squeezes my arm and asks, "Somebody you've been boffing? Should I be jealous?"

"Not as long as you have your Pawnee."

"I hope you take off your pants for her."

"I wouldn't mind, believe me."

"Well, I've got to go and collect my Big Chief. I've got very specific plans for him this evening." And off he drifts.

More than ready to leave, I wonder if I should say good-bye to Tatiana or just scoot out: what is the etiquette? I hesitate long enough to see Susan entering the apartment. Definitely, she makes one too many, and I work my way to the exit. While I'm waiting for the elevator in the hall, Susan pokes her head out of the door and waves at me, a sweet smile on her face.

"Good to see you, Susan," I say, trying to sound casual. "I've got to go."

"Take care!"

I feel a bit stupid, but I console myself with the thought that busy as I was dodging Tatiana and avoiding Susan, not to mention sparring with Tim, at least I did not think about my back once.

All the way home, I continue to think about Tatiana, though: her smile, those blushes, even that silly little white thing on her head. Even in that getup, she outshone all the other women there. Just what I need, a woman poor as a synagogue mouse plus her boy to raise. I've already raised one, and what a pleasure Eric has been. I doubt I could ever be so lucky again, or even want to be. I've got to forget about this Tatiana and her son. It's not fair to any of us.

As if to reinforce that conviction, Eric calls as I am getting undressed.

"What's up?" I ask.

"The banker is expecting payment the day after tomorrow, only there is no money. The software people seem to eat money."

"Do you need me to help?" I ask quietly.

"No," he says unconvincingly.

But I ask again. "Eric, are you sure you don't need anything?"

"Well. Would you have one hundred thousand? It would be a loan—I promise—I will repay it as soon as I collect on my first batch of receivables."

"Yes. Of course. Let me see what I can do. When do you need it?"

"As soon as possible."

I try to sound enthusiastic, but in reality, I am a bit nervous. Where am I going to get a hundred thousand? I've got the commissions from selling Shimmy Levine's portfolio for those nasty kids of his, but that didn't amount to much—maybe thirty or forty thousand. Eric is my only son. So why shouldn't he keep me working into my dotage to help him pay his debts? Sounds fair; it's better than retiring and playing golf, probably. Stick a broom up my ass and I can sweep up as I walk around, earn a few extra bucks to give him. Or I can take a night job. One thing is for sure, I won't die of boredom.

17.

The next morning I go to Ellen's dresser. I take out her jewelry box. Enough with the emotional bullshit, I need money for my boy. Why should I eat into capital when I can cash in the family jewels, which are doing no one any good laid away unused? I open up the box.

There are her pearls with her mother's diamond clasp; here, her engagement ring and her wedding band: those stay put, not for sale. I take out her diamond watch—we bought it in Geneva on one of our trips—and a pair of diamond earrings purchased in the duty-free shop at Ben Gurion Airport. I set them aside, on top of the dresser, and add two Van Cleef and Arpels pins that we bought when I made my first big hit in the market. And an elaborate Cartier bracelet, it's how I wished her a happy twenty-fifth anniversary. No tears, no emotion; she's dead, and Eric needs help. I know I have her permission.

But where do I sell these things? I am not calling Violet, or Chaya or whatever she's calling herself now, and I doubt that Charlotte is happy with me at present, as I have insulted her demigod. Myra, you can be sure, only buys from indigenous tribes, and Susan would know more about cookies. And I don't want Evelyn or Judy or any of Ellen's friends to know that I am doing this. Then I think of Tim— guys like that would know. So I call him.

Tim's dear friend Moshe Gorlick, I find out, is a jeweler on Madison Avenue. Of course, he doesn't use his real name. His shop is called Montague Garfield, as is he. Just say that I am Tim's friend, and I will be treated like family, Tim assures me.

An hour later I am alone with Montague in his shop, its walls and counters everywhere displaying the real thing. Montague looks like he might wear some of this stuff when he's alone; he caresses the pieces of jewelry in front of him, only half jokingly calls them "my children." He holds Ellen's earrings up to his ears and moves his head from side to side while peering into a mirror; he looks quite pleased. He is moderately enthusiastic about the pins, but he loves the bracelet from Cartier. He lays it on his own wrist, his eyes register his delight. He is a chubby man in his fifties, his hair blonde although his complexion is dark; he has a handsome face grown jowly.

"Tim told me about your wife. I'm so sorry. This must be difficult for you." He takes one of my hands in both of his. "But I promise you I will help you. You are in good hands." Literally.

The bell at the door announces a customer. "Oh, please bear with me—have you time?" he implores. I nod my assent, and he buzzes the door.

A short older lady, built like a Samurai wrestler and strapped into an expensive suit, waddles into the shop in a blaze of gold jewelry. Her manner is familiar. "Moshele," she says, "it's my birthday and

Murray said to come here and do him some damage and you and I are going to do just that. I'm in the mood for colored stones as soon as you are finished with this gentleman." She nods toward me. "Take out the trays, Moshele, and let's have some fun."

Montague looks at me inquiringly; he wants to be accommodating, but he smells cash. I tell them both to take their time, I'm in no rush. A grateful Montague waves his finger at me, after having kissed its tip, and then takes out five trays of jewelry set with rubies, sapphires, emeralds, and who knows what else. But no diamonds.

"Colored, I want colored," the birthday girl is declaring. "Up to fifty thousand Murray said, so fifty to sixty is all right, but not the listed price, Moshele; the real one, the Murray-and-Sheila price. The price only twice what you paid, you little goniff."

"Sheila, Sheila, with customers like you I'll starve. I'll have to leave Madison Avenue and go back to Brooklyn if I don't make a little profit, I pay one dollar, I sell for two dollars; I make my one per cent profit and I pay the rent."

They begin to examine the jewelry, piece by piece, and Sheila says, "I've always liked rubies, but I'm not sure the colors are good for me. Maybe I'm too old, too faded for rubies."

Montague demurs. "Sheila, there is no age limit for rubies. You are young in spirit, and rubies enhance your spirit."

"I don't feel comfortable in them, Moshele," she complains as she tries on earrings and necklaces. "They overwhelm me."

"Try the blue tray; sapphires are ageless. Look, here are museum-quality pieces with sapphire, chalcedony, and diamonds—a trio of color and light, a fitting tribute to Murray's love for you."

"But Moshele, Moshele, my eyes are green not blue. Besides which, I want no diamonds, as I keep telling you, just colored, that's all. I want something mysterious, fabulous, something to turn my friends green with envy. I think I'm in the mood for emeralds."

"Sheila, your wish is my command, your wish is my pleasure. Don't even trouble yourself to sort through the emeralds; I've got the one for you, the only one for you. It's still in my safe, not even on display yet—you know how attached I get to the best pieces. It was made in Paris over one hundred years ago, but it was made for you, only for you."

Montague goes to the safe, opens it, takes out an emerald bracelet, and hands it reverently to Sheila. She gasps with pleasure. Holding the wide emerald bracelet up to the light, she exclaims, "I love it! I love it! It's beautiful. My eyes, it brings out the color of my eyes. And it's pavé, I love pavé. Moshele, you're a genius, a maestro."

"I love it, too," says Montague. "Pavé is my favorite for emeralds, none of that nasty platinum showing. Just wall-to-wall green, sparkling green, like your eyes, Sheila. My God, how can I part with it? Only for you, Sheila, only for you."

"What do you think?" Sheila says, waving the pavé emerald bracelet in my direction. "You look like a man of taste. Do you like?"

"Pavé," I say, "very nice pavé." Whatever pavé is.

"It's mine. How much, Moshele? How much? Have mercy on Murray—he works for every dime, he works like a horse. Don't be cruel, how much?"

"It cost me thirty-two thousand—for you, forty thousand; for anyone else, fifty. On my mother's grave, just for you, forty. And I have earrings the exact same shade of green, the same quality also. Earrings to die for, or better yet, to live for; earrings for a queen."

"No," says Sheila. "Murray will kill me if I get two things. One thing up to fifty I can do, but two things, even if they come to less,

he'll think I'm a pig. Anything with the same color, a little more sub-
stantial, closer to fifty?"

"Only with diamonds. Emeralds and diamonds together are
wonderful."

"No, colored is what I want, just colored. And I love this
bracelet. I'll take it for thirty-eight thousand; with the tax that's
about forty. Moshele, be a sport here. I'm a sport, you be a sport.
I'll be back for those earrings, you know that. It's only a question of
time. Thirty-eight."

"You're killing me, Sheila, but I can't say no to you. This bracelet
belongs on you, it's a match! Wear it in good health. Thirty-nine."

"Thirty-eight-five." Sheila pleads, "Say yes, say yes."

"Yes, yes," says Montague. "I surrender," he adds with feeling.

Sheila puts on the bracelet. She and Montague embrace and kiss.
"Maestro," she compliments him, her voice trembling with great
affection. "Maestro."

Then she turns to me and says, "Thanks for your help." And she
leaves.

No check passes hands, no bill is drawn up. The transaction is
totally verbal. As if reading my mind, Montague says, "She's in here
at least seven or eight times a year, one of my regulars. A lovely lady.
Of course, she's built like a Mack truck, but that just gives her more
room on which to put jewelry. Did you see those shoulders, like a
linebacker?"

Returning his attention to Ellen's jewelry and our business, he
takes my hand in one of his. "Trust me," he says. "I'm going to
make this easy for you. Let me figure it out." He handles each piece
carefully, again and again, does some quick calculation in his head,
deliberates a moment, and then says forty to me.

"Forty?" I say, disappointed.

Montague grimaces. "I'm too soft," he says. "I may have to hold these pieces for a year, maybe two. All right, because of Tim: forty-two. I can't do better, believe me."

I nod my assent. "Good," he says, "you've done well." He is again holding my hand. "Just how good a friend of Tim *are* you?" he asks, his look curious, almost intimate.

"A new friend," I reply. A little confused, he tilts his head at my answer, but he presses me no further.

Minutes later, check in hand, I say good-bye, go straight to the bank, deposit Montague's check, and write one of my own in the amount of one hundred thousand for my boy. I then go over to Eric's apartment, where he is waiting for me.

"I hope this helps." I hand him the check. "But I've got to ask: Do you really think you'll get the software ready in time?"

"Yes. These guys are fantastic. Expensive but worth it. You'll see. Thanks so much," he says, hugging me. "Oh, I have some news. Carol and I have set a date for the wedding."

"You have? Did you find a rabbi?"

"Well, that's the thing. We've decided to get married by a justice of the peace." Eric pauses. I gulp for air, not able to say anything.

"After the Kugelmass fiasco," Eric continues, "Carol and I interviewed two other rabbis who sometimes officiate at mixed marriages, but they were, well, too un-Jewish, I guess. Anyway, why spend the money on a wedding when things are so tight now? We decided to keep everything simple: It's only going to be you, Carol's parents, and Della."

"I see. You seem to have everything all arranged."

"Yes. So you will come on the twentieth of June?"

"Of course, of course," I mumble. "Well, I better get back to the office."

"One more thing, Dad."

What now? I think. Sometimes it seems to me that *nachas*, that shopworn Yiddish word for the pleasure you get from children, is just the temporary cessation of worry and aggravation that you get from time to time as a parent; then you go back to pain and suffering as usual.

"Passover is coming up, and I really want Carol to experience a Seder—she really wants to experience it. Maybe we can go to a communal Seder at a synagogue?"

"What about one at home? Your mother always celebrated at home," I say plaintively.

"Whatever, Dad," says Eric, answering his cell phone, already on to the next thing.

When Ellen was alive we had big Seders at home, with many guests, and there were always children at the table. This will be the third Passover without her. Last year, just Eric and I sat down and tried our best. Della cooked the traditional foods, and we read the parts of the Haggadah recounting the Exodus from Egypt, but in the end we were sorry that we had turned down the invitations we had received. Still, I find the idea of making our own Seder with guests—and not just Carol—an appealing one.

Ellen died three weeks before Passover. All through the winter and into the spring she slowly faded away, her ability to fight off the cancer diminishing steadily, until it became a waiting game. At least she suffered very little pain, thank God for that. When finally the end did come, so did a palpable sense of relief along with all the other, more piercing emotions. Ellen very much on my mind, I change my afternoon plans.

Instead of returning to work, I get my car out of the garage and head out to the cemetery far out on the Long Island Expressway. It's not that I usually feel any closer to Ellen when I stand at her grave, or to my parents, who are buried right next to her; sometimes I simply feel the need to go.

At the cemetery, I pass three funeral corteges, three new permanent guests, before I drive onto the fortunately quiet Machpela Road, corner of Abarbanel, where our family plot is situated. I have forgotten to bring a prayer book, so I mouth what I can remember of the memorial prayer as I stand before the three graves. Then I search for three stones, one for each of the graves, in observance of an ancient rite symbolizing the acceptance of God's will. As I place the stones on the graves I find the primitive custom powerful and comforting, and I remember my parents doing the same thing a half century ago when we visited my grandparents' graves in the cemetery in Brooklyn. I remember the cemetery, too, its jumble of mausoleums and gravestones in all sorts of sizes and shapes reflecting the different tastes of all the families. Here all graves are the same—the modern minimalist look, no character, boring.

I have done what I came to do, but I linger. I am not yet ready to leave Ellen, I feel physically connected to this spot. It's irrational, perhaps, but something seems to be holding me in place—that needs to be said. Stupid to speak to the dead, embarrassing; nonetheless, I do. "It's not my fault, Ellen; it's not my fault about Eric. I don't know what to do. Mom, Dad, I don't know what to do. He's going to marry her no matter what I say. There's nothing I can do, except alienate them both." I pause; my own words surprise me. No longer cynical, no longer hesitant, I continue, "Ellen, it'll be two years soon; I have to start living again. Nobody will ever mean to me what you do, you know that, but what if I live another twenty years? Should I do it alone? I have to start living again, and you know that, too."

I hear footsteps, so I stop my chat with the dead. A nearby funeral is disbanding, and an old bearded man in a black suit with a black fedora on his head is shuffling toward me. Accompanying him, towering over him, is a youngster in his twenties with a knitted skullcap on his head. They must be headed for the car parked near mine. Our eyes meet and we nod silently at each other. I'm not at all ashamed of the emotion they must see on my face.

The old man stops next to me. He points to the prayer book in his hand, no doubt noticing that I don't have one, and asks, "Can I help, do you need a prayer said?" I suddenly need it very much and say yes, thanks. He opens the book with a practiced hand. His voice filled with feeling, his demeanor earnest, he begins to intone the *El Moleh Rachamim* prayer—God Full of Mercy—its words ancient, moving, powerful. He pauses for the Hebrew names of the dead, which I supply, and then continues to the end. As he is fulfilling the great good deed of honoring the dead, a powerful imperative for every religious Jew, the young man beside him sways to the sound of the prayer with his eyes closed and his strong young arm holding up the old man. As close as I feel to them, and as grateful, I find it hard to thank them because my voice is constrained by my emotion. They seem to require no thanks, however. They smile and walk on to their car.

Emboldened, I'm unashamed now to speak openly to the graves. I plead to my wife and to my parents. "Don't let Eric be the last of us, don't let it end with him, please don't." Pathetic and hopeless, I know, and too late, but what does it hurt to ask? You don't ask, you don't get. So I ask. "Please, don't let me down."

In the car, I mop my face and collect myself before I start the engine and begin the long trip back to reality. I decide to skip the office and head home—it's already two-thirty in the afternoon—and when I get home the sound of the vacuum tells me that Della is here. The sound is pleasant, familiar: Life goes on and requires a cleanup, and this apartment gets it every day, whether we need it or not. Bent on her work, Della is backing into the front hall when she notices me. She jumps.

"What are you doing home early?" she asks. "You sick?"

"No, I just got back from the cemetery and decided to call it a day."

"Oh, that's nice," she says. "Someday I wouldn't mind going with you. I'd like to visit my Ellen, too."

"I'll remember next time," I promise, then go to my room and sit down in my father's chair and make myself comfortable. I need no book, no television. I am content to just sit and rest. To hell with the office, it's good to be home. It's good to be alive.

Later, I go back into the kitchen to tell Della Eric's news. She holds my hand, and her eyes say it all. "Whatever God decides," she adds when I finish, "what can we do?" One tear is running slowly down her plump, dark cheek, and I love her for that simple tear, for its wealth of genuine sympathy.

Remembering to do something that I had meant to do before, I go back into my bedroom and take out Ellen's pearls from her jewelry box. When I return to the kitchen Della is busy tidying up. I make up a little story. "Ellen told me that she wanted these pearls to be given to you when Eric gets married. She wanted you to wear them at the wedding, and then to keep them. So here they are."

Della is stunned, her eyes now brimming with tears. "Her mother's old clasp," she says, shaking her head. "For me?" she asks.

"Yes, wear them to the wedding and then they are yours, a gift from Ellen and from me, with our love." The two of us stand there, in the middle of the kitchen floor, she is crying, and I'm pretty choked up myself.

She holds up the pearls. "Lord," she says. "You bless this good man and bless his boy, and I will praise You. Place Your blessing on Eric and bring him back to You, Lord, in the name of Jesus."

After a quiet moment or two, taking hold of herself, Della wraps the pearls in a linen handkerchief and places them in her handbag. "Thank you," she says as she prepares to leave. "See you tomorrow."

In the bedroom I shared with Ellen, I stand in front of her dresser and I say, "I hope you approve, Ellen. I hope I did right." Somehow, I know she does, and I will sleep well tonight.

18.

T hree or four times a year, I have to brace myself for a visit by my biggest client, Sinclair Klipper. New York is the Klippers' pit stop, for Sinclair to review his business affairs with me and for Babette, his wife, to resume her affair with Bergdorf Goodman and Saks, on their way home from Europe to Chicago. Sinc is my biggest customer in two ways. Number one, he is a third of my business. If he knew that, he would probably negotiate his commissions down to a hair above zero, but he doesn't have a clue. Number two, he is probably six foot three and easily weighs three hundred pounds—a skinny man with the biggest belly from chest to balls that I have ever seen. And I have seen it from every conceivable angle, because, in addition to providing investment advice it has unfortunately become my duty to provide Sinc with an unusual and stimulating New York afternoon experience while Babette is shopping her brains out. This one-day entertainment has assumed an importance to him that overshadows his portfolio performance. So what I have to offer is something more personal than mere money, and over the years I have become adept at discovering ever more novel experiences for him. Or for us, rather: The one glitch is that I also have to accompany him on these outings, which we then rehash by telephone in the weeks that follow. At forty, this was fun. At fifty, it was better than spending the day in the office. Now it is a pain in the ass, but a very necessary one and, having already shelled out close to one thousand dollars, I have made quite detailed arrangements for today's encounter.

As is usual on these occasions, Sinc comes to my office mid-morning, and we actually talk business for three-quarters of an hour. Then he calls the hotel to make sure that Babette is up and to tell her that he and I are attending an important seminar so he will be out of reach until around two in the afternoon. He blows a kiss or two into the phone, hangs up, and turns to me expectantly. "Another fifteen minutes and the car will be here to take us to Nirvana," I tell him. "Meanwhile, how was your trip?"

"Budapest and Prague were okay," he says. "Budapest is worth two days; Prague, two or three. But the highlight was the spa in Karlovy Vary, the old Carlsbad. Holy cow, what a place. I spent ten days there, lost sixteen pounds. They have hot baths, cold baths—first one, then the other. If you survive that, they beat you with palm fronds, wrap you in mud and seaweed, and embarrass you into starving yourself. They've got lots of food, everything covered with whipped cream and chocolate, but you're afraid to eat. They weigh you several times a day, any other time they're trying to massage you to death. They have these female tanks—they look like Stalin or Beria in a skirt; arms like hams—who massage you. They'd grab this belly of mine and twist it and push it like they're kneading dough.

Then come the high colonics and the enemas. It's cheap in dollars, only twenty-five dollars for an enema, but this is some enema. I think half the weight I lost I owe to those enemas. You don't realize what bags of dung we all are, you're hauling around pounds of it from meals you've eaten weeks before. But not after the colonic, believe me. The corned beef sandwich you had two weeks ago, it's out. The pickles, too, and every peanut festering away inside the digestive tract is gone. The old Brünnhilde in charge told me that lots of pill capsules come out, they're littering our insides. Only now I've got nothing left inside, I'm clean as a whistle: I haven't had to fart in almost a week. I really recommend it, what a spa! Sixteen pounds! Of course, it did cost me four thousand dollars, which comes to what? . . . About two hundred and fifty bucks a pound, right? But what better to spend it on than on health?"

"Well, today I have arranged something more soul-satisfying for you, a unique New York moment. So we'd better get going if we don't want to be late."

We aren't late. A woman named Valerie opens the door to an expensively furnished apartment. Swarthy and proud, of indeterminate background, she is dressed in a tight pantsuit; her walk is at once sensuous and defiant. I'm a little nervous. After all, I am the impresario here. I hope that Sinc will be pleased.

"Coffee?" asks Valerie. We decline, and she seats us on the couch, where she then joins us. "I am a therapist specializing in scream therapy," she explains. "I don't know if you are familiar with this therapy, but it consists of my beating a drum, first slowly, and then faster and louder, until the patient permits himself to totally shout and scream out whatever needs to be released. This therapy requires an acoustically protected room in which the subject lies naked. The effects are truly magical, nothing less than an emotional outpouring, as one screams everything negative out. It rejuvenates one. If at any time you wish the drumming to stop, I am also pretty good with a guitar, but I strongly recommend the drums. They are very evocative. And now, if you would follow me . . ."

Sinc looks a little scared and a lot excited, like a kid. I did my job well, he's happy. We undress together, but I can't see where he has lost the sixteen pounds. His stomach is so big that he has to sit down to take off his pants; otherwise, gravity would pull him down. We are waiting only a minute when the door opens to a room with padded walls and two comfortable-looking massage tables. Between them Valerie sits down in front of a set of drums; she holds a large clay drum between her knees. A faint smell of clove fills the room; it's probably the scent in the large green candle, which provides the only light. Humming, seemingly to herself, Valerie indicates with a gesture that we should lie down on the tables. Once we are both lying on our backs, Valerie begins to work the drum.

"Let it out," she urges softly. "Scream a little, scream it out."

Sinc lets out a sad little howl, and I manage a peep.

"Gentlemen, gentlemen, you can do better than that. Think of your problems, think of your worries."

Again, a pathetic scrap of noise pops out of Sinc, and I feel more like giggling than screaming.

"Scream, scream," Valerie urges. "Think of your marriages. Think of your wives. Think of your bills."

That evidently does it for Sinc. He lets loose with a good first scream, and then he's into it—he's really screaming. I try again; Valerie is not pleased.

"Dan," she says, "Dan, let it out, honey. Scream a little for me. Tell me, do you have children? Think of your children and scream for me." I think of Eric, I think of the hundred grand, of Carol, of

Kugelmass, and I can feel the rumbling then rising up inside me, and out it comes: a scream.

Sinc is still going strong. He's really into it. "You pig!" he screams. "You ugly, lazy, fat pig. You inherited all that money, but you're not worth the powder to blow you to hell. Your name should be Baboon, not Babette, you lousy pig!"

"Yes, yes," responds Valerie. "Yes, yes, let it all out."

"Baboon! Baboon!" yells Sinc. "You can spend millions dressing yourself up, but you're still a baboon. I should buy you bananas instead of Balmains, bananas instead of Blahniks. No more Bill Blass, just bananas. You're a baboon," he bellows, "a baboon. I wouldn't screw you with someone else's dick!" And then he begins to sob. "Baboon," he whimpers, "bananas, bananas." The drumming is softer now, softer but insistent.

"Come on, boys," says Valerie, "let it out, I want it, come on, let it go."

Sinc is in tears. Off the baboons and bananas now, he's moaning, sobbing, while I lie there silent. Valerie encourages us to rest as she continues the soft drumming and occasionally utters an "om."

An hour or more must have passed. Now silence fills the room.

"Danny?"

"Yeah?"

"This was perfect, unbelievable," Sinc gushes. "What a great experience. Thanks, you're my buddy. But, Danny, don't tell anyone about this, okay?"

"No one, I promise, Sinc."

"We're asshole buddies, right, Danny?"

"Right, Sinc. Don't worry, my lips are sealed." And I'm thinking I won't have to worry about my commissions ever again.

In absolute silence, we drive to Sinc's hotel. Before he leaves me he squeezes my hand with his, he looks worried. "Buddies," he says to me.

"Buddies," I confirm. With one look back at me he shuffles into the hotel.

I am struck by an unnerving thought. Maybe today's adventure had brought me a sign from heaven. Clearly, being single is not as lonely as being married to the wrong person, so it could be that Violet's little religious revival has saved me from a fate only worth screaming about.

19.

V iolet's number catches my eye as I'm flicking through my messages the next day at the office. The message says, "Call Chaya."

Chaya's voice peals with no less excitement than Violet's. "Dan," she says, "wish me a mazel tov. Maria and Aaron are going to get married here in New York. Which will be so much more convenient for both families."

"Mazel tov, Violet."

"Call me Chaya," she says, then continues, "I'm going to make a big wedding, six hundred and fifty people, and I hope you'll come. June twenty-seventh: Write it down—you'll need that tux again. I'm so excited. I'm rushing off now to the florist. They quoted me a hundred and twenty-five thousand for the flowers I wanted, which is a sin, but it includes candles and containers. What does it matter? I want the best for my only daughter. But listen, Aaron's parents are coming in to New York to meet me. Would it be possible for you to join me, just to give me courage?"

"What do you think I am, an escort service? You want to hire me by the hour? Remember me? Self-absorbed, shitty little me, the man without a soul. Remember when you were still Violet how I wasn't good enough for you and now you want me to meet Maria's in-laws-to-be: Are you nuts? And did I say, no, thanks?"

"Finished venting? Can I have a word or two? I'm sorry I spoke to you that way, Dan. Really. I miss you, and I think of you a lot. Can't we be friends? Shouldn't a friend do a favor?"

"Escorts are not friends," I reply. "Normally escorts are paid for their services. In this case, however, I was paid only in insults; so again—no, thanks."

"Please," she begs. "Don't leave me all alone with that first husband of mine and his Miss Piggy and the Toronto duo. That would be cruel, and I know you are not cruel, Dan. You are sweet. Even if you have no soul, the rest of you is pretty sweet. Do this one for the new Chaya. And wait till you see me—you know what *tznius* is? It's modesty, I now dress modestly. Please come tomorrow night."

I don't want to give in, but I miss her. The truth is, I'd really like to see Violet again. I succumb. "Okay, where?"

"My house at seven P.M. Look good. I told everybody how cute you are. And don't be late."

So at seven-fifteen the next evening I am ushered into Violet-Chaya's apartment, which is still monochromatic, still extravagant—at least some things don't change. Then, enter Chaya wearing a modest black dress with long sleeves, the loose bodice hiding those lovely breasts, the long skirt concealing those great legs. Thank God, her hair is still blonde, and her diamonds are on full display, so she is still recognizable.

She leads me to the living room, where her first husband and his wife stand to greet me. He doesn't look like a bum. He actually looks like a nice fellow: strong like a bull, wide smile, tight brown suit, big pinkie ring, Vince Oressto by name. His wife Gina looks remarkably like him except for an impressive set of very large, partially exposed breasts that she flaunts like a badge of honor. A gold medallion hanging from a thick gold chain bounces on their precipice. She looks a little nervous—she obviously feels out of place—so I sit down next to her and try to make small talk.

Mercifully, just a few minutes later the doorbell rings. I hear Chaya greet the newcomers merrily, and they follow her into the living room—a friendly-faced, sturdy man in his fifties and his shrewd-looking, redder-than-redheaded wife, who is dressed to the nines. We are introduced to Aaron's parents, Isadore—"call me Izzy"—and Dolly Katz. Chaya introduces me as her friend and traveling companion in Israel, details that arouse only an awkward silence. She fills it by explaining why she wants to be now called Chaya.

"My most recent trip to Israel really convinced me to look back to my roots, to reconnect with my heritage. I feel that the name Chaya, which means "Life" in Hebrew, betokens this new direction, this change in lifestyle, that I've chosen."

"Lovely," says Dolly, "but on the wedding invitation I do hope you will use Violet; otherwise, how will people know who you are?"

"By then most people will know me as Chaya," Violet replies.

"Perhaps Violet-Chaya would be better than just Chaya," insists Dolly.

"I like Chaya. I'll reconsider Chaya-Violet, maybe."

"Violet is such an elegant name, and it goes so well with an Italian name like Oressto," Dolly presumes.

"No, with Finkel," Violet corrects her. "The invitation will read Chaya-Violet Finkel and Vincent Oressto."

"What about me?" asks Gina. "Won't my name appear? I certainly helped raise Maria. I'm very fond of her."

"Well," says Chaya-Violet, "you may have helped to raise Maria, but Maria is now Miriam. Besides which, I really don't see why you, as the stepmother, should be named unless you and Vince are planning to help pay for the wedding."

"Wait," Izzy interrupts, "I'm happy to pay for the liquor and the band—that's traditional for the parents of the groom—but of course I then get to choose the band."

Gina offers, "Maybe we'll pay for the flowers, right, Vince? We'll give you ten thousand for the flowers, but my name has to be on the invitation."

"Ten thousand? That'll barely pay for the bridesmaid's flowers. Have you any idea what flowers cost? For ten thousand you'll be lucky to get a cactus," scoffs Chaya.

"I've made two weddings, ten thousand is more than both weddings' flowers cost," argues Gina in her own defense. "And we had plenty of flowers."

"They must have been reused—from a funeral, maybe," says Chaya, sounding very much like Violet.

"We thought it would be nice to have the Royal Canadian Marching Band perform," says Dolly. "I believe that they do regular music as well as marches, you know. Very chichi."

"I want traditional Jewish music," says Chaya, "and only traditional Jewish music. And separate dancing—no social dancing—only men with men, women with women. Miriam and Aaron are very Orthodox now, very strict, and we have to accommodate them."

"It's not enough that everything has to be kosher?" complains Dolly in a plaintive tone. "You know how unhappy some of my friends will be; no shrimp, no clams—there really should be some limit. And now you're telling me I can't dance with Izzy?"

"Not at the wedding, dear," says Chaya. "I'm sure you can manage that, dance all you want before or after."

A long moment of silence follows the dance decree. Gina's considerable bosom is heaving. Chaya is looking more and more like Violet, and Dolly's face now is almost as red as her hair. The husbands have been reduced to silent spectators cowering in their chairs. I'm thankful not to have to be a participant in the proceedings.

"Would anybody like a drink?" asks Chaya.

An abrupt and loud "no" resounds from Gina and Dolly—nobody drinks when they're preparing to joust to the death. The husbands remain silent, as do I.

"I pay, I have the say. There it is, out in the open: I pay, I say," Chaya says.

"Why not?" says Gina. "Easy come, easy go. You didn't earn the money except on your back."

"Oh, no, no," says Dolly. "Don't let's get personal. I have made three weddings for my daughters; I am the most experienced. All of Jewish Toronto attended, and no one failed to praise my organizational abilities. I should really be the one to take charge of the arrangements."

"You paying?" asks Chaya.

"For the liquor and band," respond Dolly and Izzy in unison.

"Who is paying for the rest?" asks Chaya.

"You are the parents of the bride. You two," answers Dolly.

"I'm paying. I pay, I get the say," Chaya says.

"But three hundred of my people will be there," says Dolly. "I cannot leave the evening solely to you."

"Who says you'll have three hundred?" asks Chaya. "Why should you have three hundred? Especially as Vince wants one fifty. That leaves me with only two hundred, and I can assure you that I have more friends than both of you put together. And it's costing me three hundred and fifty dollars a head for the damned kosher caterer—that's one-third more than the non-kosher—and you know damned well, Dolly, that Jews don't drink, so the liquor will cost you next to nothing, and I don't call that significant. So you can stop right there, Dolly."

"I need three hundred," says Dolly. "My family alone is over one hundred, and Izzy needs to invite, too. And all of Toronto wants to come. And we want our rabbi, Rabbi Sunshine, to perform the ceremony. I've already had him circle the date."

"Without asking me?" storms Chaya. "I am thinking of having the Kanczuga Rebbe himself officiate. We don't need your rabbi from Toronto."

"Aaron will be very angry," retorts Dolly. "He loves Rabbi Sunshine."

"I don't care if he brings sunshine, moonshine, or starlight," says Chaya in her most Violet way. "It's my rabbi or bust. You want it your way, you make a nice shindig up in Toronto for your three hundred closest and most intimate friends and let your rabbi gleam on them."

"Wait a minute," Gina jumps back in. "We'll raise our sum to fifteen thousand, but that's our top. Anyway, Maria is allergic to many flowers. We really should use daisies rather than big smelly flowers, so she won't be sneezing under the canopy."

"We're not using daisies," screams Chaya. "Daisies are for shit. We are using imported orchids, the finest roses in vibrant colors, stands of lilies, barrels of peonies, multicolored anemones in the aisle baskets, and the wedding canopy will be one hundred percent bright blue hydrangeas. You can shove those daisies, lady."

And at that moment, a liveried servant enters to announce, "Ladies and gentlemen, dinner is served." He is totally ignored. I get to my feet, in the hope that a gesture toward dinner will break through the tension in the room, but no one else moves.

"All right," says Gina. "Twenty, but that is tops. Twenty thousand, and I want my full name, Gina-Rosa, on the invitation: Gina-Rosa Oressto."

Dolly says, "My rabbi was the head of the rabbinical council in Canada, he's no slouch. He's been received by the Queen of England, but for you he's not good enough. The Queen, the Queen!"

"So maybe the Queen would like to contribute to the wedding expenses. If she wants Rabbi Sunshine, let her speak up," says Chaya.

"Dinner is served," repeats the waiter. He opens the dining room doors. The elegant table glitters with china, silver, and crystal. The wondrous centerpiece of roses is topped regally with a crown of daisies.

"Daisies, fucking daisies!" screams Gina. "You're telling me daisies are for shit, and look at your own centerpiece: daisies! Something is wrong with you! And I'm not staying for dinner to find out what. Also, we're back to ten thousand, and you put my name on the invitation or else. Vince, we're leaving."

They leave us gaping in stunned silence.

"You want to eat?" asks Chaya wearily. "Anybody want to eat?"

More silence. Then Izzy says, "We're not agreeing to just any old wedding you dream up, Violet or Chaya or whatever you call yourself. If we don't like the arrangements, we're not going to

attend, and I very much doubt that Aaron will either. Good night."
Without a backward glance, he leads his wife off the jousting field.

Chaya and I sit quietly. I wait for her to speak. Finally she says, "I
screwed up, didn't I?" I nod in the affirmative.

"I should have shut up, paid, and let them have their way. Maria
will be so miserable. I really screwed up. You can still call me Violet,
because I'm no Chaya yet—you can't teach a stone to sing. I'm really
ashamed of myself . . . Go home, Dan, you don't need this. I'm going
to have to call the two sets of idiots and grovel. I'll apologize. I'll plant
daisies down the fucking aisle. I'll have that rabbi of theirs come
down from Toronto and do his sunshine thing. I'll pay for all their
guests. I'll grovel. I've groveled before, and I'll do it again. But after
the wedding, after Maria hooks this big bargain Aaron, I'm going to
make that Dolly's life miserable. She'll rue the day she met me. As
for Gina, her punishment is Vince. But Dolly I will get even with.
She'll tear out every strand of that dyed red hair of hers, strand by
ugly strand. Better red than dead they used to say, right? Well, she
won't think so." Vengeful Violet may be, but mostly she looks sad.
"Go home, go home."

I pat her on the shoulder and leave her there. Before I reach the
front door I hear her crying, a wrenching sound, but I resist the urge
to turn back. Sometimes it is best to be alone.

Three days later I get a call from, according to my secretary, Violet.
She's back! And when I pick up, she sounds so happy. "You can call
me Violet, you can call me Chaya, you can call me *pisher*, but don't
call me late for dinner," she announces. "I groveled, they caved in.
The wedding is on. I'll stick a few thousand daisies in for tugboat
Gina, and we won't have anything red because Dolly-baby doesn't
want anything to clash with her red hair. I even agreed to green as

the color for the wedding, green yet—that's Dolly's favorite color. And I smiled, and I was polite and I said yes to everything. Circle the date, and get yourself a green bow tie for your tux, and I hope you are not allergic to daisies."

One thing is sure, I'm not allergic to traditional Jewish, which the ceremony, however extravagant, is certain to be. For that, I feel a pang of envy and loss.

20.

A week goes by, and I have not turned up any guests for our Seder. Violet will be in Jerusalem, Charlotte doesn't return my calls, and Evelyn and Bob are going to Florida; so it'll be just Eric, Carol, and me. Della will cook up a storm—chicken soup, matzoh balls, gefilte fish, the whole works—but the prospect of a Seder without a child present bothers me, as the whole purpose of the Seder is to retell the Exodus story and pass it on to the next generation. Then, like magic, the phone rings, and my secretary tells me it is Tatiana calling.

"Am I disturbing you?" she asks. "Is it a busy time?"

"No, no, I'm delighted that you called. What can I do for you?"

"Well, the synagogue is redoing its reception room. They hope to finish before Passover, but for now Niki cannot use the piano there. I am reluctant to take advantage of your kind offer, yet I am also anxious for him not to lose the continuity. Is it possible that he could practice at your apartment—while you are at work, of course, so as not to disturb you?"

"Absolutely. I meant the invitation. Della is there most days. And it would not disturb me, so he can come on the weekends, too. It will be great to hear the piano being played again. You can start today. Just call Della and set it up; I'll tell her it's okay."

"I thank you," she says formally. "You are very kind. It seems I am always in your debt one way or the other."

"It's my pleasure. At my age, having a beautiful woman notice me, let alone feel that she is in my debt, is a real treat."

"Your age?" she says. "Your age is just fine with me. You are at your very peak."

"Well, thanks," I reply, somewhat flattered. "By the way, do you have any plans for Passover? Would you like to join my family for Seder?"

"I would be so happy! Niki will be so happy!" Spontaneity breaks through her formality, and I am touched by the gratitude and joy in her voice

"It's set then. I want you to meet my son, and his fiancée."

"Yes, of course," she says. "And thanks again."

"And I'll tell Della to expect you and Niki for the piano practice!"

We hang up. I find myself staring at the phone, smiling.

I never thought she would call. Is it possible that she's interested in me, or is she just desperate for her kid? Her image suddenly overwhelms me: her beauty, her eyes, those wonderful lips, the sway of her body, the whole feel and scent of her—like a caress, she returns to me. Her hands, graceful, delicate; those legs. I may be sixty, but I'm not dead yet. Still, you want a woman like that, you've got to pay one way or the other, and the payment in this case is plainly too damned much. A penniless woman with a nine-year-old boy? Better to stop dreaming right now. And yet, when I call Della, I'm happy at the thought that I will probably see Tatiana on weekends, if she has the guts to come by while I'm there.

No sooner am I off the phone with Della than I get a call from Myra Forshpise. "Yes, Myra, what can I do for you?"

"Is that a joke, what can you do for me? You can strap up your lower back and come over again soon. That's what you can do for me."

"Myra, I am complimented, but I am not interested. I was crippled for days after the last round. What should I be trying for now? Do you provide disability insurance for your male companions?"

"I won't hurt you this time, I'll be gentle. I won't exercise all my rights, just my right to an orgasm. You know that in the end you'll come back for more anyway, so why argue with me? We'll be careful. Billy is away again, this time in Brazil for a few days. It's good timing, I'm in the mood. When he gets back it will be more awkward, then comes Passover; it's too long to wait."

I have a thought. "About Passover, do you need an invitation to a Seder?"

"Thank you, but no, we have a special ecumenical Seder of our own, with people of different religions and backgrounds, and we celebrate the freedom of all nations and all nature. I'm having three Palestinian students as special guests. Of course, I have to go through the Haggadah and expunge any mention of the Egyptians, so as not to insult my guests—you know, many Egyptians are Arabs, too. I invited the head of the PLO Mission in New York to show solidarity, but he didn't have the courtesy to reply. Anyway, think about my invitation. I don't call just anyone for a second round, you know."

For a moment, I am actually tempted: I figure maybe she'll be calmer the second time around, more restrained. "Well, what about tonight?" I ask, half regretting the words as I speak them.

"Oh, not tonight, I'm sorry. Tonight I have a meeting of the American Friends of Native Americans. We'll be treated first to a lecture on the historical migratory habits of the Sioux Indians, then to a songfest of Indian chants. I'm a vice chairman and I'll be presenting the annual Multi-Feather Award to our guest of honor, Congressman Dodge. He has an aide who is a Pawnee Indian, so he's very sympathetic to our cause. Maybe you would like to come as my guest?" I demur.

A few days before Passover our Seder begins to grow. It turns out that Carol's parents are coming to New York, in part to meet me, so they will join us. Then Violet calls. She has decided not to spend the week in Israel, as she's in the throes of wedding preparations, and happily accepts my invitation to the Seder. The next day it grows some more. Myra's ecumenical Seder plans have collapsed. The three Palestinian students decided it is inappropriate to celebrate the Exodus from Egypt, because if the Jews had stayed as slaves in Egypt, they would never have entered the Promised Land and thus would not now have the nation of Israel. What's more, her husband, Billy, who is not Jewish, will be in Oslo on business. My invitation to her comes with the warning that we will be reciting an unexpurgated Haggadah, so she'll have to be brave and bear up under the plagues that afflicted Egypt. I also fend off her request that after the Seder she spend the night at my house, as I'd not want to contemplate what Carol's parents might think, let alone Violet. I tell her that her soul will be nourished, not her body. She accepts nonetheless.

The day of the Seder I stay home to help Della, who has spent the week cooking and preparing. Together we boil the silver to make it ritually acceptable. We add a leaf to the dining room table and set it with the special Passover china that Ellen reserved just for the holy week. By the time the evening arrives, Della is exhausted, so I am glad that I accepted Violet's offer to have her butler help serve. At seven sharp, Eric and Carol arrive with her parents. Cora Hoffman, a pleasant-looking, thin woman with faded blonde hair, is wearing a pantsuit and one ladylike strand of pearls. She has a warm, contagious smile. Her husband, Dick, in a maroon blazer with a pair of plaid pants comprising most of the colors of the rainbow, has combed his hair carefully over a large bald spot, but he in no way disguises his open, friendly demeanor.

Though unfamiliar with the rituals of the Seder, or any other Jewish service or celebration, for that matter, the Hoffmans appear to be genuinely interested and eager to participate. "We know all about the Exodus, we are Bible-reading folks," Cora notes, "but I have to confess ignorance about Passover observances. I know you are restricted in what you eat, Carol told me, so I brought flowers instead of a cake."

She brought daisies, which Violet would not thank her for, but I do as I pass the bouquet to Della to put in a vase. We sit down in the living room, where Cora is issuing a chorus in praise of Ellen's wonderful taste when Tatiana, Niki, Violet, and Myra arrive all at once. I make the introductions, and there is a perceptible pause as my guests—decidedly a disparate group—assess one another.

Tatiana, ashimmer in a long black dress, looks lovely, young, wonderful, like a flower among the thorns. Myra, of course, has come in native garb, her Native American dress embellished with massive pieces of silver and turquoise jewelry. Violet is aglow with jewelry of a more international character, not the least of which is the large diamond rose clipped to her hair. Accompanying her is the butler, who immediately joins Della in the kitchen, and we all enter the dining room to begin the Seder.

In the center of the table sits a lavish floral arrangement—no daisies—sent by Violet. Myra has brought a plant and Tatiana a box of Passover chocolates, which Della places on the sideboard. I distribute copies of the Haggadah and announce that we will read most of it in English, but with a Hebrew song occasionally interspersed between sections of the text. Very soon, we arrive at the Four Questions, which set the tone for the Seder and which are asked by the youngest person at the table. It is Niki's moment, and he surprises us by asking the first question—"Why is this night different from all the other nights?"—in Hebrew. Tatiana happily rewards him with praise, and he then recites the balance in English.

As we read round-robin the answers to his questions—"We were slaves in the land of Egypt and God led us out with a mighty hand and an outstretched arm . . ."—I notice that my guests are in very different states of mind. Tatiana is beaming with pleasure. Violet proudly very slowly reads some lines in her newly learned Hebrew, while Myra seems annoyed and anxious. The Hoffmans follow intently every word and ponder every symbol; they are determined to have a cultural experience. Eric looks bemused, Carol deeply involved. But it is Niki who shines, his pleasure evident, his excitement level rising even higher when I tell him that before we eat I will hide the *Afikoman,* a broken piece of unleavened matzoh without which we cannot finish the meal, and if he finds it he can negotiate for a present from me.

Repeatedly examining the symbolic foods on the Seder Plate, Niki can't seem to resist handling the bitter herbs and the parsley, but he eyes the dish of *haroset* warily. "I know why we have the herbs, because slavery was bitter. And the parsley, because it is spring. But what is this?" he asks, pointing to the *haroset*. "It looks like glue."

"It's supposed to look like clay, like the bricks our ancestors had to make as slaves. I think it's apples and wine and nuts, but you can check with Della, she made it. We'll get to eating it later."

His eyes shine with happiness. "We eat unleavened matzoh because we left Egypt so fast that the flour didn't have time to rise," he announces, and Cora thanks him for the explanation.

"How wonderful that you know so much about your people's history," she says. Niki beams with pleasure at her praise.

We arrive at the Ten Plagues. "Custom dictates that as we recite them, we spill a drop of wine for each plague to symbolize our sympathy for the Egyptians who, although our enemies, were human beings for whom we feel sorrow," I explain.

"Sorrow, indeed," says Violet. "They get no sympathy from me. They got what they deserved."

"But is it not fitting that we feel sorry for our enemies? Certainly it is Christian," says Cora.

"In that case, I'd be busy day and night feeling sorry, I've got so many of them. Half the world is anti-Semitic."

"Three-quarters," adds Tatiana, "and about ninety percent where I lived, in Ukraine."

Myra sits upright. She bangs her hand on the table. "How dare you condemn the world that way! My Guyuteras certainly are not anti-Semitic, and the Tagalus, what's left of them, hardly know what a Jew is. You can't include them in your blanket condemnation. And these plagues! The poor cattle had to suffer—for what? And all those frogs? And what about the firstborn Egyptian males? Why was the plague limited to the males? I'll tell you why: Because even God discriminated against the women. They had so few rights they weren't even worth killing off. Chattel, they were just chattel. This Haggadah is very disturbing. Where is an ode to Miriam, who helped save Moses? And to Pharoah's daughter, who pulled him out of the reeds? Women were the real heroes, and they are not even mentioned. It's a disgrace."

"Oh, my," says Cora. "Surely you cannot think God's word is disgraceful."

"What God?" storms Myra. "It must have been a bunch of rabbis who wrote this stuff while their wives were busy cooking and cleaning and having their babies. Not one word in praise of women."

"You wind a man up, you send him out, and back he comes each day with money. Tons of money," Violet goads. "You pat him on the head, spend the money, and then outlive him by a couple of decades. I like our gig."

"Women perform essential duties. We are vital, engaged in careers." Myra is outraged.

"What do you do?" asks Violet. "Are you in the Indian jewelry business by chance?"

"I don't work, I don't have to, but I donate my time to all sorts of causes."

"And your husband, what about him? Is he all decked out with feathers, or does he work for a living?" Myra glowers but says nothing. "I rest my case."

"Ladies, ladies," appeals Cora, "we're at a religious service, let's respect the word of God. This would never happen in Saginaw."

"Nothing would ever happen in Saginaw," says Violet.

"Not true," snaps Myra. "Saginaw is, I believe, an Indian word. I think it means alfalfa, or maybe it was the name of an important chief. Have you any Native Americans in Saginaw?"

"I really never noticed," admits Cora.

"Never noticed the indigenous people? Well, you can be sure they notice you. And while we're on the subject, why are we not all acknowledging the suffering of so many native peoples? Isn't that the lesson to be drawn from the poor Egyptians and their plagues?"

"No, Myra dear," says Violet. "The lesson is that we cannot stand idly by when people are enslaved. And we cannot allow ourselves to be enslaved ever again."

"My point precisely," Myra retorts. "Aren't most women enslaved, condemned to boring little lives, second-rate existences? Don't you agree, Mrs. Hoffman?"

And at that moment, mercifully, the first portion of the Seder ends and dinner is served. A long silence accompanies the traditional first course, a hard-boiled egg in salt water, symbolizing the circularity of life and its tears. Less solemnly, we continue with the chicken soup and matzoh balls.

"Great food," says Dick.

"High in cholesterol," mutters Myra.

Niki skips the food. He is rummaging around the apartment in search of the *Afikoman*, which I have hidden in the living room bookcase where he should be able to find it fairly easily. When he does, he and I begin our negotiation in earnest. Excited, without thinking, he sits on my lap as we talk. He waves the precious bit of matzoh triumphantly before my eyes, his until I ransom it with a reward. He wants some computer game; Tatiana, embarrassed, tries to stop him, while Eric roots for him openly. In the end I surrender, and he, laughing and victorious, hands over the matzoh. And Tatiana is looking at me with feeling . . . What is it? Gratitude maybe? Whatever the emotion at its source, her gaze, though fleeting, is so penetrating that I feel as though she has touched me physically. I find it hard to keep my eyes off her.

The mood has lightened by the time we begin the second part of the Seder. I fill the Cup of Elijah to the brim with wine and explain to the Hoffmans and to Carol that we now symbolically open the door for Elijah, the precursor of the Messiah, and sing him a song of welcome. As I go to the door, I tell Niki to watch the cup to see if the invisible visitor takes a drink. I wink at Eric, who will see to it that the table moves, so the wine in the cup will splash. Which it does. Niki is half disbelieving, but thrilled: After all, he saw it with his own eyes!

All the while we are reading the service, I notice the concentration with which Carol is participating, with every word striving to absorb the mood and message of the Seder, whereas Eric, his manner relaxed and careless, is hardly paying attention much of the time. Despite myself, I feel a surge of gratitude toward Carol for her attentiveness, for her regard, and I see very clearly tonight the qualities that caused Eric to fall in love with her.

As the Seder ends, we proclaim the ancient vow, "Next year in Jerusalem," except for Myra, who says, "I have really restrained myself tonight, but, in all honesty, how can we say that 'next year' business? I have absolutely no interest in being in Jerusalem—I much prefer the Amazon or New Mexico, or, for that matter, Ramallah. And you, Violet, you are definitely more Paris or Milan, admit it."

"I'd like to be in Israel next year," Niki chimes in, "it's where my family lives."

And Violet answers vehemently, "Wrong, Myra darling. I may look like Paris, but Jerusalem is in my heart. It may not be in yours, although God knows you have the map of Jerusalem on your face."

Tatiana steps in between the two warring parties. "It's time to say good night," she says, then turns to me. "I know that Niki and I will never forget your hospitality and your kindness. This has been a truly memorable evening, thank you so much."

"Don't leave just yet," I say, not ready to see her go. "I've been so busy being the host that I've barely had a chance to speak with you."

"You've been the perfect host, but Niki must be getting to bed, and I think you've got enough on your hands tonight without worrying about me. But may I give you a kiss for being so good to invite us?" She reaches up, she brushes those fabulous lips of hers against my cheek. "Good night," she says, with one flash of a flirtatious look. Is she toying with me? Does she sense my attraction to her?

Niki has warm hugs for everyone, shy only with Eric, with whom he shakes hands very formally. Hero worship is clearly budding, and we all smile when Eric pats Niki on the head and praises his performance at the Seder.

As Tatiana and Niki leave, Myra takes me aside, only in part to thank me for the evening. Her fervor now deflected from the Haggadah and onto me, she asks, "Do you want me to wait around?" With Violet's gaze focused upon us, I say no as clearly as I can, and guide Myra to the door as efficiently as possible.

Violet's butler emerges from the kitchen with a tired-looking Della, their cleanup completed. After Violet very charmingly says good night to the Hoffmans, then to Carol and Eric, I accompany her to the front door. In the minute that we are waiting for the elevator, with Della and the butler standing in hearing distance, she asks, "Danny, dear, when you were a little boy did you ever dream of rescuing a damsel in distress—a poor suffering beautiful brunette damsel, by chance? You may need to be reminded, dear, that children's dreams are not quite as charming in sixty-year-old men as they are in little boys."

She enters the elevator, then turns for one last comment.

"Better start learning a little Ukrainian or Russian so you can defend yourself, comrade." Before I can respond the elevator door closes in my face.

I return to the living room and to my guests. "It's been great to meet you and your friends," Dick says to me. "Thanks for this special experience. Cora and I feel that Carol is in the best of hands, and we are very happy about that."

"Our children seem anxious to be married and intent on doing it without too much ceremony," Cora adds. "Of course, I have always imagined a church wedding, with Carol in white, bells ringing, but I do understand that it's not going to happen that way, that it's going to be a justice of the peace instead of a minister. Well, it's just that . . . It strikes me as so sad, so empty. How do you feel about it?"

"I'm sorry, too," I admit. "But there seems to be no other sensible alternative. The kids have interviewed ministers who would be willing to marry them, but find them unsatisfactory—and not without reason. We will have to make do."

"I just can't imagine my grandchildren not experiencing Christmas or Easter, and I'm sure, after the service tonight, you must feel the same way about Passover as well as your other holidays. Mixed marriages are not very frequent in Saginaw. I'm afraid I'm not used to the idea."

"Me, neither," I agree. "New York or Saginaw, it's the same issues. It's hard for us both, but I don't see that we have any choice."

"You don't," interjects Eric, "and you shouldn't. Carol and I feel we have the right to do what is comfortable for us, although, of course, we want you to approve of our choice."

"Okay," I agree. "But we, your parents, have rights, too. We have the right to approve or disapprove, we even have the right to walk away if we choose. We are not required to automatically accept whatever you do."

"I agree," says Dick. "What you are planning now may be okay for the two of you, but if you have kids, what then? Won't you then, for their sake, have to choose a religion and raise them in it? You want unity in a home, in a family, and a clear moral focus. Only religion can give you that."

Silence for a minute or two—then Carol says, "Look, we can't solve all our issues tonight. Eric and I hear you, and we respect your opinions, but we are going to get married in a few weeks, without a ceremony and with no religious service. You are all invited—we want you all—to attend, and I'll let you know when as soon as we set the date."

So that's that. Cora and Dick look at me, and with just one glance we acknowledge each other's unhappiness. If there are grandchildren, then one side or the other will ultimately be the loser in the religion department—and the odds are not in my favor. Children are usually raised in their mother's faith, and anyway, we Jews are a small minority. Carol's parents are lovely, fine people and fair-minded; their concerns, their hopes of perpetuating their way of life through their grandchildren, are no different from mine, yet . . . How can there be any real happiness here when it is so much rooted in disappointment?

I search for some empathy in Eric's face for me, but I find nothing. He is holding Carol's hand, he's smiling broadly. I perceive this as a moment of defeat, and I feel that downdraft of emotion that usually accompanies such moments. Still, I do my best to keep the conversation light and friendly until the Hoffmans get up to leave. Again they say their thanks, and we exchange good nights. Cora gives me a formal kiss. Dick shakes my hand.

The next day Tatiana calls to thank me; she seems to know that I'm in a bad mood. I blame it on a little cold, unwilling to discuss anything more personal with her. Myra calls a few minutes later. Happily recovered from her Seder rantings, she again expresses her thanks, and she suggests that I come over to her place—she has hidden a little matzoh for an *Afikoman*, and if I find it, she is my present. She adds that it is quite findable, by the way, in full view on her front hall bench. I decline. I'm not in the mood for either sex or pain, both of which Myra is likely to supply. Besides which, Eric is coming over tonight. Carol had to go to Boston on a case, so he and I will have a quick second Seder, just the two of us.

Later that evening, Eric and I sit together skipping through the Haggadah and rather enjoying ourselves, while Della enjoys hovering over us to make sure the food is to our taste. Eric remembers lots of the Hebrew words and songs, and tonight he leads me through the service. His happy mood reminds me of him as a child at our Seders, his excitement, his pleasure at finding the *Afikoman*, his laughter. As we end our Seder Eric bellows, "Next Year in Ramallah." We both laugh.

Then, in a sudden change of mood, Eric says, "Dad, despite everything, I haven't really forgotten Jerusalem. Maybe you won't believe it, but it's true. I guess you drummed it into me pretty deep. If you have grandchildren, I promise you that they'll sit with you every year at the Seder. I'll take them to see Jerusalem, not just once, Dad, but lots of times. Carol is really into the Jewish stuff intellectually, we're halfway there. Don't worry."

Sitting there, still holding the Haggadah in my hand, I take one last shot. "You never know how things will turn out, Eric. Are you reconsidering Carol?"

"No. And I won't reconsider. But I promise you, I'm going to do my best with any kids we have. That's the most I can do."

"Next year, maybe we'll really go to Jerusalem for Passover, you and Carol and me," I say, and we shake hands on it.

"Maybe Tatiana and Niki too, huh, Dad?" he asks with a twinkle in his eye. "Do I detect a certain interest on your part in our pretty Russian refugee?"

"Sorry to disappoint you, but you are wrong. It's only two years since Mom died, I'm not ready for commitment just yet, and when I am I'll be looking for something a little less complicated. What did you think of Violet?"

"I'm not commenting on any of your ladies, Dad. But both Carol and I noticed the way you were looking at Tatiana at the Seder: you couldn't take your eyes off her." More seriously, he adds, "Careful, Dad, you better find out more about her. She may be after a green card or something, you never know. From where she is situated, you must seem like God's gift."

"Well, when you take my advice on which woman to marry, I'll be glad to listen to yours. Meanwhile, at least all of my prospects are Jewish. I don't have to hunt around for some crackpot to perform the marriage or look forward to the Municipal Building as my wedding chapel. If and when I ever decide to remarry, I'll invite you to a restaurant, introduce you to her, and expect you to celebrate—sound familiar?"

"Okay, okay, I get the message. I surrender. No more advice."

Eric gets up to leave, and I remember one more thing I've got to do—if not now, when?—so I tell him to wait while I go into the bedroom, there to open Ellen's jewelry box one more time. I'm keeping her wedding band, but the engagement ring I should give to him. I take the ring out of the box, and hesitate. Maybe I should wait awhile? Giving him the ring is like giving his marriage plans my seal of approval. And I don't approve, I don't, and I won't. Yet what will he think if I don't make the offer? I remember the day I gave it to Ellen—the way she looked at it, the way she looked at me. . . .What good does it do here in a box?

I take the ring to him in the front hall. "Mom's," is all I say. "Give it to Carol if you like."

His face pales, and he clenches his jaw. "Thanks," he manages. We hug, avoiding each other's eyes. Then he puts the ring into his jacket pocket and leaves.

For a little while, I just stand in the front hall, lost in the past, until Della's cheerful voice calls me back to the present.

21.

A few weeks later, Della and I stand with the Hoffmans in a little semicircle behind Carol and Eric in the Municipal Building while a city official marries them. He tries his best to inject some warmth into the proceedings, and Della, resplendent in her pearls and a big white hat, is genuinely moved. Cora, Dick, and I play our roles with no real enthusiasm. But the bride and groom glow with pleasure, their smiles radiant, their eyes sharing with each other that magical concentration of interest and desire that cannot be simulated.

After a flurry of congratulations among all of us in the busy hall following the civil ceremony, Eric and Carol rush off to their honeymoon weekend in Nantucket. I know Eric is unable to take any more time than two days because his one remaining company is still on life support, but I haven't pressed him for details—it's his honeymoon, let him enjoy himself. Della and I then put the Hoffmans into a taxi for JFK, and we take another one home. I remember my promise to "bring" my mother in some way to Eric's wedding, but there wasn't even time for a quick glass of champagne, let alone a toast in which to mention grandparents. Everything was done one-two-three, mechanically. Aridly, without ritual.

And talk about rubbing salt in your wounds. A few nights later, I attend the wedding of Maria-Miriam Oressto to Aaron Katz in the grandest ballroom in the city. For weeks, Violet has been on the phone with me incessantly, venting and asking advice and complaining her way through every detail of the evening. "All of New York will be there," she'd declare frequently, "and most of Toronto." "Everything will be perfect," she'd assure me and herself. She'd review her decisions regarding the main course with me. It's evidently considered tacky to have a choice of entrees, and Violet had decided upon veal, but Maria wanted salmon. A transatlantic food fight ensued by telephone. Toronto meanwhile preferred roast beef. The idiots, Violet pointed out, no one eats red meat anymore, at least not in New York. When she learned that Vince too wanted veal she began to lean more toward Maria's salmon: "Why should he have his way? Is he paying?" And then, that "vicious old bag" in Toronto objects to the color of the Grand Ballroom drapes, which are crimson and clash horribly with her fire-engine red hair. Although, in Violet's opinion, it would be a lot cheaper to change the old broad's hair color, preferably to its original gray, she dutifully speaks to the hotel staff who are not at all shocked at the request and agree to cover the offending crimson with an over-drape of beige and gold—available for a mere seventy-five hundred dollars for the evening. "Because of her I have to wear green, which clashes with my skin tone and does nothing for my eyes, and because Maria is so religious I have to wear it up to the neck and down to the wrists—green, everywhere green. On the other hand, when I'm finished with this evening all of New York will be green with envy, so it will definitely be the color of the season. And I'm wearing Finkel's Folly, that's what Irv used to call it. It's so valuable that a bodyguard has to attend the function with me for it to be insured while I wear it, and it weighs a ton. But if not for Maria's wedding, when? Just wait until two-ton Gina and that Toronto twit get a load of me in my crown jewels. The old saying is true: Living well is the best revenge."

So as I enter the Grand Ballroom I am prepared for grandeur, for glitz, for glamour, but not for the twelve-foot torrent of daisies in the shape of the Canadian maple leaf that fills the anteroom. And not for the waiters on the staircase landing offering drinks and canapés in case you can't wait to eat till you get to the ballroom. And not for the great suspended bowers of peonies and roses that hang from the ceiling, not for the wedding canopy made entirely of hydrangeas, not for the hedges of daisies that line the aisle down to the canopy. And certainly not for the full symphony orchestra playing background music. And not for Violet. She is aglitter with Finkel's Folly. Every movement of her head produces a dazzling cascade of light around her neck, which is augmented by her giant diamond pendant earrings.

"Am I too green?" she whispers nervously, and I assure her that the refracted light from her diamonds makes it difficult to even notice the color of her dress. "Am I beautiful?" she asks, and I assure her that when I learn of a more superlative word I will use it. Then I take her right hand in mine; I kiss it gallantly, and get a mouthful of diamonds. "Stick by me," she says, and I join the bodyguard accompanying her as she greets the guests.

When Dolly appears, her hair ablaze and her body swathed in

green, Violet greets her with vociferous, seemingly heartfelt enthusiasm, and Izzy gets kissed on both cheeks. "My dear, dear family,"
Violet intones as she embraces them, "now we are one."

"And dear Vince," she exclaims, "our little baby Maria is all grown
up." She kisses him, and he begins to cry with emotion. "And dear, dear
Gina," says Violet, doing a double take as she eyes Gina's green dress,
which leaves little to the imagination. Beginning at the very tips of her
extraordinary breasts and proceeding downward, it clings as tightly as
possible to every sumptuous curve of Gina's remarkable body.

"God, I've brought the Kanczuga Rebbe from Israel," Violet whispers to me, with a quick nod toward Gina's breasts, "how is he going
to deal with those?" She opens her evening bag, rummages around
in it, and extracts a little lace handkerchief. "Gina, darling," she says,
"I've got just the right touch to finish off your stunning outfit," and
she tucks it right in the center of Gina's considerable cleavage. "Perfect, darling!" exclaims Violet.

She squeezes my arm, and I pick up my cue. "Yes, that's just perfect." Gina stares down at the addition to her wardrobe.

"Did you notice the daisies," Violet asks Gina, "are you pleased?"

"Yes, but I can't imagine how in the world you managed to get so
many in one place—there must be thousands."

"I did it to please you, Gina. All ten thousand of them, just for
you, even if I did have to corner the world market. Almost six thousand had to be flown in yesterday from Amsterdam, where they were
gathered from all over the world, and all for you, darling. Because
you so particularly wanted daisies. Anything for family."

"A la famiglia," toasts Vince approvingly.

"Exactly," replies Violet.

"Are those real?" asks Gina, pointing to Violet's necklace.
"They're so beautiful."

"Think of them as my daisies, everybody has to have a favorite thing," Violet says and sweeps away to another cluster of arriving guests.

At that moment, Maria enters the room with her bridesmaids. She is radiant with happiness. She is wearing a simple white gown, in accordance with Jewish custom, her veil is thrown back from her wonderful face; she wears no jewelry. She seats herself in a white wicker thronelike chair on an elevated platform, where she is soon surrounded by Violet and Dolly and Gina. A minute or so later, a burst of trumpets calls us all to attention. Then a merry Jewish wedding tune fills the room as Aaron, accompanied by Izzy, Vince, Rabbi Sunshine, and the Kanczuga Rebbe as well as a number of young men dancing with interlocked arms, makes his way through the crowd and up to Maria. When Aaron stands before the bride, and with her exchanges a look as exalted as it is emotional, silence descends on the gathering. Aaron veils Maria, and again the music blares. Reluctantly, Aaron rejoins the men, and the guests proceed to the room where the wedding ceremony will be performed.

Throughout the evening—during the processional, the traditional ceremony, dinner, and even as I dance in the men's circle to the old tunes—my mind keeps wandering back to the Municipal Building, to Eric and Carol, and further into the past, to my parents, but most of all, to Ellen . . . And how I wish that Eric were here to witness such a celebration. How could anyone turn his back on such tradition? I shake my head in dismay.

As the main course—salmon—is being served, Violet tells me that the Kanczuga Rebbe, seated at the table of rabbis next to ours, has asked to see me. I walk over wearily. What now? When I approach he rises slowly and painfully from his chair, takes my arm, and asks me to accompany him. We leave the ballroom together and sit down in the almost empty anteroom.

"If you will forgive me," says the Rebbe, his eyes focused on me, his hand on my shoulder, "I must ask you to do me a favor. Sometimes when I look at people, I am possessed by the need to speak with them, to share with them a particular insight or even an intuition. Frequently it is a verse from our holy books. I am always reluctant to do so but sometimes I feel I must not be silent. I see in you a certain sorrow. I asked Mrs. Finkel, and she said that it has to do with concerns about your son. I felt that about you, too, when you visited me in Jerusalem. May I share with you a verse from Jeremiah?"

Without waiting for my reply, the Rebbe continues, "Thus says the Lord: Refrain your voice from weeping and your eyes from tears; for your work shall be rewarded, says the Lord . . . and there is hope for your future, says the Lord . . ." I hope this speaks to you, to your heart, that it has meaning for you. I see you are in pain, but I believe these words of our ancestor will help you, will give you great hope."

I feel that I am in the presence of greatness, in the presence of a pure soul. My mind is confused, my heart is sad, my defenses are down, and I am very moved by his concern but find it difficult to respond. Then, from deep inside me, arises the question. "Will my grandchildren be Jews, Rebbe?"

He shrugs in answer to me: He cannot know.

"My children and my first wife were killed in Auschwitz," he says, "and yet here I am. With five children and thirty-one grandchildren. I married again after the war, and I have lived to see Jewish grandchildren after all. Who can understand what happens in this world? A religious person accepts. We complain, we wrestle and argue with Him, we worry, but we in the end accept. Try your best to inspire your son and his wife. Don't give up. God willing, maybe you will succeed. I will pray for you."

He looks very tired, yet this wise old man takes the time to be kind to a relative stranger. When I thank him, he admonishes me. "We are brothers," he says, "brothers comfort one another."

I help him return to his chair, then I return to mine. Violet searches my face. "So?" she asks. I shrug; I am unable to share this with her.

The evening passes pleasantly after that. My spirits rise. The moment comes when the Rebbe gets up and goes slowly over to the bride and groom, who are now sitting in the middle of the dance floor. Perfectly still, he stands before them. And then, as best he can, he dances for them. For them, he performs the great good deed of "making the bride and groom happy." I join him, as do others, and together we dance joyfully arm in arm. It is a moment of joy I will never forget, for I am dancing not only before Maria and Aaron but before Eric and Carol as well, and with me dancing are my parents and my grandparents and their parents, and I have finally "brought" my mother to a wedding.

22.

I wake slowly from a deep sleep. The dream is still with me. Weddings. White dresses, chairs in the air, people dancing all around me. I think it is Eric and Carol in the air, I think it is Miriam and Aaron. In the dream. But I am the one aloft in the chair. And when I try to see who is facing, who sits in the opposite chair, the face is blank; and then the chair is empty.

I crawl out of bed. I get some orange juice to elevate my blood sugar; I need to clear my head. As I look out the kitchen window, Tatiana and Niki wander into my head. The boy has been coming to practice every day, except on weekends, so I haven't seen him or Tatiana since the Seder. Della can't stop raving about the boy, and she seems to be developing a rapport with Tatiana. From her, I get little tidbits of news about them. So I know that Niki will be going away for two weeks to a summer camp subsidized by the Jewish Federation, and he is a little scared of leaving home. I know that in

Della's estimation he plays the piano beautifully and that he should be taking more lessons than Tatiana can currently afford. I'd like to know more.

So I call Tatiana.

"It's Dan. I must tell you—I'm a little insulted."

"What have I done to offend you, Dan?" Tatiana asks, concerned.

"How come you and Niki never come over on weekends?"

"We don't want to disturb you. It is more than enough that we take advantage of your generosity during the week."

"Please come by. What are you doing today?"

"Well, nothing yet."

"I would love to see you," I say and add, "the two of you."

She accepts my invitation, apparently with genuine pleasure.

By three o'clock, it's dark and rainy; a real downpour has begun. I am pacing the front hall, wondering if they will come, when, to my relief the doorman rings up to announce them. I open the door and wait. Wet and laughing, the two of them come out of the elevator. Niki throws off his raincoat, and with great enthusiasm he runs over to me and hugs me for all he's worth. I lean over and hug him back. With a big smile, Tatiana watches us both.

By the time I take her wet coat and umbrella, Niki is at the piano playing away. Tatiana and I sit down in the living room so we can listen to him. While the skill he demonstrates is evident, the emotion he infuses into the music is remarkable for a boy not yet ten years old. I feel a peculiar surge of pride that's almost paternal, but I discount it as the simple pleasure of hearing music fill the room again the way it did when Ellen was alive. For more than half an hour, the music pours out of him. He works hard at the keyboard, his face filled with intense concentration and his entire body moving with the rhythm.

Suddenly he stops. He turns to Tatiana and asks something in Russian. She replies, then digs into her bag to produce a small thermos. "Chocolate milk," she explains to me as Niki gulps it.

She is still damp from the rain, her hair hangs limp and moist. Her body held straight, her face happy as she watches her son, she is sitting next to me, and I don't want her ever to leave, not ever—I want her just to stay right here with me. I could do so much for the two of them; the boy needs a father, and she looks so tired, burdened. I could turn their lives around. And she could change mine. She makes me feel strong and needed, and I have to resist the urge to reach out and hold her hand. What would she do? How would she feel if I did that, if I took advantage of her being here at my invitation? . . . I'm sixty, what could she ever feel for me, except maybe gratitude?

Niki has finished, and still we sit there. He comes over to me, asks, "What did you think?"

"Great," I say, "really superb. You will be a star someday." Beaming, he sits down between Tatiana and me, but he leans up against me, and I smile, surprised, with pleasure.

"Do we have to go home now?" he asks. "Couldn't we stay a little longer? It's so hot at home."

"No air-conditioning?" I ask.

"We don't have the capacity," says Tatiana. "Even a fan sometimes knocks out the electricity. But the rain should help, it should break the heat."

"Della made some cookies yesterday," I say to Niki. "Would it be okay for him to have them, Tatiana?"

She agrees, but when she takes him to the kitchen I remain in the living room, in my chair, and become increasingly annoyed with myself. Tatiana attracts me, she moves me, and the boy is a pleasure—but what could this possibly lead to? I don't want to start all over again, it's not what I need. Not at sixty. In a few minutes, Tatiana returns, and when she suggests that they leave I do not try to dissuade her, however much I may want them to stay.

"See you next weekend," we all say to each other. I give Tatiana a key. I tell her that I have already arranged with the doorman to admit her, even if I am not at home. Then they go back into the rain.

23.

I decide to be out the following Saturday, when Tatiana brings Niki over to practice, so after two in the afternoon I stroll over to the Whitney Museum to visit a special exhibit of American painting. The place is busy. While I'm waiting for the elevator I get that vaguely uncomfortable feeling that someone is looking at me. I turn to my right and there stands Susan Kleiness looking a bit non-plused, our encounter obviously as unexpected and awkward for her as it is for me. Still, we manage to make small talk, and when it becomes evident that we are both here alone we therefore resign our-selves to being pretty much stuck with each other. As we stroll together through the exhibit upstairs, she proves to be much more knowledgeable about art than me, and I appreciate her commentary. I also enjoy her company, and our mood lightens. I invite her to join me for some tea in the restaurant downstairs. She accepts: "I'm game, they have great desserts down there." She would know.

As soon as we have ordered, she says, "Let's get it out of the way. I feel like I need to say something about the night we were together. I want you to know it was very unusual for me, as I told you then, I can understand why you didn't call me again. That's entirely your right, of course, and I am not angry. So let's start this over again, as friends."

"Wow, you're quite an original character. I like your directness. Let me say first of all I really enjoyed that night. It was fireworks for me, but it made me realize I'm not ready for very much more than that at present. That's the reason I haven't called, in case you want to know."

"Well, I can assure you that you're safe here. I have never yet attacked a man in a restaurant," she says, smiling.

So we begin to talk business. She launches into an explanation of why her stock has recently gone down, when a bizarre-looking woman walks over to our table and Susan lets out a surprised little yelp and, after the two embrace, I am introduced to Herta Searing. A woman in her fifties, she speaks with a slight German accent; her pale blonde hair is essentially uncombed, her remarkable blue eyes bulge out, her intensely red lipstick overshoots her lips, and her huge dangling earrings taunt the eye with numerous variously colored stones. All of her fingernails are painted in different colors, and her hands are smudged with what look like ink stains.

At Susan's invitation she joins us. "Herta is my dear, dear friend but also my favorite psychic, which is how we met," Susan tells me. "We speak at least once a week, and I depend on her very much. This is a lovely surprise."

Herta, though, is not listening. She seems to have decided to focus all her psychic energy on me. "You don't believe in such

hocus-pocus, do you?" she asks, and when I do not reply she continues, "Who is the woman with the E beginning her name? The
letter E, who is she?"

I respond, "Maybe my late wife."

"Yes. So that's why I see her with a halo. You are still in touch with
her, you speak to her sometimes. She hears you, don't worry. Now,
what is a Feck or a Funk, a name with an F? A woman. Difficult, very
rich, very powerful. Snip-snip to your masculinity; not good for you.
Run from this Fenk. Do you know who is indicated?" I nod affirma-
tively, wondering how the hell she knows, who told her all this. It
can't be a setup, not here with Susan.

"Lots of women: What's going on? A shame, at your age. You tend
to your business, never mind the women—too much of a strain on
you." She pauses, leans her head forward; her eyes, narrowing, focus
on some distant point. "Your watch," she says, "something about your
watch. Who got it for you?"

"No one. It was my father's. I inherited it from him."

"It's good, very good. Yes, your father. When you are in trouble,
hold it tight, you will be helped. A good aura, don't give away the
watch. You should be ashamed to do what you do with the women
while you wear the watch. You certainly are a busy boy."

She pauses again. Her look softens, and she smiles with
pleasure. "Are you an actor?" she asks. "I love the theater. I feel
you are an actor."

"No," I reply.

"You thought about becoming an actor, no?"

"No."

"You have the talent—I'm never wrong on these things, almost
never. One day perhaps you will take up acting."

"I don't think so, I'm a broker."

"Ah, it's the same thing, the same talent. You like music: All around you is the piano, pounding away."

"My piano," I assure her, "but not me playing on it."

She waves her hand dismissively. "I hear the piano, who plays is of no consequence to me. So much piano noise I begin to get a headache. Also, I am quite hungry. Perhaps they have a hot fudge sundae here?"

"I'll order one for you," I offer, and while we're waiting for it, Susan and I watch Herta, sitting now with her eyes closed, massage her forehead vigorously. It is a much appreciated pause in my first experience with a psychic.

Our waitress brings the sundae, Herta slurps it up. "Nuts on top," she says, "I love the nuts." She doesn't mind the whipped cream either. With a slight white mustache over her upper lip, she turns to Susan, then points to me and asks, "Is this the one you told me about? It is, isn't it? Forget it, he is with the other women. He has moved on. No future, but it's nice to be friends. Right?" And she dips into the thick fudge sauce and starts shoveling the ice cream into her eager mouth with loud and appreciative slurps. Susan is meanwhile polishing off some biscotti. I find it hard to concentrate on my tea what with the outburst of Delphic pronouncements.

"No more fooling around together for you two; a good man is coming for Susan, a big man who loves her, big like a tree. And for you no Fenk either," she says, pointing at me. "You already have met some other woman. You can swim, I hope. Because this woman, she is drowning without you, she grabs you like a lifesaver. All this I give you for free—next time you want Herta you'll have to pay. I'm a *Geschäft*, a business, not a free university. If you want to know more, you must become a client, and then you get the *echt* reading, the real thing. Enough for now, I earned my sundae. Here's my card. Call only between ten P.M. and two in the morning, that is when I am at my best; one hundred dollars a call. You mail me the check immediately after the reading. I know so much more about you, but I tell no more now: from this I must make my living. Now I go to prepare for a séance that I hold this evening. I am hoping to chat with Charles de Gaulle, or at least with Pétain; I am interested in the period. Good-bye, Susan; good-bye, Mr. Gelder. Until we meet again." And she walks off briskly and determinedly.

"Dan, isn't she amazing?" asks Susan, and I acknowledge that she is, but disturbing too.

"I don't want to know all that stuff, even if it's true," I say. "Aren't you afraid of being influenced, of being sucked in?" I ask.

"Of course, but I'm more afraid not to hear it," Susan admits. "I'm more afraid to be all alone without a hint of what direction to take."

An awkward moment arises when we leave the museum. I am clearly welcome to walk her home and visit, but I claim to have a pressing appointment and walk quickly away. By the time I arrive home, Tatiana and Niki have gone. I am disappointed. In the front hall, I catch a whiff of Tatiana's alluring perfume, which mingles disappointment with desire.

24.

Sunday morning, I am awakened by a call from Eric.

"Dad, can you come over to my office?"

"What time is it? Isn't it Sunday?" I ask, momentarily confused.

"Yes, it's Sunday. But I need your help."

"What has happened?"

"It's the software. It's not working. All that money—" I hear panic behind his voice.

"Now, don't worry. We will figure it out. I'll be right over. Where are you?"

"At the office," he says shortly and hangs up.

When I arrive at Eric's office, the place is quiet and empty. At the peak of business, he employed more than a dozen people; today it's only Eric, his secretary, and two software people. Eric explains to me why the software is not operational.

"Well, how much money would it take to get it right?" I ask.

Eric looks over at the two software guys and says, "They think they need about five months at about seventy-five thousand per month."

"That's three hundred and fifty thousand dollars!" I say in shock. "What happened to the rest of the money?"

"I didn't buy a car with it!" Eric says defensively.

"I know, I know. It's just—"

"I know, Dad. You're worried."

"I'm not just worried, but there is only so much I can do for you, son."

He and I go over the financials. It is evident that there is not enough liquidity to allow the company to survive for the minimum time necessary it needs to get its software product integrated into the systems of its large but so far only potential customer.

"Game over," says Eric, "unless the bank frees me of financial covenants and advances some more money. And I would say that the chances of that happening are about as good as my becoming the lead dancer in the Royal Ballet. It's all over."

I can't disagree. Since the potential customer will not make a cash advance or even sign a solid contract, bankruptcy looms as the only sensible possibility. This will allow Eric at least to make an attempt to squeeze out a few pennies from the value of the software. So I suggest, "Maybe you should file for bankruptcy before you are down to the last penny. That way, you'll have some liquidity, and you might be able to salvage something."

Eric has aged visibly in these last few months; he has lost his buoyancy, and he is obviously not sleeping well. He doesn't look like a young man who has just married. Defeat has diminished even that pleasure for him.

"It all hinges on the bank. I begged them for six months for more funding, but no dice. The guy in charge of the loan, Lemon is his name, is a real hardnose; no socializing, all business. I can't seem to get through to him."

As sorry as I feel for Eric, it does no good to show it. Frustrated by my own inability to help, I can only listen sympathetically.

I have no reason to be in good humor when I leave Eric at noon. Yet my spirits begin to lift as I walk toward home. It is a really spectacular day, sunny and breezy; the mood in the street is lively, bright. Still preoccupied, wondering whether I have any connections at Eric's bank, I am startled when someone puts a hand on my arm.

"Hi, dreamer," says Violet. "What are you doing roaming around the streets in a daze?"

"I'm AWOL. Please don't report me."

"There are many things that I would like to do to you, but reporting you is not one of them."

"Gee, a guy can't walk on Fifth Avenue during the middle of the day without being solicited."

"You wish. Instead, let me buy you lunch."

"I'm not going to be very good company, Violet. I've just spent the morning with my son. His business is in big trouble. So I don't have much of an appetite for lunch, except for maybe a little ground glass or some hemlock."

"Stop it, you're about to have a fabulous lunch, and it's on me—we'll have wine, even champagne, if you want. I'll get you drunk, and then I'll take advantage of you."

She leads me down the block to a restaurant where she is evidently well known. We are treated like royalty, and one excellent glass of wine later I am telling all. Her mind sharp and her grasp of the business situation impressive, she probes for the details. Then she surprises me.

"Listen, Dan, we're not really lovers, not too often anyway, and you know I'm not looking for a husband, but if I were, I would consider you seriously. What you lack in soul you make up for in other ways, and one of them is the way you love your son. God knows why, he sounds even worse than my Maria. Now, you know better than most that I have many negative characteristics. But I am loyal to my friends, who, by the way, are few and far between—I guess it's my occasionally overbearing personality—so when I find a good one I value the relationship. Plus I have another winning trait: Irv left me so rich that all I have to do is wake up to find that I'm delightfully richer each day. In short, I would like to save your son's ass, which I surmise means about three hundred and fifty thousand dollars. I would like to make that offer to him. I want all the intellectual property to secure my loan. Don't worry, you're off the hook emotionally, because I could lose it all and it wouldn't spoil my dinner. Feeling any better?"

I'm stunned. If on the one hand I am delighted, on the other hand I'm uncomfortable. "Look, in this tech business three hundred and fifty can go down the drain before you finish your coffee," I tell her. "I really appreciate what you're trying to do. Nobody has ever been so generous to me, not ever, but I don't know that I have the right to let you do it. Certainly, it was not my intention in telling you. And I have no idea how Eric would feel about it."

"Dan," she says, "let me do this for you. I need to do it, I want to do it. I seated you next to me at my daughter's wedding; I am very fond of you in my way, and if I want to piss away my money, that's my business. Now, write down Eric's number and I'll call him. Or better yet, tell him the good news and have him call me. Tell him it's a wedding present. He can have little Miss Michigan write me a thank- you note like she would for a vase or a cake knife. So it's set- tled. Finished, off my mind. End of discussion."

My feeble protestations fall on deaf ears. I allow myself to enjoy the good news for a few minutes, then rush to a phone to tell Eric. He whoops with joy and pleasure, compliments me on what he assumes is my prowess in bed: "Nobody ever gave me even dollar one for *shtupping*," he says. "You should write a how-to book!"

That night Violet calls me to tell me that she and Eric have agreed on all the details. Papers are being drawn up. She also instructs me, "I don't want you to change one iota toward me. I like you prickly, not compliant. If I annoy you, tell me. If I want you, don't oblige unless you want to. Three hundred and fifty is not enough to buy you; remember that."

"I promise. However, I do have a price and for three million five hundred thousand dollars, I'm yours body and soul—oh, I forgot, I don't have a soul, still interested?"

"Now that we know what you're going for, I can always negotiate the price down."

"Last time I say it, Violet"—and I mean it—"I'll never be able to thank you enough. Thanks again."

25.

The following weekend, summer truly arrives in New York. The air is still and sultry, the pavement glistens, and the odors of city life begin to waft through every open window. I have the itch to leave. It's high time that I opened up the country home that Ellen and I bought more than twenty-five years ago in the Berkshires.

I haven't set foot in the house since Ellen died. Every time Eric encouraged me to go up, I'd put it off—work to do, plans in the city, hay fever. Of course, we both knew I was making excuses, but I just couldn't contend with another wave of sadness prompted by stirred up memories.

Ellen had redecorated every inch of the stone and shingle house, to restore and preserve its nineteen-twenties charm. It was Ellen, too, who attended to the multicolored slate roof, which needed repair after every winter. We spent many weekends up at the house with Eric when he was young, but once he got older it became our romantic hideaway. There was something liberating about being in the old house then, and the two of us would carry on like young honeymooners. We would often stay in our pajamas an entire day; we'd plant ourselves in front of a roaring fire, cuddle, make love, eat, sleep, and then repeat.

For two years, the thought of going anywhere near the scene of those memories hurt, but I feel more fortified now. Something inside me has changed. I am ready to make the drive north.

It takes two and a half hours, and as I drive down the long driveway toward the house all sorts of conflicting emotions hit me. Ellen and I planted many of the trees and bushes on the three-acre property; it's been awhile since I've seen them, and I take real pleasure in them as I do in the garden abloom with the bright flowers that Ellen loved. The caretaker has been doing his job well.

When I open the front door, more memories rise up and punch me in my chest. For a moment, I find it hard to breathe. I sit down in the small screened-in porch off the living room and try to get hold of myself. Ellen's touch is everywhere, on every lamp, in every chair, in every piece of art on the walls. The large watercolor of an English garden we bought for a song still hangs where she placed it, above the mantel, and dominates the living room. The metal dog she used for a doorstop still stands secure in his habitual spot near the porch door. And for the first time since she died I hear myself asking the question out loud that I have asked silently many times: *Why did you leave me? It would have been more natural for me to go first.*

It's the wrong question, of course. A question that has no answer. Ellen didn't go willingly, she fought hard against the cancer. We both fought hard against it, and we both lost. And when I finish shouting at the injustice of it, I don't feel foolish. In fact, I feel better. I make a quick trip through the house to see if everything is in order, then head out to get some groceries. I drive toward the small town of Lenox, but just as I'm pulling into the grocery store parking lot, I realize I can't do this, not yet. I'd rather be in the hot city, anywhere but here. Here there are no distractions, here there are only memories. Here I am alone with exactly what I am, a tired, lonely sixty-year-old man.

When I get back to New York, back to my apartment, before I even enter I hear the piano. Of course, it's Saturday. Niki is hard at work, and neither he nor Tatiana notices me when I walk into the living room. I think he is playing Beethoven. He is playing with such intensity that I feel a pang of real affection for him: He's so little, so innocent, so talented. In his less than ten years, he has lost his father, been uprooted and taken to a new country, been separated from most of his small family, and yet he is full of love and full of music. I wish I could be as brave as he is, I wish I had his adaptability. Proud of him, engrossed by the sight of him at the piano and by the sound he is making, I am a little startled when Tatiana turns and greets me. Then Niki jumps off the piano stool and runs toward me. He wraps me in a hug as tightly as he can. He warms my heart.

We all sit down, and I tell them about my house. I even admit that I had intended to spend the weekend there but changed my mind; I don't tell them the reason. Niki tells me that when his father was alive they had a small dacha just a short train ride from Kiev, where they stayed in the summer. Tatiana says it was a shack, but a shack that they all loved. They swam in a lake nearby, they grew vegetables. Their memories are sweet to them, important and cherished, like mine. And here they are in a new country, in a city steamy with summer heat: living in an unair-conditioned walk-up, stuck in someone else's small apartment.

Tatiana looks at her watch. "It's time to go. I have to prepare supper."

"So soon? But I just got here," I say plaintively. "And I'd really rather not be alone. After all, it's Saturday night. And it's hot out there. We have tons of food in the apartment, Della cooks up a storm on Fridays. So why not stay? Please."

Tatiana looks at me, then at Niki, who is nodding his head in encouragement. "Okay, then. We will stay."

"Can I watch TV?" asks Niki.

Tatiana gives her assent, and she and I go into the kitchen. She motions for me to sit at the table, then she begins preparing our meal. Obviously very much at ease at the task, absorbed in the process, she moves with assurance back and forth, and her every move delights me. She is not dressed like most New Yorkers on a very hot summer night. She is wearing her usual simple black outfit, accented only by her red high heels, which do wonders for her superb legs. She brushes past me, and I catch the fresh, clean scent of her perfume.

"Making dinner in an air-conditioned kitchen is such a luxury. You are very fortunate."

"Yes," I say, admiring her from behind. And I think again how amazing it is that I feel so comfortable with this woman who is so different from me. Outwardly, we appear to have little in common, yet our rhythm together is so easy, so effortless. I feel so relaxed. Every now and then, she glances up from her preparation, as if to acknowledge my presence, but she seems to feel no need to fill the gaps of silence. I like this: both the silence itself and her comfort in it. I like that we can share it; it's a rare thing to find with someone new.

Still chuckling at something he was watching on TV, Niki joins us a little reluctantly when called. We sit at the kitchen table, we're eating happily together, when lightning flashes and a loud clap of thunder rattles the windowpane behind us. Tatiana pales; obviously frightened, she puts down her fork. The thunder crashes again, and now Tatiana is clearly terrified. Niki gets up and hugs her; looking at me with manly pride, he explains that his mother is scared of lightning. At the third bolt, Tatiana jumps up and, moving away from the table, she urges me to do the same. "But there's no danger whatsoever, we're perfectly safe," I try to reassure her.

"I know, I know, but I can't stand it, I can't," Tatiana whispers.

So I, too, hug her. With Niki standing on one side of her and I on the other, the three of us wait it out. She leans into me, her hair against my face and her hand tight on my chest, my heart is beating fast. Excited by her presence, I am also shaken by the strange intensity of my desire for this woman. The way she fits into my arms, we might have been made for each other; it's the way I felt when I held Ellen in my arms. The storm soon relents, its din yielding to the soothing sound of a heavy summer rain.

By the time we finish our coffee, the rain has stopped, and I accompany them on their way home through the freshened, wet city streets.

Niki holds my hand. I'm telling him a silly story while we walk, but I'm only half concentrating on it, as I am watching Tatiana through the corner of my eye. When we reach their building, Niki gives me his now customary hug, and I, already lost, already defenseless, kiss Tatiana lightly on the cheek.

And why, I wonder on my way home, don't I simply surrender to what is beginning to feel like an inevitability—my illogical, irrational need for this woman. Because it means at least ten more years of hard labor, if I live that long, I tell myself. College for the kid, music lessons, trips, God alone knows what else; and yet I feel happy with them. I feel desperate, too, for even if I am willing to work and work hard, do I have a chance with her? In Tatiana's eyes, am I any more than a kindly uncle, an older guy—too old a guy?

An uglier thought enters my head: What if she is playing me? You hear the story all the time. Older guy falls for younger woman, and a month, a week, into the marriage, older guy discovers all the woman wanted was his money, his house, his assets. Maybe that's what Tatiana is after.

Then I remember how wonderful it felt to be with her in the kitchen, to hold her in my arms, tonight.

26.

No good deed goes unpunished," is the way Violet begins our phone conversation. "I accept that," she continues, "but why isn't there some time off for good behavior? I was so nice to the sister of the Toronto witch, the fat one from Scarsdale with the same red hair as Dolly: Oh my God, do you think it might actually be natural and run in the family? Can't be, that red has got to have come out of a paint can. Anyway, the Scarsdale redhead, Barbara Farfell, has invited me up to a cocktail party in honor of Maria and Aaron before they return to Jerusalem. I've got to show up, and I can't face it alone. It's next Sunday. You might even end up enjoying it, it will be at their club on the water. Don't say no, or you'll have my suicide on your conscience. Just wear a nice blue blazer; no tie, the country look is fine—and bring your fabulous smile. I'll pick you up at four o'clock. Please, please, please, say yes."

"Yes," I say obligingly. "Shit," I add.

"I know the feeling. But be sure to wear that blue blazer; I'm wearing pink so we won't clash. See you." For that three hundred and fifty grand she gave my kid, I'd wear a pink suit if she wanted.

The next Sunday is the hottest, most humid day of the summer so far. As Violet's driver whisks us off to the Argyle Harbor Beach Club, she explains her outfit, "It's my summer country look." Violet is indeed all in pink; even her diamonds are pink. "I plan to clash as much as possible with Barbara's hair—I'm hoping she's as obsessed with it as Dolly is."

Throughout the forty-five-minute drive, the sky darkens, rain clouds appear, and Violet mutters. "Why couldn't Maria and Aaron have gone on a honeymoon like other people? Oh, no, they had to have the ultra-Orthodox *Sheva Brachot*, the Seven Blessings—night after night of dinners hosted by friends, each one ending with the same special blessings. I must have gained ten pounds. I never knew there were that many kosher restaurants in town. Eating, eating, all they do is eat. Doesn't anyone screw anymore? And now they're going home. I begged them to stop for a few days in Europe, have a little fun, but no—they have to attend Aunt Barbara's cocktail party, at which, by the way, they cannot eat a morsel, evidently it's not kosher enough for them."

The skies open, and the rain comes down in torrents driven by a high wind. Surprisingly, an act of God can silence Violet. We are forced to drive slowly, the monotonous whoosh of the windshield wipers the only sound in the car as we all concentrate on the visibility problem. When the rain slackens, Violet's mood has changed. She takes my hand, holds it firmly, but she avoids my eyes.

"I'm getting used to you," she says. "Don't change, don't ever develop a soul, just stay the way you are: old reliable Dan. If I could ever love another man, it would probably be you. Big if, so you're lucky, you're safe. But promise me you'll stay single and won't fall for some boring little broad. Promise me you'll stay just as you are."

Violet's timing, her intuition is startling. I don't reply, I simply squeeze her hand in mine. It would be just my luck to have Violet falling for me despite all odds, at exactly the same time I might be falling for someone else. Part of me would like to confide in Violet, as I did when we were in Israel, but another part of me pulls back. And I keep my thoughts, my doubts private.

As we draw up to the club entrance, the harbor stretching out in front of us, I marvel at how filled with surprises life is. To prove me right, a seagull passing overhead chooses that moment to dump a load that with perfect precision hits me in my right eye and splashes onto my shoulder.

"Shit," I yell.

"Precisely," says Violet, now laughing merrily. Surrounded by scores of other arriving guests, she helps clean me up as she sings a little ditty she no doubt learned in her Brooklyn childhood: "Birdy, birdy in the sky, why did you make a doody in my eye? Next time from the sky so blue, please try aiming for my shoe." Then we both proceed happily into the party.

A lavish array of food awaits us. At the center of the room is an ice sculpture in the form of a maple leaf, which competes for attention with a mountain of chopped liver carved in the shape of a seagull. Surrounding these works of culinary artistry are stations with sushi, crepes, smoked salmon, and sliced meats. Armed with champagne and a fixed smile, I make my way through the party and watch my sparkling Violet charm everyone in her path, except for the Farfells, whom she mesmerizes. I wonder what life would be like with Violet—despite her imperious, often annoying nature, she would fit into my life and meet my needs more naturally than . . . Tatiana and

Niki: I see myself working long hours, coming home more tired than not, for what? Why? Again, my doubts. I am not fabulously rich like Violet, but to someone like Tatiana, I must look like a prince.

And all the way home, as Violet naps beside me, I weigh Violet against Tatiana. There are so many pros and cons, so many pluses and minuses. Finally, mercifully, I am dropped in front of my building and go straight up to bed.

27.

I hope he rots in hell," begins the woman on the phone. "I hope he burns, him and that Mexican strumpet of his."

I think it's Myra, but I ask.

"Of course it's me. Myra Forshpise, wife of Billy Cox, one thing I never got much of during our marriage. God, I'm glad I never took his name—a woman should never give up her name for a man. You are all a bunch of alley cats; you'd screw a snake, given the chance. If it wasn't for the occasional orgasm you provide, none of you would be worth the powder to blow you to hell. Where I hope he writhes in lakes of fire."

"Myra, Myra, what's going on? What's the matter?" I ask, both concerned and annoyed. All women sound like Violet when they're angry.

"The matter! What's the matter?" she sobs. "The matter is that my Billy has been inserting his pathetic little dick into Gloria, my maid.

And she's pregnant. I should have known it was Billy months ago. He burst into tears when I told him about Gloria, her pregnancy, and took the next flight home—from Helsinki. But who would have guessed? I mean, she's barely four feet tall with gold front teeth, and she usually smells of silver polish. It's so insulting! This is what he chooses over me? Once my divorce lawyer gets through with him, *he'll* be four feet tall, and I'll own his gold teeth. Almost twenty years I lived with him, with him and his open marriage and open fly, while I had to find pleasure with strangers, and did I ever complain? He and his human rights missions—those Third World trips, the mosquitoes, the heat and smells—all of that I went through with him, and he leaves me for an enchilada, for a tortilla chip."

"Myra, should I come over? Do you need some help?"

"No, I don't need help. I need my hairdresser, I need my manicurist. I don't need anything from any man," she shrieks, then hangs up.

Evidently, Billy is having fun. Dave's had his. Everybody is jumping on top of one another. Except for me. I couldn't get laid in a whorehouse it seems. Violet, Myra, Susan, Charlotte—they try me out once, twice maybe, and then move on. What do I have, bad breath?

And at that unpropitious moment, Tatiana calls. Her co-tenants are away for the week, and she would like to reciprocate my kindness. Do I like Russian food? She invites me to dinner on Friday night, and I accept. We agree that I'll come over with Niki after he finishes practicing at my place. I call the florist and arrange for flowers for the table to be delivered on Friday afternoon to Tatiana's apartment, and I make a mental note to wear my navy suit. I always feel I look my best in that suit, and that's how I want to look for her.

* * *

Midweek, Eric and I have a light lunch together at a coffee shop. His face beams, as he details for me some of his achievements toward perfecting his software product. He is once more brimming with confidence, and I'm only more grateful to Violet for giving him this opportunity. When Eric is happy, I can always see a lot of Ellen in his face: the same quick, wide smile, the same dimple in the right cheek, the darkly luminous eyes. He tells me that he would like to start going to the house in the Berkshires on weekends, and he urges me to join him and Carol on the one coming up—so that Carol can have the opportunity to get to know me better. I have to turn him down, as I've got Tatiana cooking for me

On Friday afternoon New York is suffering from one of the worst heat waves in memory. The sidewalks are hot, everything is sticky. People on the streets look exhausted and sloppy. The occasional young man is strolling shirtless. Niki and I walk the blocks to his home slowly, but we're both drenched in sweat by the time we reach the dreaded stairs of the walk-up. I should not have worn my navy suit—any suit—and by the time we climb the stairs I'm sure, too, that I should not have accepted the invitation. The hall is blisteringly hot, and the apartment is barely better, its single fan scarcely even moving the tepid air. The heat in the kitchen is nearly intolerable, and not surprisingly, Tatiana is wet and frazzled when we greet her. She thanks me for the flowers, which sit at the center of the table, and begs me to take off my tie and be comfortable.

Comfortable, I think to myself, pressing my handkerchief against my forehead, and still it beads with sweat. I couldn't be more uncomfortable.

Tatiana reenters the room with two little brass candlesticks and two short white candles. I have not witnessed the lighting of the

Sabbath candles since Ellen died; it was the one ritual Ellen faithfully observed. After she lights the candles, Tatiana covers her eyes for a minute, mumbles a few words, and then turns to Niki and me. "Good Sabbath," she says, and Niki echoes her. I ask her whether she began practicing this ritual when she came to New York, but no, she tells me, her grandmother had always lit the Sabbath candles, although her mother abandoned the practice. Tatiana cherished the little candlesticks, and she resumed the practice after she married. She had never learned the appropriate prayer, and still doesn't know it, but she makes of the ritual her moment to pray for the fortunes of her family each week.

The meal is excellent but heavy—hot borscht, pirogen, blini, and stuffed cabbage—not really suitable for a humid, hot summer evening. As Tatiana is clearly anxious that I enjoy the food, I eat more than I want or should. By the end of dinner the combination of my body heat from overeating with the hot air flowing from the fan has made me uncomfortable, and I can see that Tatiana feels the evening has not been a success. As we finish, Niki asks if he can turn off the fan so that he can watch television, since the electricity is not sufficient for both. Tatiana hesitates, her eyes on me, but I say I'll be fine. So we two sit in the now breezeless room, and despite my compliments on her cooking she looks miserable. My hair plastered down, my shirt soaked, I am so sweaty that I am past caring, but I can't bear the sadness in her eyes, like that of a person who has presented someone with an unappreciated gift.

"Tatiana," I say, and I can hear the sympathy—no, the love—in my voice. I stand, I lift her up, take her into my arms. I kiss her. There is no resistance. Then I look straight into her eyes; she is crying silently, and I wonder if I have offended her, have overstepped the line. But she does not pull away. A long minute passes. And she says one word: "Finally." She repeats it: "Finally." She clings to me, and I to her, and I don't know how long we remain that way. I do know that at last I feel perfectly at home in a way I never thought I would again.

We stir the slightest bit when we hear a noise at the door. It is Niki. Wide-eyed, surprised, he looks at us until Tatiana beckons to him. When he's at her side, she wraps an arm around him and presses him close to her, to include him in our embrace. For the first time since I met her, I feel no regret and no hesitation. I don't know exactly what is going to happen next, but, whatever it is I am now to some degree responsible for this woman and her son. So it is with absolute assurance and authority that I tell Tatiana to clean up quickly and to pack up a bag. "The two of you are coming home with me tonight, no arguments accepted," I tell them. "At least until this heat wave is over, you are my guests."

Once Tatiana has put Niki to sleep in Eric's room, she comes into the small library off the living room. She is dressed in a light pink bathrobe and negligee, and she's wearing silly-looking little slippers. With confidence and determination, she walks toward me, and says, "Niki is asleep, Della is gone." She takes my hand, and leading me into her bedroom, she tells me, "This is our night to be together." I am glad it is not to be in my bedroom, in the room I shared with Ellen for so long.

Tatiana takes off her nightclothes and tosses them onto a chair. Turning toward me, proud of her beauty, her eyes steady on mine, she stands before me with no embarrassment evident. I can't help but stare; I am simply floored by her beauty. Her breasts are large but firm; her rounded hips more alluring than I had imagined; her thighs, maybe a little thick at the top, a slight imperfection—but an imperfection that touches me and only heightens her desirability.

I am astonished at the intensity of my desire, and for some reason I freeze in place. Without a blush she comes close to me and starts undoing my belt. My throat is dry. I want to tell her how beautiful she is, how I've longed for her, but I can't say a word. My navy blue trousers drop to the floor. This is absurd; pathetic. Some Don Juan I am: I can't even take off my own pants and my knees are weak.

Her eyes, her magical eyes, tease me with a mixture of flirtatiousness and irony. "Can you manage the rest?" she asks as she reaches up for a kiss.

I don't really know quite how, but within seconds we are on the bed—me on top of her, with my damned underpants now wrapped around my ankles, my shirt and tie still on. Her mouth is open like a gasp, her eyes are shut, and whatever she's whispering, moaning, in Russian, the sounds are encouraging. When we finish, I stay on top of her, my face pressed against hers, our legs still tangled together.

Her eyes open; there is a question in them. She's asking for something with those eyes, but I say nothing. There will be no postcoital declarations from me tonight, no words of love, nothing to regret later on. Maybe I haven't outgrown sex, but at least I've learned to keep my mouth shut.

"I love you," she says tentatively. She's still young, she doesn't yet know how easy it is to confuse an orgasm with love. Or maybe she does, maybe she has other more practical reasons for her declaration of love.

I have to say something. "You're wonderful," I say, "splendid. You are my dream come true." Her eyes search mine, but I turn away. I bury my face in her hair.

28.

U nexpectedly, of course, Violet calls me at the office and invites herself up for lunch. I order in some salads and grilled salmon, which my secretary, Tina, sets out on the side table in my office. She leaves a thermos of coffee and another of tea as well as a large pitcher of ice, and with a glint in her eye she tells me that she'll hold my calls, "so you and Mrs. Finkel can have a tête-à-tête, undisturbed." Well, I'm disturbed already. How do I tell Violet about Tatiana and me? What will she think? Why do I care what she thinks?

Looking expensive and pretty, Violet breezes in. "Yum," she says as she glances at the set table. "Just what I wanted—you and food." She sits down and unfurls her napkin—it is obvious which comes first—and I join her. The fact that she is avoiding my eyes no doubt means she has something to say. She chooses her words carefully.

"I want to suggest something," she says. "If it's of no interest, don't be afraid to be blunt. I soon leave for Europe for my usual summer escape, and I will also make a quick visit to the kids in Jerusalem. I come back here in the fall, then go down to Palm Beach for the winter—boring but socially correct." She pauses, to shift her mental gears a bit. "You and I have been slowly circling each other like two sumo wrestlers looking for an advantage, and, like two sumos, each time one grips the other, the other slips right out of the hold. Occasionally, very occasionally, we find ourselves in bed, where we each perform rather well, I think. Every once in a while, I call you to come to my rescue, but you never, or almost never, call me." Silent for a moment, Violet then looks up at me, her eyes shrewd and inquisitive. "You began to actually fall for me in Safed, didn't you, and in Jerusalem I could have bagged you, if I hadn't paused in my campaign to win you. I know you blame the Rebbe for that, but it wasn't what the Rebbe said about you so much as how I felt about myself after my meeting with him. I felt unworthy, I felt empty. I knew that my charities were important, but I realized that giving away money I hadn't earned myself was not enough; I recognized I had some spiritual growing up to do. So I pushed you away, I told you that you lacked suffi-cient soul—that was me talking, by the way, not the Rebbe, who actually seems quite fond of you. And you went away like a gentleman and waited for me to come crawling back. Which I guess I did, sort of. Every time I needed a man, I came running, and every time you agreed, then off I'd go, I'd run away, I'd hide, until the next time I needed you. So now I've come here to hash it out with you, to figure out with you what we are to each other. Are we friends? Are we occasional sex partners? Are we more? Was it mostly my money or my facelifts that attracted you to me, or was it me? And is it too late for either of us to care?"

Is she coming after me now? If I say the right words, will she want me now? Is this a test of some sort? And what about Tatiana?

I have a few questions of my own, as I wonder if she is resuming her campaign, if she is out to buy me now. Sometimes, it seems, everything is merely a matter of timing, of chance. Or are all of our apparently random experiences actually preordained so that ultimately some unknowable goal is achieved, or left undone? Or maybe I'm so mixed up that I don't give a shit anymore. Tatiana or Violet— who cares? Maybe Tim has the right idea if not the right sex: Be fickle, go from flower to flower, take your pleasure, and run for the hills. I have more than a few questions, but I don't know what to say, now, to Violet. So I concentrate on spearing a cherry tomato in my salad with my fork.

"Oh Christ," she says, picking up the tomato with her fingers and popping it into my mouth. "After you swallow, let me know what's on your mind, if anything."

But I remain silent.

"Who is she?" Violet asks. "Obviously, there's a new player on the field, so who is she? God, I hope it's not that self-righteous camp follower of the Earth's oppressed, the one with all that cheap jewelry. If it is, I quit. If she scores with you, I don't want to play."

"It's not Myra," I say.

"But there is someone, isn't there? Do I know her? Is it that Russian you were mooning over at the Seder?"

"Why are you talking to me this way, Violet? Do you have some claim on me? Have you ever expressed the slightest interest in laying some claim? Haven't you always told me that we are not for keeps? No strings, you said. So what the hell are you doing?"

"I don't know, Dan. I don't want marriage, but I would love to know that you'll be there, available. That's what I want."

"Rent-a-Dan," I say. "Rent-a-Dan is what you want. You really are something, self-centered is too kind a description. You live in a Violet world, with the rest of us just orbiting around you. I'm too old

to orbit, Violet. I want something more permanent until they cart me
off, someone I care for, someone to take care of me if I ever need it.
Are you interested in applying for that job?"

My question goes unanswered. Violet finishes her salmon, wipes
her mouth primly, and then, poker-faced, she pours us both some
coffee. "I'm starting in London next week. I'm skipping France this
year—they are too anti-Semitic and too anti-American. To hell with
them, they won't get a dime from me. Instead, I am going straight
to Milan, then to Abano. I'll send you my itinerary. If you want to
join me at any point, you're always welcome. I think I am crazy to
walk away from you; I'll probably regret it, but I won't be pinned
down by anyone. Only Irv was able to make me surrender myself to
him, to our love. I don't know if I have room in my heart for
another great love."

We sit together companionably now, my anger gone. Without
realizing it, I have taken her hand in mine. "You've changed a lot
of lives, Violet. Look what you did for Eric. Don't make light of
yourself."

"Tell me, Dan, just for the hell of it, was there ever a time, even a
minute, when you thought you might really love me? Tell me the
truth, Dan."

"Yes," I admit. "When we walked to Maria's house in Jerusalem
that Friday evening. I'll never forget that walk, never. And later that
night, when you came into my bed, that was a special time."

"Well, I had my chance," she says. "I'm sorry it didn't work out—
for both of us." We fall silent again. Then, out of the blue: "What's
her name, Dan? Who has the inside track?"

"You know who, you guessed it—Tatiana, the one with the little boy."

She is sad—I can see it in the shadowy cast of her eyes—but she
makes no comment other than to ask if it is serious.

"Maybe," I reply, knowing that she doesn't want to hear the truth right now.

"Well, if things heat up, let me know. I'll come back for any happy occasion. Have plane, will travel."

She gets up to leave, and we hug each other. Once again, she promises me her itinerary. She leaves quickly then. She turns round once, sees me standing in the open doorway, waves at me from the corridor. Things will never be the same between us again.

I spend the afternoon under a bit of a cloud, and I get home in a down mood. Niki is watching television, which he abandons long enough to welcome me home with a hug. Tatiana and Della are talking in the kitchen, the murmur of their voices affording me a certain comfort. Yet the presence of Tatiana and Niki in my life, in my home, also comes with a price: the loss of spontaneity. While Violet, aggressively free-spirited, will be exploring Europe and Israel, I will be working at my desk in the office and returning home each night to pretty much the same routine, though admittedly a rather enjoyable one. I call out my hello, but the women in the kitchen don't hear me. I retreat to my bedroom, still my private sanctuary because of Tatiana's sensitivity regarding our relationship.

I sit down and assess my situation. The thought of Niki and Tatiana leaving the apartment even when the summer heat breaks is now out of the question. Niki seems really happy here, even goofy at times. He loves me a little already, but he loves Eric a little more. He's picked up many of Eric's gestures, and he agrees with everything Eric says; we all laugh about it. Eric visits much more frequently these days so that he can take Niki to the park with him when he goes jogging. Every once in a while, I wonder what Ellen would think about the changes taking place in her home, about all that's happening to her family. Would she approve? She was jealous of me when she was alive, no question about that. Yet it all seems to be going so smoothly, it all feels so right, that I can't help but believe that she's somehow in on it with me.

I've considered bringing Tatiana and Niki to the country house, though I haven't mentioned it to them. I consider it again as I pull off my jacket and tie, but stay seated in my chair, in my sanctuary, where I know full well I'll soon be found. And Violet intrudes on my thoughts again, Violet and the peculiar friendship we've evolved in our short but extraordinary time together, Violet and the tempting opportunities she offers me. It has gotten a little dark by the time Tatiana finds me. "There you are," she says and switches on the light. "Why are you sitting in the dark?"

"No reason, just thinking," I tell her, admiring her—in her T-shirt and slacks she looks about eighteen years old.

"It's after seven, no more thinking allowed," she says as she pulls me up from the chair. "First we'll eat, and then I'll fix it so you won't want or even be able to do much thinking tonight." We'll eat but I'll be looking forward to the rest of the evening.

A few days later, I am plagued again by thoughts of Violet. She has sent me her itinerary, and I know that she is leaving tomorrow evening, on British Air to London. I think it appropriate to wish her bon voyage but I've dreaded making the call. Still, I'm relieved when it's Violet who picks up the phone, and not her maid.

"Hi," I say, "it's your soulless friend Dan, calling to wish you a good trip. Enjoy it and be safe, Violet."

"Thanks for calling, Dan. I've been thinking about you, about what friends we have become. Maybe in some previous life we were already close, because I have rarely felt so at ease with anyone as I do with you."

"Don't tell me you believe in previous lives. God, I hope we don't have to do this over and over; once is plenty."

"You're right, Dan, I agree. You got my itinerary? Join me any time the mood strikes, and if another Cold War sets in and she sends you to Siberia, just hop a plane to wherever I'm lolling. It's where you'll always be very welcome."

With that, I wish her a great trip, and we hang up. It takes me a little while before I get up, turn the office lights off, and head home.

29.

T he worst of the heat wave seems to be over. Now New York is just hot, and we contend with the ordinary summer sizzle. Niki deals with it by staying in the air-conditioned apartment and practicing the piano day after day. Della thinks he should get away from the piano some of the time, that he should get out and associate with other kids his age. When I suggest day camp, he doesn't want to go, and he begs Tatiana not to send him to the two-week subsidized sleepaway camp either. He won't know anybody, he's no good at baseball, and nobody here plays soccer, he argues, teary-eyed. Tatiana is reluctant to send him, she confides to me, as there is finally some routine in his life—so why force him to do new things just now?

The ideal solution would be the country house. Ellen's old upright piano is there, maybe a little out of tune now, but that can be corrected, and Niki and Tatiana could take advantage of the swim club nearby. I could join them for long weekends, Thursday through Monday. I weigh the invitation before extending it, because I'm still apprehensive about returning to that Ellen-filled environment, but it seems foolish not to try. To my pleasant surprise, Tatiana is conflicted when I make the offer. On the one hand, she thinks it will be wonderful for Niki; on the other, she says, she will miss me during the week. Maybe she means it. I know I'll miss *her*.

After a day or two, Tatiana makes the inevitable decision, and I drive her and Niki up to the house the following Thursday. We can't really settle in until we stock up on groceries, so we visit a nearby supermarket. Walking up and down the aisles with Niki, I allow him to select whatever he wants, while Tatiana attends to the basics. It's fun to watch the boy happily grabbing sugarcoated cereals and junk foods from the shelves, although both of us dread Tatiana's reaction when she sees the dubiously healthful contents of the selections heaped in our cart. React she does. "Sugar and more sugar," she complains, and Niki looks at me conspiratorially. When she smiles, we know we have won.

The shopping, bed making, dusting, and the sweeping keep the three of us busy, but when I do take a moment to catch my breath, I marvel at how different the place feels with them in it. The house has come alive, the way it was when Eric was young, only now it's Niki who's got the television blaring, and it's Niki's quick footsteps sounding loudly on the old wooden floors. The piano does need tuning—Niki laughs himself silly at its distorted sounds. As I gaze out at Ellen's patch of dahlias, her favorites, carefully tended by the gardener, I remember how during the summer months she'd decorate our Friday night table with these colorful flowers. I can almost see her graceful figure kneeling at the edge of the flowerbed.

Only it's Tatiana now, leaning over to pick them, and it's a bit of a shock. I almost shout out to stop her, in fact. I catch myself before I commit the ridiculous. She comes back into the house, puts the dahlias in a glass of water, and places them at the center of the kitchen table. In that moment, I accept fully what is happening in this house and in my life: We no longer are captive to the past. It is a bittersweet acknowledgment, and I would like to believe that Ellen too accepts my new relationship and approves of it. I *think* she would, and that will have to suffice, for now.

I'm a little surprised in the evening, when Carol calls to ask if she and Eric can come up for the weekend.

"Carol, this is now your house, too; you do not have to call to ask. I'm always happy for your company."

"Thanks, Dad," she replies. I've got to get used to that Dad thing. "Dad," she repeats, "since I'm learning to live with New Yorkers, can I exhibit a little chutzpah here? That's the right word, isn't it, when you say something you're not quite sure you have the right to say?"

"Uh-oh. Maybe you should stick to your sweet Saginaw ways," I tease her. "But let me have it."

"Well, Dad, every couple needs to have some time alone together, and in my opinion you and Tatiana have seemed a little ragged around the edges lately—so here's the chutzpah part: I think you two should go away somewhere together this weekend and let Eric and me stay with Niki. Trust a woman's intuition. Do it. It'll be good for you both."

I'm touched. "Thanks," I say, "that's really sweet of you, Carol. Let me think about it." I put down the phone. Then I pick it up again. Such a thoughtful gesture from a girl I've not exactly welcomed with joy into the family—Eric would never have come up with that idea—deserves more proper thanks. "Carol," I tell her, "that was a wonderful idea, and I'm going to arrange it. But the nicest part of all is that you were thinking of me. I'm not very used to that anymore, but I'm grateful, and I want you to know how much I appreciate your kindness."

She pauses in the face of my paean. "Dad," she says, "I'm very fond of you, I respect you very much, and I want to be a good daughter to you. You can be sure I'm going to try my best."

After a little awkward silence, I say, "See you tomorrow," and we hang up. "Choice," I say to Tatiana. "Two nights at a spa or at a country inn, just the two of us: choose."

"But Niki—" she begins, but I interrupt her.

"Carol and Eric will babysit," I explain.

She beams with pleasure. "Oh, how wonderful. I've always dreamed of going to a spa. Massages. Manicures. Yes, I would choose."

The following evening just before six o'clock we're driving up to the impressive pillared entrance of the Fair Hill Spa. The modern building, perched on a hill and surrounded by manicured, verdant grounds, commands a splendid view of distant mountains. While I'm happy to see Tatiana so excited, my own previous spa experiences limit my enthusiasm considerably. Eight hundred dollars a night will buy me very measured quantities of uninspired spa cuisine, scores of athletic possibilities and nutritional lectures that do not particularly interest me, a high probability of constant flatulence, and possibly the loss of two pounds in as many days. "Have a nice stay," says the parking valet.

"Have a nice stay," says the porter. "Have a nice stay," says the reception clerk. "You are going to have such a nice stay," says the activity coordinator, a buxom Amazon in a lavender gym suit with green hills embroidered across her considerable chest. Tatiana selects a manicure, a pedicure, a seaweed wrap, a massage, and a Dead Sea mud bath, the last a whopping $250. Figuring I can get mud for free in the backyard of my country house, I limit myself to a massage and a session with a personal trainer.

Tatiana comments favorably on the décor, which is contemporary in style, all polished wood, glass, and rough stone fancied up with flowery fabrics as well as rather amateurish paintings of flora and fauna. Every two hundred feet, or so, there is a water station together with a large sign reminding you to drink a minimum of eight glasses of water a day. Numerous little, highly decorated toilets allow what goes in to also come out. Maybe ten percent of the guests scoot around, trim and fit and energetic, while the rest of us lumber about in our little-used gym outfits. Everyone discusses the latest nutritional finds and decrees: the relative merits of cherries versus grapes, the importance of watercress in pain reduction, the startling claim that beans are wrongly accused of causing gas. Large painted wall panels everywhere offer uplifting advice. "The best weight loss comes from sharing your food with the hungry," reads one; or "The prettiest mouth is that which is formed by a constant smile," another. Some of these panels contain outright lies, like "The surest way to have good friends is to be one yourself." Right . . .

As Tatiana and I stroll down the endless corridors, we are constantly and effusively greeted by everyone we pass—smiles, smiles, and more smiles; some manic, some shy, some just peculiar. I fix my mouth in a small half-smile and leave it at that; in response to all the good evenings and goodwill, I tender what I hope is a pleasant enough grunt. Exhausted by all this good cheer, we reach the dining room, where we join a long line of voluble, hungry people waiting impatiently for their food.

The dining room has a warm country look, with huge glass walls facing the grounds, wrought-iron chandeliers cast in an elaborate floral design, pastel-colored carpeting and tablecloths, and green plaid chairs. Scattered around the room are several salad bars and fruit stations, each of which displays discreet signs indicating the caloric contents of the foods on offer. A young woman with very large thighs and a memorably commensurate rear end rushes to our table. "Welcome," she says with a flourish, "I am Lindsey, your server. May I tell you about our specials tonight? Our vegetarian delight platter, a potpourri of steamed vegetables served with eight whole-grain noodles, two hundred and ten calories; our six-ounce grilled salmon with soy and tarragon sauce, three hundred calories; our five-ounce grilled chicken breast garnished with fava beans and baby bok choy, two hundred and eighty-five calories. Our whole-grain pizza of the day is topped with marinated peppers, zucchini slices, and halved baby onions." I dutifully order the salmon and head to the salad bar for consolation. After our meager entrees, we nibble on lemon and poppyseed cookies as we sip mint tea. Tatiana suggests that on the way out I should take a banana or a pear back to the room for energy.

"What do I need energy for? It's almost seven-thirty and they're showing a movie at eight."

"I have decided to help you lose weight tonight the way it is done in Kiev: the natural way," she says, blushing a little. "No spas in Kiev, very few gyms, many dangers if you stroll about after dark. We share apartments, so one must obtain one's workout in one's bedroom. Silent but steady exercise in a confined space," she teases.

"Hey, I'm an old guy and I'm half-starved. Have some mercy."

"I'm too hungry to feel any mercy," she replies enigmatically. "Better take a banana." I grab two.

"Have a nice evening," intones the headwaiter as we leave, and I think I just might.

In our room, the beds have been turned down and a small carob candy rests on each pillow. Tatiana goes straight into the bathroom, where she certainly takes her time, and I'm meanwhile dancing around trying to contain a bladder that would very much like to empty itself. The sound of water running in the sink increases my urgency, and when she finally emerges—in a little pink and yellow nightie—I rush past her, slam the door, and reach the toilet just in time. As I'm noisily relieving myself I notice that the door has not slammed shut.

"How romantic," Tatiana says, "the soothing sound of water splashing."

"Don't make me laugh mid-pee," I warn her, "otherwise you'll have to mop up after me." It's an instant in which I realize how at home we've become with one another, how at ease.

When I've finished, she is seated on the bed. Beckoning, she raises her arms to me. I sit down next to her, we embrace. "This is so nice," she says, as I look into her astonishing eyes. Holding my gaze, she pulls off her nightie, and with a provocative mix of shyness and seduction she helps me out of my gym suit. "Hurry," she says to me, "lie down on your back. I'm doing the work now, but don't worry, you'll get a workout too. You'll work off a few hundred calories before I'm finished."

She starts nibbling on my toes and slowly, with arousing attention to detail, works her way upward. I'm a little surprised, even a little taken aback, by her seeming abandon, but soon an overwhelming wave of pleasure erases everything else. I hear the headboard pounding against the wall in a telltale pattern, and I hear myself, as though from afar, whimpering and then letting out a sound something like a whistle, something between a moan and a scream. Tatiana doesn't stop. She doesn't pause. It seems shorter, but it must be hours before we finish our third round. Finally, she rolls off me, and I can stop and think—and my God, I forgot to take my Lipitor and Toprol after dinner! I've got to take them before I again forget, but when I try to sit up, Tatiana objects. "Not yet," she says, "don't move."

I try to explain. "Lipitor, shmipitor," she says. "I'm better for you than any medicine. Anyway, with all the water in you, you'll be fine." They must have spiked her water with something, I wish they'd put some in mine.

After one more romp, in which I participate only passively, she gives up. "Okay," she says, "go take your pills and come back to me. I'll be waiting." She lies back on the pillows, her thick black hair spread out behind her. I stumble out of bed; my right knee aches and my penis feels sore. When I look in the bathroom mirror, I see, in a rare moment of lucid self-examination a tired, bleary-eyed image of myself, hair askew, looking every year of my age. I grab my pills and down them. I feel a little dizzy. I lean against the wall; I wait, I listen. Silence. Hoping maybe she'll fall asleep if I take my time, I wait some more, and when I finally open the door—slowly, quietly— thank God, she's lying there, her eyes closed in bliss. My penis aches more; I wonder if she bruised it, but I'm too tired to look. Instead, I crawl quietly into the bed and nestle against her. She moves her foot along my leg in a familiar way, secure in her sleep with my presence. Such a remarkable woman, and mine for the asking, apparently. Who knows what her motivations are. My money, maybe; and maybe she's halfway in love with me too. If God knows, He's not telling. But meanwhile, she and I have begun to be happy, and if I don't die from overexertion, I may just start to enjoy living again.

The next morning, we get up early. Breakfast is served until nine A.M., and if you miss it, you may be malnourished by lunch. Dozens of happy morning people greet us as we trudge toward the food, and after we've eaten our whole grains, fruit, and white omelets, Tatiana heads for a manicure. Totally and deeply exhausted, but grimly determined, I go to the gym.

"Good morning," Todd, my personal trainer, welcomes me. "We're gonna have some fun this A.M." With glistening white teeth and an unrelenting smile, he beams at me. I follow this picture of health to the locker room, where he examines me clinically as I undress and put on my shorts. "Not bad," he says, "but those abs need work. We'll get them firmed up for you." Unconsciously he pats his own very firm, flat ones. "We'll get you looking and feeling fit again," he announces with fervor. Meanwhile, my knee hurts, I can hardly keep my eyes open, and my penis is killing me. I can't very well examine it now, as Todd is leading me into the gym.

"Have a seat here," he says, indicating a mat, "while I get your health stats from the computer." Another wave of exhaustion flows over me, and I lie back on the mat to relax for a split second—or however long it is before I am being shaken awake by Todd. "Mr. Gelder," he says with a note of professional concern in his voice and a computer printout in his hand. "Are you all right? Do you feel all right? Shall I take your blood pressure?"

"No, it's just that I didn't sleep much last night, maybe three hours. I'll be okay." Except I can't get up from my prone position. I roll onto my side and try, but Todd has to help me up.

"Too much stress," he opines. "You brought your worries with you. You should exercise now and take the two o'clock yoga class."

"Good idea, but could I just sit down somewhere for a minute or two, maybe on that bench over there, against the wall." He helps me over to the bench and I try to assure him that I'm fine if not fit. "All I need is just a little catnap," I explain. I sit down on the bench and lean back against the wall.

"I'll get you some juice," Todd suggests.

"Thanks, Todd, please do." Go for the juice, take your bloody time, and let me rest. Todd is no sooner off on his mission of mercy than my eyes begin to close. Maybe I'll get lucky, maybe he'll have to squeeze the juice himself, I'm thinking as I nod off . . . It has to be twenty minutes before he returns with a glass full of pale yellow liquid, about as inviting-looking as a urine sample.

"What is it, Todd?"

"It's our special Fair Hill Lemon Frappe, packed with vitamins and minerals. It'll perk you up."

I dutifully drink the concoction and can hardly conceal my joy and relief when Todd regretfully informs me that my forty-five minutes with him are up. "We'll try again tomorrow," he suggests, and I stagger toward the locker room.

I get into a shower and turn it on full blast. Maybe it's the frappe or maybe it's the nap, whatever, I begin to revive. But the water pelting my penis really hurts. What the hell did she do to me last night? I dry myself off and look around: The room is empty, here's my chance. In a mirror over a nearby sink, I discover a decidedly black and blue appendage down yonder. On a glass shelf above the sink stand various pump bottles, among them Fair Hill Body Renewal Lotion. Sounds perfect. I pump out a goodly amount onto my right palm and apply. Relief is virtually immediate as I gently rub it in. Embarrassment is not far behind, as I'm suddenly aware that someone else has entered the locker room. Startled, I turn, and Todd, bearing another glass of Fair Hill's yellow surprise, stops midstride.

His wide, astonished eyes fixed on my groin, he asks, his voice tremulous, his face red, "More frappe?"

"Thanks." I let go of my penis and reach for the glass. "Very thoughtful of you."

His gaze still riveted on my groin, he backs away. "Not at all, sir. Have a nice day."

"You too," I reply. "Have a nice day."

While I'm dressing, I hear gales of laughter coming from the gym. So much for my plans to exercise. I'll have to strengthen my abs Tatiana's way.

That evening Tatiana and I whisk through our supper of vegetarian mushroom burgers, caramelized onions, and caraway-coated carrots. On our way back to the room, I grab two bananas—this time for Tatiana. Because tonight I will take charge.

The minute we're in the room I launch my assault. Tatiana giggles nervously as I help her unzip. "Take your time," she says. "There's no pogrom."

"I can't wait, I'm ready." I pull off my pants.

"How about your Lipitor?" she says with a sweet leer as I'm pushing her down on the bed. I climb on top of her, lick a stray caraway seed out of the corner of her mouth, and after a few rather noisy minutes I roll off her.

She nuzzles up to me, her eyes shiny and pleased. "Wow," she says, "maybe we should stay at this spa a bit longer." Holding each other, we lie together in silence, naked and sweaty and very much at peace.

Time indeed might have stood still, but then she turns to me. "Oh, Dan, I almost forgot. There's a favor I must ask of you."

I have a sudden sinking feeling. Two romantic nights together and now she needs a favor. I wonder how much this will cost me, but I smile and say, "Of course, anything I can do."

"You know all about what I do at work," she proceeds, "and by the way, I want you to know that Rafael has already had two sessions with the orthodontist, thanks to you. You also know how many tragic cases we have to deal with. We're drowning under the weight of it all. So some of my fellow caseworkers and I want to volunteer to work weekends on the more extreme cases. We are told, though, that we face all sorts of legal liability issues, even as volunteers, and we need some guidance. I thought you might be able to suggest a lawyer who could advise us."

And I thought she was going to ask for money. What's wrong with me? Yet strangely, guilty though I feel, her goodness, her compulsion to do good, irks me and evokes a perverse reaction. "Miss Goody Two-Shoes," I tease her, "Saint Tatiana. So now you want to spend your workweeks *and* your weekends doing good deeds. Will there be any time left for Niki? Or for me?"

She is taken aback. "Don't worry about Niki. He's my whole life, and he knows it. But why do you ask about yourself? I've already told you that I love you. It is you who have not reciprocated. Are you so sure that you want me to spend my weekends with you?"

The discussion has become serious. "Of course I do. I enjoy your company," I reply with some annoyance. "You're young and beautiful and kind. But why me, Tatiana? Do you find me young or beautiful or kind? Or just . . .Why me?"

She looks at me quite steadily, but her expression is difficult to read. "Why do you think I'm with you, Dan? Your air-conditioned home? Your Bechstein? Your money—oh, maybe it's your money."

She pulls the covers up over her nakedness and turns her face away from me. My face is burning with anger at myself, at my insinuations and insecurity. What happened to me? How could I be so unfeeling, so cruel? How could I do this to her? My throat is dry, hot. "My God," I say to her, "what an idiot I am. Please forgive me. You have to forgive me for this stupidity."

For a long minute, she doesn't reply. It feels like an eternity, but then she turns back to me. "I love you, so I guess I have to forgive you," she says. "But now I have a question to ask you. If you didn't think I was beautiful or sexy, would you want my company? If I were truly a saint or a great intellect and you did not find me attractive, would we be here tonight? Would we?"

A rhetorical question requires no reply.

"You want the truth?" she continues. "It's okay for a man to choose a woman for her looks, that's fine, but for a woman to find attractive a man who can care for her properly—that is not okay? You want the truth? I'll tell you the truth. It always surfaces anyway. I've loved you since your return from Israel: All of a sudden, without any warning, I found myself in love with you. Maybe you're not young, but to me, in my eyes, you will never be old; never. But what if you were poor? What if you needed my help? Would I marry you? Maybe not. I have a child, I must protect him. He is my primary concern, above my own happiness. So the fact that you are a rich man is a blessing. It makes us a possibility. If you can one day love me enough to want to marry me and be a father to my son, that day I will be a happy woman. If not . . . I will be okay, and so will Niki. I buried my parents. I buried my husband, my beautiful, young husband. I left my country and my language and my home, and I came here for the sake of my son, and I did it without help from anyone. So I don't break so easily, you need not worry. If you think I am only after your money, then, fine, leave me and don't worry about it. I suppose you are suspicious of me because I slept with you. I knew it was a mistake, but it was hard to resist. Don't you know, can't you tell, that you are the only man I have been with since my husband died? And believe me, you were not the first to try, and certainly not the youngest, and God knows, not the kindest. Lucky me, I fell in love with you; lucky, lucky me. Tatiana, always the lucky one."

"What do you want me to say, Tatiana? What is it you want me to say?"

"Don't say anything, Dan. Don't say anything you don't want to say. There's no fire. You are obviously not ready to make any decisions right now. Fine, you don't have to. I am not afraid of your decision, that's all I'm saying, but I do want you to tell me as soon as you have decided either way."

She averts her face again. I want to say something kind, something to soften the moment, something that conveys the respect and affection that I feel for her. By the time I've sorted out my thoughts, she is already asleep.

The next morning, Tatiana behaves normally. We eat our breakfast of groats and berries. We swim in the warm indoor pool. We take pleasure in each other's company. On the two-hour drive home, conversation is desultory, but the mood is light and companionable. I'm off the hook, if I want to be.

30.

My first call at my office on Monday morning, comes from Tim Wells. "Hi, it's been a while," he says. "How the hell are you?"

"Fully zipped up," I reply. "What can I do for you?"

"I've got someone I'd like to bring by your office—we need some financial advice on an idea he's dreamed up. His name is Miguel Sanchez, you'll like him. I'd also like to bring along a potential investor, an Iranian named Parvash Khalerian. I'd really appreciate your help." So we book an appointment for the next day at ten.

Tim and his friends arrive promptly. Sanchez, a big man with a wide smile and a strong handshake, is dressed informally, with little apparent regard for his appearance. On the other hand, Khalerian, slight, and dark-complected, is as meticulous in his dress as he is formal in his manner. We get down to business. Miguel explains his idea to me.

"I grew up in Washington Heights," he says. "Now it's mostly

Hispanic, but plenty of old European Jews still live there, like our next-door neighbors when I was growing up, Fritz and Lotte Wertheimer, and the lady down the hall, Selma Lehman. She used to help me with my math homework, she was a wiz. They were all refugees from Hitler, so most of them spoke English with an accent, but I got along fine with them, and I always got good advice from those old people. Whenever I had troubles, *tzuris* they called it, I would go to Selma or to her friend Sophie downstairs, and they would give me great advice. So I've come up with a great business idea, but I need financial backing, investors: I want to create a phone service you pay for by the minute, its name will be My *Tzuris* Line, and you'll be able to call in, twenty-four/seven, and on the other end of the line will be an old Jewish person with an accent, man or woman is up to you. You tell them your *tzuris*, your problems, and they listen, they advise you. You ask about your basic *tzuris*, you know, children, making a living, marital problems, your mother-in-law—no matter how old these people grow, they never forget their mother-in-law. I've arranged for a room in an old-age home where the phones will be manned around the clock. You can't imagine the wisdom of these people—don't forget Kissinger comes from Washington Heights, maybe we could get him as an advisor. The thing is, I need at least fifty thousand dollars as seed money, there are fixed costs, and I only have twenty-five, so I'm looking for investors. The return will be huge. The only problem is, the labor source keeps on dwindling: They die. So we have to move quickly."

"It sounds interesting, but my own son has a company that's sucking me dry. I don't have the extra cash to invest."

"No, no, listen," says Miguel. "First, before you make any decision, do me a favor, try it out. I have a Mrs. Bettelbaum waiting for your call. Just give it a try. No strings attached."

Khalerian chimes in. "I urge you to make the call. For me it has been a life-altering experience." I ask him to explain.

"My own dear father is dead," he begins "so when I found myself recently in a confusing personal situation I had no one to confide in. I told this to Tim—he is my next-door neighbor—and he recommended that I speak to a lady of a certain age, a Mrs. Bettelbaum, whom I finally called after great hesitation. It was not very promising in the beginning; the lady is hard of hearing and kept misunderstanding my name despite my attempts to correct her. But she sounded so kind and seemed so eager to help me that I decided to tell her my woes. All my family fled Iran; I am the only one of us to settle in America, the rest are scattered the world over. For generations, we had owned and developed businesses and properties in Shiraz and in Teheran, but we succeeded in leaving with only a little cash and jewelry. I was sent ahead here, to New York, with the jewelry, to find and buy a business that would support the family. At the time, I knew only one person in the city, a former partner of my father, a Mr. Manozian, who lives here with his daughter, Soraya. I explained to him my mission and asked him to help me dispose of the jewelry and he introduced me to a buyer, a Mr. Montague Garfield. I received a very paltry sum for the gems, much less than I thought was their true worth, and my business opportunities dwindled. Meanwhile, Soraya and I had become attracted to one another and began talking about marriage. I told Tim one day about the jewelry, and I mentioned Montague Garfield's name, only to discover that Tim knows this Montague very well. He made inquiries and learned Montague had paid Soraya's father more than three times the amount that he had passed on to me—more than three times! I was in shock and in great distress, my family depends upon me and yet the thief was Soraya's father. Should I tell her? Should I confront

Mr. Manozian? I didn't know what to do. So finally, frantic and confused, I called Mrs. Bettelbaum, and soon I was telling her everything; I emptied my heart to her. When she spoke, it was a revelation to me. She told me first of all I should bite my tongue, which I believe is an expression requesting silence. Then she asked me whether a dowry is usual among my people; I told her that it is. She asked me whether I was sure of my love for Soraya ,and I assured her that I was. She told me never to mention the thievery to Mr. Manozian but to subtract the amount he had given to me from the amount I now knew he had obtained from Montague and to ask for that difference precisely, exactly, from Manozian for my dowry. That way, I get my money and Manozian knows I know about his thievery and knows better than to ever cheat me again. Brilliant. I asked her how she so quickly knew what to do, and she told me that when she was a little girl in a place called Salant, almost the same thing happened between the kosher butcher and her great uncle. The whole world is Salant, only larger, she said. To a worm in an apple, the apple is the whole world, she said. And speaking of apples, she said they don't fall far from the tree, so I should keep a close eye on my Soraya. God forbid, maybe she inherited her father's tendencies. I was overwhelmed, I needed no further convincing. I want to invest in this service, I want to expand it to include Farsi-speaking grandparents as well; also others, Spanish, Italian, we could open a Web site. I hope you too will be enthusiastic and will consider joining with me in expanding this service, because I believe that My *Tzuris* will be a worldwide phenomenon."

Intrigued, I agree to speak with Bessie Bettelbaum, and I'm soon shouting into the receiver while she's encouraging me to talk louder. I'm embarrassed. What should I say?

"*Nu, nu,*" she says. "Don't be shy. I'm eighty-eight years old, I lived through the Germans and the Lithuanians. You think there's much I haven't heard? Tell Bessie, you'll feel better."

"My wife died," I start. "I'm alone now for two years, it's hard."

"Don't I know," she says. "My Max is gone more than twenty years. You live with it, it's like losing an arm, a leg, but you live. What else can you do? Are there children?"

"One, all grown up, married."

"Oy, mazel tov, see? You can be happy again," she replies.

"He didn't marry a Jewish girl."

"Oy, I'm sorry, I'm so sorry. It hurts, I know. Were they at least married by a rabbi?"

"No, a justice of the peace."

"You tried everything—guilt, yelling, everything?"

"Everything," I assure her.

"Is she a decent girl, a decent person?"

"Absolutely," I say with conviction.

"So it could be worse. Nowadays we have Jewish girls who are not so decent, you could have ended up with one of those. My cousin Irma, she has three boys; one found a non-Jewish girl from Peru, a dentist. They married also with a justice and they have two children, and would you believe, every Friday night they come by Irma and have the Sabbath meal. The girl is an angel, she comes to me and does my teeth for free. So you can't tell what God has in store, you should hope for the best."

"Mrs. Bettelbaum," I ask, "after only two years should I be looking for a wife already? Is it too early?"

"Listen, a man without a wife is lost. Can you cook? Can you boil water even? And who cleans for you? No, it's impossible. Of course you need a wife. A man without a wife is like a horse without a rider. But be careful, choose like a good businessman, weigh the pluses and minuses," she admonishes me.

"Well, one woman is a little crazy but very, very rich, and the other one is poor but beautiful," I summarize.

"Don't call the rich one crazy. Rich ones are never called crazy; they are called eccentric. Money makes everything turn to honey. But I'm thinking from your description you've already fallen for the poor one, so why are you asking? Look, my Max was not a rich man. First we lived through the camps in Europe, then we made a three-year stop in Caracas, where we had a cousin, then we came to Washington Heights. He never learned Spanish, he never learned much English either—what did he need with English, he was a tailor—but we produced a corporate lawyer and a film producer. Those two boys speak English like the Queen. And all from a sewing machine. Of course, even if you are poor it's nice to have money, but you're already in love. Give in."

"Thanks, Mrs. Bettelbaum," I say, "you've been wonderful, a real help to me." And I mean it, too.

"It's nothing. With my arthritis and the pains in my legs I hardly sleep. I can hardly eat. The best thing for me is to talk, especially to a nice young person such as yourself. Good luck to you."

"I'm in for fifteen grand," I say upon hanging up. "She sold me. What a lady! She's better than Prozac, cheaper than a psychiatrist." Parvash says he's in for ten, and we all shake hands: It's a deal. I pour four glasses of seltzer and offer a toast to My *Tzuris*. It certainly feels like a sure thing.

31.

When I return home that evening, a note from Della informs me that Violet has called from London. She's left her number, but I don't call, because of the time difference, so I am not surprised when the phone awakens me at seven a.m. and it's Violet.

"Wake up, Danny boy," she says. "The early bird catches the worm."

"Are you referring to yourself?"

"It's a Russian worm I'm referring to, the Kiev bug—it can last a long time and leave you tired and poor."

"Well, the Kiev bug is up at my summer house, I'm all alone," I tell her. "What can I do for you, Violet? Is everything all right?"

"Absolutely. London is always nice, but I passed the Ukrainian embassy today and thought of you. I just wanted to hear your voice."

"That's it, Violet? My voice? You used to prefer other parts of me, as I recall." I can't seem to stop flirting with her.

"Hold on to those memories, cling to them, when you find your-self up to your nipples in borscht and kasha. Think of me dining on Scottish salmon while you're chewing your way through her blinis. I'll soon be in Italy, where anti-Americanism and anti-Semitism seems to be fashionable again, but the food is so good and the men so attentive that I can almost forgive them. How about coming over and protecting me from the new Fascisti?"

"Sorry, Violet, the answer is *nyet*. I'm happy slaving away here in the heat. Why trade that in for a Tuscan villa? Absurd."

"All right, all right, next you'll be singing the Ukrainian national anthem, I assume they have one. No marriage talk yet with Miss Green Card?"

"Not yet, Violet, but I make no promises or predictions. I may be hooked."

"If you get bored, remember that I will make you very welcome in Italy, only try not to look too American or Jewish. No skullcaps, no baseball hats, no prayer shawls. Dye your hair blonde like I do. We're out of fashion this year, it's those gentle, kind Iraqis that are now all the rage here. Nobody in Europe likes us anymore. We'll have to stay undercover."

"I wouldn't mind being under a cover with you."

"Dream on. Phone sex is all you'll get from me. Keep in touch."

Before getting up to face my day, I lie in bed thinking how pecu-liar my relationship with Violet is. If it's not love of some sort, what in God's name is it? Unquestionably, Violet has become a presence in my life. From the first moment we met, she assumed her power to alter my life, she's continued to confuse and amuse me like nobody else. I remember that crazy psychic, Herta something. I have her card somewhere; maybe I should spend a hundred bucks to find out how she might elaborate on her comments about Fink or Fenk or

whatever it was she called Violet. I could certainly use some guidance, even if it comes from left field.

At ten P.M. sharp, the first of Herta's best hours, I sit by the phone
with her card. I'm still debating with myself as to the value of consulting any psychic, let alone Herta, but finally dial the number.

"Herta Searing here," she answers.

"Dan Gelder. We met at the Whitney. I am Susan's friend," I
remind her.

"You are not Susan's friend, that is not a proper description. You
got too close to her once; it did her no good, so hands off. She is
ready for better things. You are heading elsewhere, too. What happened to that Fink woman, the snip-snip lady who leaves you high
and dry? Is she gone yet?"

"Yes, she's traveling."

"Good, very good. Tell her, go round the world, just so she stays
away from you. She is not good for you, too much noise. She is a
whole orchestra in one woman. You need only some piano music not
the drums and the bassoon. You need lots of attention, you are very
needy like most men. Do you have any questions?"

"My son—his health, his business. My business, my health."

"Wait, wait, too many questions all at once. Your son, handsome
boy, problems in business, I am not sure that his business survives. It
will be months before you know. He has a woman, perfectly nice.
Why are you not happy with her?"

I hesitate. I'm supposed to tell the truth to this German lady?
How will she understand? I don't reply. She's a psychic, let her
figure it out.

"You're not pleased, I don't know why. I see grandchildren. But
why would you be lifted on a chair, lifted up, your head almost at the
ceiling? What does it mean to you?"

"It doesn't mean anything to me."

"Who is Esther?"

"I don't know. Oh, I have an old Aunt Esther."

"No, no, young and blonde. You do business with an Esther?"

"No."

"Well, don't worry. Maybe it's Hester—or Lester?"

"I don't know a Hester or a Lester."

"Well, I'm never wrong. You'll see, it may take years but I'll be proven right. Now I see a pretty woman, very pretty, and quite determined. She is after your money."

"Yes, but I don't think she is after my money. We've become very close," I reply, disturbed by the implications.

"Listen, money in a man is like beauty in a woman," says Herta. "At your age, your pocket is your most attractive feature. You think she fell in love with your manly figure? She is younger, no? But it's all right; you love her, so it's okay. I have no negative vibrations here. She is entitled to security; I approve. Cash, you will spend cash: new furniture, new clothes for her, and pearls, she dreams of pearls. Big ones. Oh, the furniture you will buy. Bye-bye, cash; hello, big pearls and rugs and couches, all new—you'll be busy."

I'm stunned. I don't believe a word she says. It was a mistake to call; now I'll feel the influence of her words, and what for? To what good?

"Your business will flourish, new opportunities present themselves," she goes on. "You will work until old age, no rest for you—it is good, it will keep your mind young. All around you people retire, but not you. They are tanned, you are pale. Any other questions?"

I tell her no, and she reminds me to send her a check. After we hang up, I sit there, crushed. I shouldn't have called. She is all wrong about Tatiana but what she said hurts. I consider how things started with me and Violet, so much of it based on the fact of her money—its attraction and power—yet a real, loving relationship developed between us. I comfort myself with the thought, the certainty, that no matter what role money may have played at the outset of Tatiana's interest in me, she has grown to love me. Then I see me. When I'm undressing and catch a glimpse of myself in the standing mirror: an older than middle-aged man, gray hair, paunchy, some prize, a real beauty. No wonder Tatiana fell for me, who could resist? With that sardonic thought I climb into bed, grateful that at least I am alone tonight.

I'm still shaken the following morning, Making my way to the office later than usual, I wander in at almost ten-thirty, and I'm still hearing Herta's voice in my head. Doubts have overcome my tenacious certainties about Tatiana's sincerity, her love, her motives, and I'm sure only that I need to spend some time alone. I call Tatiana in the country.

"Hello, there," I say.

"Dan, Dan—when do you arrive?"

"Well, actually, I think I am going to stay in town this weekend. I have lots of things at the office to catch up on. Besides, the two of you will have fun without me."

"That's just an excuse," says Tatiana sagely.

"I promise, my sweet, this has nothing to do with you. But I do have one favor to ask: Will you and Niki come down on Monday? I have something to show you."

"Of course. A surprise?" she says, sounding excited. I make no further comment.

A plan is set in motion. Maybe I'll understand Tatiana's motives a lot better by Monday afternoon.

* * *

Among a slew of messages, I find two from Myra. It's time to be clear with her about Tatiana and me, and to tell her that I have no interest in continuing our relationship, which mostly demands that I listen to her exhausting confidences. But when we speak she sweeps me immediately into her tale of woe.

She has just returned from Detroit, where she attended an international convention of pro-Palestinian groups. "I knew Billy would be there," Myra informs me, "and I wanted him to see that I am continuing my political involvements quite independently of him. But the most extraordinary thing happened. The keynote speaker at the major event on Sunday was to be Karim Fahkaki, a lawyer from Jenin and a close friend of Billy's. On Saturday, Karim invited me to supper in his suite, and of course I was delighted to accept. Much to my surprise, I discovered I was his only guest. Which I considered a great compliment until I realized that he was making a pass at me. The man is no beauty, but how could I turn him down—you know how anxious I am to cement intra-Semitic relations, and I figured it also served Billy right, although I didn't really think he would ever know. It actually required a bit of maneuvering, but we finally succeeded in finding a workable position on the bed. I was absolutely determined to make the occasion memorable for Karim. Unfortunately, he must have a back problem similar to yours, only worse, because as I became more vigorous he began to mutter things in Arabic, which at first I simply presumed were words of love, of encouragement. But then he started screaming, he was yelling, and I became confused. Still, I plowed on. It was only when he began to cry that I realized I was hurting him. In shock, I pulled back. Karim, though, was literally bent out of shape, his rear end pointing upward and his face buried in the mattress. He seemed unable to move, and when I tried to help him straighten out, he screamed every time I touched him. I couldn't leave him that way, so I dressed hurriedly and in a state of panic ran out of his suite and down the hotel corridor to get help. I tried knocking on doors but no one replied, and then, I don't know, I froze or collapsed until I heard the chambermaid screaming. She was standing at the open door. I ran back, Karim was now on the floor, his legs askew and his face very red. When he saw me, he began yelling angrily at me. Over and over, almost accusatorily, he was shouting, *"Itbach al Yahud! Itbach al Yahud!"* I knew *Yahud* means Jew, and I was sure the *Itbach* couldn't be complimentary, so I deemed it best to maintain some distance. Fortunately, the hotel doctor arrived, together with several Palestinian notables. The last I saw him, poor Karim was still writhing on the floor, and warding off all attempts at assistance."

Myra pauses; her voice catches, and she almost sobs before she continues. "I went directly to my room, where about an hour later I was visited by the convention chairman and a very mean-looking associate. They informed me that they had now ascertained me to be a Zionist spy who had used my body to prevent Karim from speaking the next day. I protested at this calumny, but they warned me that I had better leave first thing in the morning, as I might otherwise find myself the victim of an angry mob. Certainly, this ranks as one of the saddest moments of my life: My reputation in the movement ruined, all my good intentions twisted out of shape, and the assembled guests cheated of their primary speaker. All I could think of as I hastily packed and fled from the hotel was how to make amends. At least the incident did not get televised by CNN or the BBC; for that I'm truly grateful. You know how they love to blow everything out of proportion when it comes to Palestinians. Anyway, all this just to tell you that I won't be around New York this summer. I feel like a marked woman, so until all this blows over I'm hiding out in the Navajo tribal lands. Only my divorce lawyer will know my exact whereabouts, you know, Mervin Kreplach of the firm of Shuttlesworth & Kreplach. If you need me, he will know how to reach me."

32.

Eagerly though I awaited Tatiana's return from the country on Monday, only after Niki settles in for piano practice, do I say to Tatiana, "I have a surprise for you."

I then take her to Montague's shop. She hesitates in front of the store.

"Jewelry?" she asks me.

"Yes, my dear."

"So fancy," she complains. "It's Madison Avenue. We could go to the jewelry district, why here?"

I explain that I have confidence in Montague, that he's basically a good guy and I've done business with him before. Montague greets me like an old friend, warmly, with a hug, and asks after Tim. I introduce him to Tatiana, who is standing awkwardly at the counter in some awe of the surroundings. "This lovely lady," I explain, "is my close friend, and I want to buy her something special, something wonderful. Pearls, diamonds, whatever she likes, although I'm counting on you to give me the Murray-and-Sheila price. Have a little mercy on a sixty-year-old who still has to work for a living."

Montague is crushed. "How can you say that to me? Even in jest. I wouldn't make enough profit from you to buy myself one good meal. You'll walk out of here with a Tiffany piece at a Woolworth price, I guarantee. A beautiful woman deserves beautiful jewelry, so don't worry that I'll stand in her way. Tatiana, a Russian name; my family originated there. Where are you from?"

"From Kiev," says Tatiana, "in Ukraine."

"Me too, me too," exclaims Montague. "One set of my grandparents came from Kiev: We're family. Only the best will do for you." As proof, he lays some trays of necklaces and bracelets before her, fifty or sixty items, each more lavish than the one before.

Tatiana seems taken aback, overwhelmed. "Oh, no," she says. "Nothing this grand. Only perhaps some pearls, a little string of pearls would be nice. When we left Russia, they searched everything, and my grandmother's pearls were stolen from my hand luggage. It would be nice to have pearls of my own."

"Pearls, pearls," intones Montague, "perfect for beautiful girls." He whisks away the diamonds and presents Tatiana an array of pearls. "Everything from these South Sea big mommas, at two hundred and fifty thousand dollars a strand, down to little itsy-bitsy ones for under two. Gray ones, yellow ones, pink, black, wonderful white—you name it, I've got it. With your dark hair, white, pearly white, is best. Earrings will add nobility to your face, earrings and a necklace make you look like an empress. The Empress of Kiev."

Tatiana looks at me helplessly, searching for her cue. "Which do you like?" she asks me.

I take my life in my hands, I make the bet. Let's see how she behaves, let's see if she takes advantage of the moment, if she goes for the jugular. "These are beautiful," I say, pointing to the South Seas. "Expensive but special." There is a long moment of silence, of hesitation, and then I see that Tatiana is not going to make a decision. Her face is white, her eyes moist, as she pushes away the trays.

"I apologize," she says to Montague, "but I cannot do this today. It is too overwhelming. I thank you for your time." With not a word to me, she turns and leaves. I rush after her into the street.

She seems angry at me. She walks briskly, I walk beside her. "What's wrong?" I ask.

She stops and glares at me. "What was that all about?" she asks me. "A man who wants to buy a woman jewelry does so; he sets a price range, a budget. He doesn't spend a fortune when there is no commitment. What is this all about? Am I for sale? Are you paying me for services rendered? Have you finished with me? I don't want your jewelry. I want you, for Niki and for me. I have lived forty-three years without baubles, and I can live another forty-three without them, too. You want to buy me jewels, pearls? Marry me, and then shower me with whatever you want, but not until then. What do you think I am?"

And there, on Madison Avenue, surrounded by scores of people, Tatiana can no longer control her tears. She begins to sob out loud. It's New York, nobody stops, but a lot of people are noticing. I stand there, ashamed, defeated. I thought I was being clever, but she has trumped me.

"Niki and I will go home today. You can send us our things from the house. I won't bother you anymore. You don't need to pay me anymore," she sobs, her voice now subdued, as she becomes aware of the attention she's attracting. She turns away from me then, and at a rapid pace heads toward the apartment with me in pursuit.

We stand silently at the elevator. But once inside I pull her close to me, I hug her, and in my arms she begins to sob again; it's a sound that I can hardly bear. When we reach our floor she regains some control; she must face Niki. Still, she is barely holding herself together. I open the door, she precedes me into the apartment. She goes into the kitchen where Della is baking cookies and Niki is nibbling on them. Standing to the side of Tatiana, I can feel the effort she is expending to appear composed. She swallows hard, takes a breath, prepares to speak.

But I say "Niki . . . Niki, I'm asking your permission to marry your mother. I'll be good to her and take care of her and try my best not to make a fool of myself with her too often. What do you say?"

"Wow," Niki says. "Wow, I'll be Eric's brother!"

"And you?" I ask Tatiana. "What do you say?"

There is a pause. Her face regains its color, her cheeks redden. She looks at me and whispers, "Yes. Oh, yes."

Della hugs Niki, then Tatiana. "God bless you all. This is a happy day for me. I've been praying for this."

Tatiana has never looked more glowing. "Now we can go back to Montague," she says merrily. "You can buy me a ring so I'll have proof. Now you can shower me with pearls, but you better not point at those big ones again or you'll be looking at them day and night. I'll be all beautiful and glittery for you, only for you." She kisses me with such gusto that I stumble backward a little.

"I've got to call Luba," she says. "It's seven hours later in Jerusalem, I'll call her now. Niki, come with me to the phone. We'll tell them together: You have a father again." The two of them rush to the library, and Della and I are alone.

"Della," I say, "have I done the right thing? How can I be sure that it's not just the money, the security she wants for Niki and for herself? How can I be sure?"

"You can't be, and you won't be. But so what? You have money, and you'll be a good father for that boy, he needs you. Why shouldn't she marry for that? You have to be practical. It's good for both of you, for the three of you, so it must be right. So don't look back now. Remember in your Bible what happened to Lot's wife when she looked back—you don't want to turn to salt, do you?"

Niki comes running in. Luba wants to wish me a mazel tov. As he's pulling me away I say thank you to Della. "You're right as usual. Get those pearls and that hat out, you're going to need them again." When I pick up the phone, Luba is crying from joy. She speaks to me in some jumble of languages, but it's the mazel tov that I hear most. Mazel tov, mazel tov. And then more mazel tov.

With all the congratulations still ringing in my ears, I set out again with Tatiana for Montague's. He buzzes open the door, and his face lights up the moment he sees ours. "What's up?" he asks. "What's happened?" When he hears an engagement is what has happened he bellows with pleasure. "Mazel tov" he yells. "Rings, we want rings. Oh, do I have rings. Bargain-basement prices, my contribution to the joy. Square, round, emerald cut, pear shape. What do you like?"

In the next half hour, I make two people very happy; I don't know which is the happier, Tatiana or Montague. Tatiana chooses a ring and some pearls, medium-sized ones, then, "Earrings!" shouts Montague. "Earrings with a pearl and a diamond, it will be perfect. It will repeat the motifs of both the necklace and the ring. You must have it. If not, I'll have to give it to you as a gift, you'll look naked without it."

It's time for me to step in and stop the music, but just as I am about to Tatiana puts on the earrings. They look perfectly splendid. Her face is flushed with excitement, and joy dances in her eyes. "Too much," she says to me. "Not everything must be bought today," she adds, and does not mean a word of it.

"Wrong," I say. "Today's the day. Today, I wouldn't be able to turn you down for anything, not the way you look now. Montague, let's settle on the price. I'm a volume purchaser, so I'll need a good discount, several discounts—one for volume, one for Tim, one for repeat visits, one for Kiev, one out of mercy. Write down a net net price that I can afford, a Murray-and-Sheila price. Add to our pleasure, be nice." I don't blink when he hands me the paper, although I know I'm eating into my savings as I write him out the check. "Don't cash it for three days, I need time to get money into the account. We'll pick up the stuff when it clears."

"Absolutely not," says Montague. "You take the jewelry now. I trust you one hundred percent. Take it and enjoy it, and when the check clears I'll have my money. Walk home with all of it on, Tatiana. Flaunt it. Let the world see it. It gives me pleasure to see you both so happy." Who knows, maybe he even means it.

As excited as a schoolgirl, Tatiana catches glimpses of herself in the shop windows on our walk home. Watching her, thinking how lucky, how proud of her I am, I want to shower her with every good and beautiful thing until the day they carry me out. And when Niki comes running to hug each of us as we enter the apartment, I feel a happiness which I have not felt for so long that it feels almost totally new.

33.

D on't tell me," Violet screams over my office phone. "I know why you're calling, and it's not to find out how I'm feeling, not to tell me you're joining me in my Tuscan villa— nothing that kind, nothing that sensible, that sybaritic. No, you're calling to tell me about you and that clever little Russki. You want to grow old together, she in a babushka cooking her cabbage soup and you—you can learn sweet nothings in Russian, or Ukrainian or something, to whisper in her Slavic ear. You call that living happily ever after? Go ahead, tell me. I'm prepared for the worst. She'll get fat, you know, they all do. She'll get big in the hips. You'll see. So talk."

"We're engaged."

"Engaged. Engaged in what? Engaged in tying yourself down until old age. Engaged in falling for that oh-so-sweet-butter-wouldn't-melt-in-her-mouth little conniving broad and her one-track child. I sure hope you like the piano, because for the rest of your life someone is going to be *klopping* away at one wherever you are. I know: I'll buy you earplugs for a wedding present, that way you'll maybe survive the noise. Just be sure you make the little faker sign a prenuptial agreement, to protect Eric against her, or she'll eat you out of house and home and his inheritance too. A prenuptial, definitely. And make sure there's a Russian translation, she shouldn't claim later she didn't know what she was signing. Boy, she knew when to strike. You were unprotected with me in Europe; I should have stayed home, I could have saved you from this gulag of a marriage you are going into voluntarily. Hard labor for the next ten to twenty years for you; no golf, no leisure. Salted herring for breakfast, black bread for lunch. Dinner you'll have to take her to restaurants for. Oh, I should have protected you, it's all my fault."

"Finished?" I ask when she pauses. "Are you finished screaming and ranting, or is there more venom to come? You didn't want me. Why do you care if I marry or not? I know a few guys who can serve as an escort for you, I'll fix you up. Or we can apply to Actors' Equity for a stand-in."

"Stop yelling at me," says Violet. "You're yelling because what I say hits home. You know deep down inside that I'm right. You want to live it up, not work like a horse for the rest of your life. So I don't want to marry you, but with me there would be pizzazz—lights, action, camera, fun. Ever hear of fun? Villas, parties, Jerusalem, Milan for shopping, a rebbe here or there. Galas. You could relax. You need activity, you could help me count my diamonds, my Treasuries, my stocks and bonds. Okay, I'm not saying another word. It's your life, if you're happy, great. Mazel tov. You should grow old together. Sounds like fun. Mazel tov."

"Violet, we've set a date. We're going to be married on the twenty-fourth of August by a justice of the peace up near my country house.

You wanted to know, so I'm telling you. Almost everyone is away for the summer anyway, so we'll have the civil ceremony and then be married by a rabbi in New York later in the year."

"A justice of the peace yet, sounds marvelous. Unfortunately, I won't be able to attend, but I will certainly be thinking of you. What I will be thinking, I don't care to say. Bye." With a thunderlike clap, the line goes dead.

I'm both annoyed and sad. Maybe I'm a sap, thinking that Violet's got it all wrong. Maybe I am just another sucker like some of those men my age you see hauling a baby carriage up Madison Avenue — the kid's father, not the grandfather. What if Tatiana wants another child to cement the deal? It's not inconceivable. Dear God, that would be my death sentence. I'd climb out the window and hope not to hit an innocent pedestrian down below—I wouldn't even stop to argue, just go straight to the window and leap.

A good hour passes before I again turn my attention back to work, and then Tina tells me that Tatiana is on the phone, that it sounds like something is wrong—she's crying.

I grab the phone, and Tatiana is half sobbing, then mostly yelling at me in what I assume is Russian. "Wait, wait," I plead with her. "Tell me what's wrong in English. Wait, honey, wait." Only she doesn't wait, she just keeps going until she's blabbering and crying, which needs no translation.

I continue pleading, she continues crying, and so it goes for a little while. Eventually, I get the translation. "It's your Violet. It's Violet. She called me all the way from Italy to tell me that if I mistreat you, she'll tear me to shreds. She threatened me. She called me a green card. She called me a chicken Kiev, and she told me that if I'm after your money, I'll be disappointed, you don't have that much. And she said you hate piano music, that we're a mismatch. That if she wanted you, I wouldn't have a chance in hell. And then she hung up on me when I answered her, when I told her what I thought of her and her facelifts and her make-believe blonde hair. My Aunt Tzipka, who worked as a street cleaner back home, was twice the lady Violet is, but she had a temper and she could answer a mouth like Violet's, so I quoted her, Tzipka, and said, 'I wouldn't piss on you, even if you were on fire.' But I think that I said it in Russian, I hope I said it in Russian. I said a lot in Russian. Tell me she doesn't understand Russian."

"She doesn't understand Russian," I assure her. "I'm not sure how much English she understands. She had no right to call you, and I'm glad you yelled at her, whatever the language was. I'm going to do the same. Don't worry. Forget her. As soon as I hang up she'll get hers back, in spades."

The hotel operator puts me through to Violet. *"Pronto,"* she answers sweetly. "Oh, hi, Danny; dear Danny. I apologize for hanging up on you earlier. I must have lost my temper. I'm sorry, sorry, sorry. Say you forgive me."

I don't say word one, I'm too angry: let her writhe with guilt. "Oh, come on, Dannele, talk to me. What did you call for, to give me the silent treatment? Talk to me. If you're the least bit aggravated with me, tell me. Let it out, I can take it. I probably deserve it."

I wait one more minute. Then I tell her. "Violet, if you ever even once call Tatiana and upset her again—ever—I'm going to make sure that all of Jewish New York, especially your friends, know each and every one of your sexual habits, real and alleged: what kinky sex toys I'll claim we used, how many times we did it, and where, and in unusual positions, as well as every sound and whimper you made or didn't make. I'll invent a few other shockers, too, that everyone will believe—how you dye your hair, for instance, and what you use;

which of your diamonds are real and which are certified fakes; how many facelifts you've really had and why you've got those surgical scars on either side of the bottom of your ass. All those 'facts' will appear in whatever Jewish publication can be bribed into printing them. I have loads of information that your new Toronto relations will be panting to hear, and details of your past erotic life that will capture the attention of the entire Kanczuga Rebbe's court and yeshiva. The only plaque they'll put up in your honor when I'm finished with you is over the toilet in the men's room. Do you hear me? Have I penetrated what you laughingly call your brain?"

Violet is not exactly daunted. "All this because I called Tatiana with the sole intention of saying mazel tov? For that she yells at me, and now you, too. Maybe it was the language difference. I made a little joke, and she goes crazy, huffing and puffing at me in Russian or Ukrainian or something, like a fishwife, like a yenta. The woman obviously lacks a sense of humor."

"Violet, you've crossed the red line. This escort service resigns. Have a nice life and, most of all, screw off."

"You don't mean that, Dan. We'll always be friends. We're soul-mates in a way, although I'm not sure either of us has much of a soul. We're buddies. Didn't I save Eric's ass? Doesn't that count for something? Didn't I wipe bird shit out of your eye? Didn't I sleep with you? You can't just forget me; I'm addictive. I don't give a shit whether you tell the whole world about our sex life together, and anybody with the eyes to see knows my face is lifted and my hair dyed. I don't even care about my diamonds. But if you ever breathe a single word about my ass lift, if I ever hear even a flicker or a snicker about my *tuchas*, I'll hire some of those Russians in Brooklyn, probably relatives of your delicate little flower Tatiana, and have them slowly, ever so slowly, bit by bit, break you into little pieces, while talking to you in Russian, just to make you feel at home. You make my ass infamous, and your ass will be grass. They'll find you floating in Sheepshead Bay with a note in Russian pinned to a very personal part of you. Now, do you hear me? And will you allow this very real threat to enter into your decision-making process?"

"Good-bye, Violet." And finally I get the opportunity to hang up the phone on her.

I'm angry, sure, but I'm also smiling. What a character Violet is; never a dull moment. I've got to call Tatiana, to reassure her, but first I want to replay my conversation with Violet, relish the repartee. What a woman! One thing certain, she makes me feel alive—and keeps me alive and kicking. Nine out of ten, she calls to apologize within the next twenty-four hours, maybe even within the next twenty-four minutes. My secretary buzzes: It's Mrs. Finkel and it's urgent. Twenty-four seconds, more like.

"Dan, I'm sorry, I'm sorry. This is Chaya now, not that foul-mouthed, bitchy Violet. It's Chaya, and I apologize. Everything I said was wrong, everything I did was wrong. I don't know what came over me. I was jealous, I guess—you're so cute and I may never have you again, it's not fair. Why did you ruin everything and fall in love? We could have had so much fun. I promise you, I won't attack the Red Army again, and you damn well better not mention my ass to anyone, including her. But let's be friends. You are one of the few I've ever had. Please, please, forgive me. I'm groveling."

"I know about your groveling, remember? I'm familiar with what it means for you to grovel."

"This is *real* groveling. This is not a put-on. I'm on my knees. I'm taking off all my jewelry, real and fake, I'm throwing it aside, and I'm getting into my sackcloth and ashes. I'm begging. I have sinned. Forgive me."

I try to calm down. "All right. Let's forget it. We forgive each other. Let's start over."

"Thank you, thank you. Oh, I'm so relieved—but remember, no mention of my you-know-what lift. You promise?"

"I promise."

"Do I really need a retuck? Tell me the bitter truth."

"No, you have a great ass, Violet." With that lie, I reseal our friendship and head home to comfort Tatiana.

Tatiana looks pale but composed. She has been Violeted: an experience for which there is no possible preparation; only repeated exposures provide immunity. I cheer her up as best I can. We go strolling on Madison Avenue, and I buy her a white handbag, something she's been searching for, for the wedding day. I feel like sending the bill to Violet for reimbursement, but I keep that thought to myself.

At supper, Tatiana again expresses her concern that I won't feel really married by vows exchanged before a justice of the peace, and agrees with me that we should have a rabbi solemnize our wedding in the autumn, when most of my friends will be in town. A rabbi's study will be fine, and we'll invite maybe thirty people to mark the occasion. I leave it in her hands, on the condition that we have a real rabbi, not one of those ultramodern types with no rules or limits. I want someone who knows the Law and follows it. If we're going to do it, let's do it right, I tell her. Let's do it the old-fashioned way.

34.

Two days later, on my way home from the office, I've just turned onto Park Avenue when I am startled by a loud clap of thunder. The sky has turned suddenly dark, and we are clearly in for a storm that nobody had predicted. With neither umbrella nor raincoat, I scurry to the nearest building and find shelter under its awning with two other equally unprepared pedestrians. The rain comes down in buckets. Buffeted by a sudden high wind, it falls in sheets across the sidewalks, and the streets turn into rivers; water courses toward the occasional drains. The doorman considers us with a disapproving eye. We're on his turf, but he's powerless to remove us. One of my fellow victims, a woman in her fifties, asks him if we couldn't wait out the storm in the lobby. "Sorry," he replies, looking not at all sorry, "only residents and their guests are permitted inside."

"What nerve," the woman says. "I'm on the board of my building, and we make every effort to train our help to be polite to the public. Obviously, this building can't be bothered."

Unperturbed, the doorman replies, "I'm sorry. I don't make the rules. Mine not to wonder why, mine only to comply, as the saying goes. This is the policy of Mr. Drury, our manager."

Our fellow stranded pedestrian, a man in his thirties dressed in jeans and a now very wet T-shirt, adds his two cents. "The fish stinks from the head. Sure, it's Drury's fault, not yours, but this poor woman and this elderly gentleman are getting wet, so please reconsider."

The elderly gentleman being me. I'm about to take offense—who asked him to open his big mouth, anyway?—when a taxi draws up to the curb and splashes all three of us liberally. The woman screeches, her skirt close to soaked, as the door of the taxi swings open. Out come two thick female legs, followed by an ample midriff, huge breasts, and a familiar face.

"Dan," Susan Kleiness exclaims, "are you tailing me? Have you become a stalker or is this encounter again pure chance?"

"It's the rain that has brought me to your doorstep, where I am getting thoroughly soaked while your doorman bars entry."

"Oh, Rupert," she says. "Why don't you let these people wait inside? How thoughtless of you."

"It's Mr. Drury's rule, madam. Had I been aware that you know this gentleman, I would have certainly made an exception."

"You're wet," says Susan to me. "Come on up and dry off. I promise that you will not be molested."

"Okay," I agree, a little embarrassed to leave the others stranded, but what the hell, this is New York. I follow Susan up to her apartment.

"Off with your wet clothes," she says. "I'll get you a bathrobe. Come on, strip. I've seen you before in all your glory."

As I comply I'm hoping that the price of admission does not include a sexual performance, which is definitely not the ticket today. I pull off everything except my shorts, and she hands me a man's bathrobe. I go into the bathroom and towel myself dry.

"Where did you get this robe?" I ask as I return to the living room. "It must be for a giant with arms like a gorilla."

Susan blushes. "It belongs to my boyfriend. Remember, the psychic said he'd be big as a tree, and he is."

"How's he going to feel about finding me half naked with you if he comes in?"

"Oh, he's a gentle giant. Besides which if he gets out of line, I'll fire him. He works for me, he's a salesman in my company."

"You're living with an employee? Sounds dangerous—maltreat him, and you'll have the union after you," I tease her.

"Believe me, I'm not going to maltreat him. He's the best thing that's ever happened to me. For him I've lost thirteen pounds so far, although he likes me large. He revels in my plentitude, or so he says."

"Don't forget to give him a raise."

"I do better than that. I give him a rise. He loves me, something you may have once heard of or even possibly experienced at some point in your long, long life."

"Okay, okay," I say. "Lay off, I'll be good. Over one of your famous cups of coffee and stellar cookies, tell me what's up."

"No more cookies," she apologizes, "only rice crackers, for those desperate enough to eat them. From the taste, it's hard to distinguish between them and the container they come in. I'm on a diet, no more goodies."

So we have only coffee, and she talks about Josh. How kind he is, how polite, how caring. What a good father he is to his kids, and considerate even of the woman who divorced him and married one of his friends. Susan's eyes shine with pleasure as she speaks, and if I am slightly envious of her certainty, I'm happy for her, too.

"Susan," I interrupt her, "you're in love, that's great."

"Well," she says, "nothing is easy. Josh is a salesman, not even a sales manager. He makes one-fifth of my salary, and he's not very intellectual. He rarely reads, to tell the truth. I'm not sure he even looks at the *Journal* or the *Times*, I've only seen him reading a paper when he's looking for a movie. Nothing is perfect, I know, but he should know what Albania is. The other day I mentioned a possible business deal in Albania, and he asked me what state it was in. He's not the sharpest knife in the drawer, but he's good to me, so loving, and he finds me attractive—all of me. I don't know what to do about him, but it sure feels pretty wonderful."

"I'm in a similar spot," I commiserate, "falling for a woman who has absolutely not one characteristic I was looking for, except that she is pretty. She's so utterly defenseless that I've become protective; I think I've got to solve all her problems, or most of the time I do. Every once in a while, I feel like taking off and running for my life. Only now I'm engaged."

"Mazel tov, Dan, all my best wishes. Josh wants to marry me, but . . . Seriously, Dan, is it possible that he does love me, or do I just assume the worst? Do I listen to all the objections my friends are raising, or do I go for it? Imagine how humiliated I'll be if it all goes wrong, if in a year or two he takes a walk. Yet he's such a good man, I really don't believe he will."

"It's easy for me to tell you to go ahead, take the shot, and you probably should, but I've been grappling with a similar decision myself, so I understand how you feel. Net, net? I'd go for it if I were you. I am. Otherwise, what's life about? Just to play it safe? And you'll die of boredom; it's better to die from aggravation. What's that old Jewish expression? 'Life is with people.' In some ways we might be better off living alone, but we're just not made that way."

"You know something, Dan, I think you're in danger of becoming wise. Maybe it's your advanced age."

"Screw you."

"No, thanks, that's part of Josh's duties nowadays."

"Well, sounds like the rain stopped. If I can't have cookies, I might as well get dressed and go." Susan brings me my clothes. As I climb into them, I think how extraordinarily at ease I feel with her, considering the little time we have spent together. I share the thought with her.

"Well, people who sleep together should be friendly," she says, but I can see that she's touched by what I say. "I feel at ease with you, too," she admits. "Maybe when things get sorted out, we'll all be friends."

"I believe that," I say, and give her a kiss on the cheek. "Thanks for letting me dry off."

The doorman opens the door deferentially for me as I leave. It's now a sunny afternoon, and not just because of the weather. I've got a new friend.

35.

I f Myra's indeed been hiding in the Navajo tribal lands, she is
also on the phone, my secretary tells me. I doubt that I really
have the inclination or the energy for it, but I take the call.

"Why haven't you checked up on me?" Myra asks peevishly, not
sounding like herself at all.

"I have just been busy, my dear. But actually, I do have some
news: Tatiana and I are to be married in August."

"I see," she says flatly. "So the Russki got you? I guess I can't be
surprised. What may surprise you is that I meanwhile have sworn off
sex entirely."

"Why is that?" I ask, in an indifferent attempt to be polite.

"I have just learned that I have been blacklisted regarding all
future pro-Palestinian gatherings. It appears that poor Karim had to
undergo back surgery and now wears a brace. I think I should write
to Hanan Ashrawi. She seems quite nice and rational on CNN, and

she has such a gentle voice, maybe she would intercede on my behalf. The people at the BBC think she's a saint. So she may be my best bet. After all, she's apparently a modern woman, no veil, no black robe, and she also has a crew cut—so she must be thoroughly modern. My lawyer Kreplach is framing a letter, I'll just have to keep my fingers crossed. I'm also keeping my legs crossed, no more sex for me until I figure out what I'm doing wrong. I've had too many complaints, too many men wounded. Maybe that's why Billy avoided me for so long. A woman asserts herself, and the whole world resists, nothing ever changes. If I were a man, they'd call me a tiger, but what they're calling me is an obstacle to the peace process. I used to speak at peace rallies, and now I'm persona non grata—because I gave my body for the cause. Why is life so unfair?"

I try to sound sympathetic. "Life without a peace rally sounds hard. You'll have to bear up."

"Oh, the peace rallies are the least of it," Myra replies. "Who sponsors them, in the U.S., but professors and students, and they count for nothing. But I do miss my human rights meetings. I've been blacklisted at them, too. I attempted to attend one last week and was barred at the door—some activist from California recognized me, and that was that. He called me an infiltrator, among other things. However, I'm full of hope that I will be allowed to attend a forthcoming environmentalist meeting near here. The subject is trees, so it should attract a different kind of crowd, a gentler sort—their bark worse than their bite, so to speak."

I wish her good luck, promise to keep in touch through Kreplach's office, and return to my work. But not for long. Violet is calling from Abano. When I pick up, her voice seems faraway, half lost in the splash and lapping of water.

"I'm in the spa, darling . . . wonderful spa, marble everywhere in all sorts of colors, you know the Italians, marble and chandeliers, and the food, the food! I've been massaged every day; I've been wrapped in seaweed, plastered in mud, boiled and chilled, whipped with fronds, pedicured, manicured, facial'd, and I'm perfect now, perfect, or as perfect as I can be. Even my behind feels firmer. No nasty lift for me, I'm so tight I bounce when I sit down. You want to see, come on over and bounce along with me. Today is the first of August, in three weeks you're nailed down. This may be your last chance."

"Thanks for the invitation, but I'm working on fidelity, so I'll say no. How about you bouncing over this way and attending my wedding? I could do with the presence of a good friend that day—and I consider you that, my good friend."

"I am, Danny. I know I'm nuts, but I'm a good nut, and you know I wish you well, but crawling up to the Berkshires and watching the local dogcatcher marry you to the Ukraine in a five-minute ceremony in town hall is just not my thing. I'll wish you well from afar, drown my sorrows with a splendid bottle of Italian wine, and, if I get lucky, with a fine specimen of Italian manhood at the very moment you say yes. That's my survival plan."

"Understood. Take care." After we hang up, I feel little more than amused: no regrets, no pangs over loss. It's over. I'm committed now to Tatiana. I turn back to my work without a qualm, though not without relishing my season as a middle-aged Don Juan.

36.

There is only one week to go before the wedding: seven days until our Thursday afternoon appointment in Lenox, where the deed will be done. I am in the city, but Tatiana and Niki are up at the country house, from which I am banned; it is apparently bad luck for the prospective bride and groom to see each other for one week before the day itself. I don't know if it is a Russian custom or a Jewish one, or both, but it demands that. Even Della agrees with Tatiana—too much tension, too many nervous moments, she says, better that you don't collide with each other at all the whole week.

So I spend the weekend pretty much alone, and it turns out to be good for me, because I am actually spending it with Ellen. Over the past two years, I've learned that when someone you love is dead you can find consolation inside yourself, in the reality that your beloved is always there in your heart, your soul, whenever you want them.

I walk to what were our favorite spots in Central Park. I sit where we sat to watch the joggers, the sunbathers, the little kids playing on the grass. I'm not crazy enough yet to talk to Ellen out loud, but I share my thoughts with her as I retrace our steps. I enjoy the feeling of her presence. I'm not saying good-bye; there will never be a good-bye between Ellen and me. We virtually grew up together—what one wanted, the other wanted; we finished each other's sentences. It's different with Tatiana. Age, circumstances, experience—they make it different.

On Sunday night, I am driven by the need to find Ellen's Bible, the one she carried on our wedding day. It had a bright white cover with her named emblazoned on it, and I'm sure it's in the library, somewhere high up on the shelves, I think. It takes some time to find it, mostly because the cover has yellowed into a dull ivory. Decades have turned its pages brown. I leaf through the book. I remember the white orchids she held with the Bible as we stood under the wedding canopy. The book falls open to a page that maybe Ellen often used to read, or maybe it opens there merely by chance. It reads, "I remember your devotion when you were young, the love of your bridal days, how you followed me through the desert, through a land unsown . . ." The words resonate with me. Because they're true. Because Ellen indeed married me when I had nothing, was no one. She pinned her destiny to me when mine was unknown. She trusted in me. We had some rough spots over the years, but I never allowed myself to forget that from the beginning she was prepared to follow me wherever I should go, that she believed in me. I hope I never let her down, or that she never felt I had. I lift the musty open book to my lips and I kiss it, the way I'd learned to do when I was a kid in Hebrew School. But it is not only the holy book that I kiss. It's all the memories that flood over me: the guilt, the loss, our marriage, our love.

I put the book back on its high shelf. I'll try to remember to take it the next time I go to the cemetery. But whether or not I do is unimportant. What is important now is that my love for her is still alive and that she knows it. The rest I hope she understands.

Twice during the night, I wake up but quickly fall back to sleep. Once, I remember, I'd been dreaming that I was explaining to Ellen what happened between Tatiana and me. Whether she was agreeing or arguing with me in the dream I can't remember in the morning.

I function at least minimally in the office on Monday and Tuesday. By Wednesday I can't even get dressed. I roam around the apartment two steps ahead of Della, who shoos me out of one room after the other. That evening Carol and Eric join me for a feast prepared by Della, and topped off by her carrot cake, Eric's favorite. Our mood is cheerful, although I'm surprised that absolutely no one, not a soul, has called me to congratulate me. We sent out announcements, not invitations, to all my old friends, and not everyone can be away for vacation. It's begun to bother me; someone should have called. Perhaps I have offended them by not inviting them, but why should they want to feel obligated to schlep up to the Berkshires for a five-minute civil ceremony in the boondocks?

Eric tries to calm me down. "Don't worry, Dad," he says. "Everything will be fine. You'll have the religious ceremony in New York in a couple of weeks. That's when they will respond."

"But not even Evelyn and Bob called, and I know they're in town. Something's wrong, maybe I insulted them."

"Well, we'll be there tomorrow, and that's what counts. We'll pick Della and you up at noon. We'll drive straight to Lenox, do the dirty deed, and then we can all relax. I've got the wedding ring; the flowers for Della and Carol are being delivered here before ten A.M.

Everything has been taken care of. So get some sleep. I know it's tough, but try to relax, Dad. Della's sleeping over tonight, right? Keep the old guy from going crazy, will you, Della? He's looking a little cross-eyed with fear."

"It's not fear, it's anticipation," I reply. "I have nothing to be afraid of."

There's a short pause, and then all three of them break into laughter—raucously, genuinely—as if at my expense, as if they enjoy my discomfort in my last anguished hours as a free man. Eventually I join in, but in fact it's not easy to laugh, not tonight.

The next day, we drive north to Lenox. We get to the land use office at twenty to two, but Tatiana and Niki have not yet arrived. Seated in the little waiting room, we find ourselves in the company of an angry local resident.

"I've had two coyotes roaming on my property for months. I've complained to the selectman, but nobody does anything. My dog is afraid to go out, she's messing up all over the house. So I set a trap of my own. What else can I do? Then, wouldn't you know, my neighbor's dog wanders over into my yard and gets caught in the trap. I ran out and tried to get the dog out of it, but the coyotes were already there, circling. I had to call the police who then slapped me with a fine for an unauthorized trap. Is that fair? No fine for the dead dog, but my neighbor is a lawyer, so you know what's next. I'm not leaving here until they rescind the fine. What are you here for? Them's nice flowers."

"A wedding," I answer. "Mine."

"Congratulations," he says, looking at Della and wondering.

"I'm waiting for my bride-to-be to arrive."

"Well, I hope you won't mind giving me one minute with the justice of the peace. I've got to straighten this out. I left Ramona, that's my dog, home alone, and who knows what she's making on the floor, 'cause she just stands by the door moaning and whining when I try to let her out. Besides, I was here first."

Tatiana, Niki, and the justice of the peace ("call me Peggy") arrive at the same moment. Our unhappy dog owner grabs the woman and repeats his tale of woe. "Nothing I can do, Hank, a fine is recorded. I can't just erase it. There has to be a hearing, but first these nice people have to be married. Give me a break here. Hank, you be one of our witnesses, and I'll get my secretary, too. Let's do this wedding right, then we'll deal with your fine."

Two or three minutes later, Tatiana and I are standing together in front of Peggy's desk. She faces us. Behind us are Eric, Carol, Della, and the two witnesses. Peggy begins to read the vows, and we are almost at the magic moment when the phone rings. Her secretary grabs it, explains that Peggy is busy marrying someone, and yes, she'll definitely keep her hairdresser appointment. "Not until she gets my fine canceled," adds Hank. Peggy completes the ceremony, leans forward, and with a big smile wishes us a long life together filled with lots of happiness.

"Please, Peggy," says Hank. "Do something for me quick about this fine. Ramona is alone, and I'm going to need my boots to wade through the you-know-what in my house—you gotta help me."

Tatiana and I kiss. First Niki, then everyone else hugs us, and that's that.

We leave the land use office to the drone of Hank's graphic description of Ramona's last few homebound weeks. I feel nothing, absolutely nothing. Maybe I'm just numb. But that was a wedding? Stuck in between Ramona and the hairdresser? I should have planned something more. Despite the pathetic ceremony, Tatiana is glowing with happiness. She looks wonderful in her new dress, and once my ability to talk is somewhat restored, I tell her so. We follow Eric's car into our driveway, and I can't help but notice the huge blue and white striped tent on the lawn. Or the unusual number of parked cars.

"Eric, that could hold hundreds of people," I say to him as we get out of our cars. "Couldn't you get a smaller one? What's going on, you hosting an army in there?"

"The small ones were all taken, Dad. Besides, you don't want to squeeze a hundred guests or more into a pup tent," says Eric, as Tatiana leads me by the hand to the entrance of the tent. A loud mazel tov greets me. It's shouted by a crowd of assembled guests. There's the Kanczuga Rebbe and maybe thirty of his students. There are Luba and Gregor, their kids—how did they get here? Evelyn and Bob; all my old friends. Ellen's sister and her kids. Tatiana's former apartment-mates. My God, even the Hoffmans, and everyone from my office.

"How . . ." I say to Eric. "This must have cost a fortune! How could you do this without consulting me?" I'm looking at him as if he's lost his mind, but Eric simply smiles. Before I can say anything more, I'm meeting the embrace of more than one hundred people.

Soon the Rebbe's students are shushing everyone into silence. Then Luba brings Tatiana a white veil, which she places over her head but leaves her face exposed, and a band strikes up a lilting Jewish tune.

"Let us have the marriage contract witnessed, then you can veil your bride," says the Rebbe. "And let us bring God into this occasion, let's invite Him to join us and to sanctify your marriage."

Still dazed, I've only now begun to realize the Rebbe is going to marry us, but how did Eric manage to get him here? I follow the Rebbe's instructions; I veil Tatiana, and we then proceed down the aisle toward a small wedding canopy on a raised platform. Tatiana circles me the traditional seven times, the band now playing a haunting tune while the guests are seated around us.

The Rebbe begins the ceremony. Men are called forward to recite the Seven Blessings, and in what seems to be barely a few minutes Eric is handing me a wedding ring, which I put on Tatiana's finger.

I recite the ancient declaration, "You are hereby consecrated to me with this ring according to the laws of Moses and of Israel." A glass wrapped in a napkin is placed on the floor before me. I step on it, and shatter it in memory of the destruction of the Temple in Jerusalem, and on that cue the band strikes up Hasidic music. Our guests gather around us to offer their congratulations, but I'm too stunned to understand any of it: the enormity of the expense, the attendance of Luba and her family, the Rebbe.

Before I can collect my wits, Tatiana and I are led into the house for the traditional *yichud*, a period when the couple sits privately together, alone and undisturbed. I am wet with perspiration, I drink several glasses of water. Tatiana seems remarkably composed. Figuring that Eric and Carol must have confided in her, I ask her how they had managed all this.

But Tatiana replies, "I don't know. All I know is that this is their present to us. I left everything in their hands. I didn't want to ask for anything in particular, I didn't know their budget. But I am overwhelmed. Did you see the flowers? Peonies and roses, barrels of them; I cannot imagine the expense. The catered dinner, the Jewish band. And most of all, my Luba: To bring my Luba, and her family, how can I ever thank them enough?"

Peonies and roses! Now I'm really angry, is Eric nuts? I'm steaming. Sure, it was well meant, even loving of him, but what kind of fool is he to spend money on such frills? God, I hope he didn't use

Violet's money for this, God help us if he took some of her investment and spent it on peonies. If he did, I'll . . . I'll fix his wagon if
he did, I'll . . .

Enough with the solitary confinement, I have to find Eric and sort
this out. He's standing just inside the tent, surveying the activity and
talking to Della.

"Eric," I say to him, "I love you and I am grateful to you for the
party, but I've been tallying up the amounts you must have spent on
this Broadway production here—and I'm very concerned. This isn't
like you: Have you flipped your lid? Did you win the damned lottery?
Explain yourself."

"Dad . . . Look, Dad, if you promise me that Tatiana will never
know, I'll explain it all in one word. Promise?"

"I do." I urge him, "Tell me."

"Dad, I'm serious, Tatiana must never know."

"Tell him, Eric," urges Della.

"I promise. Come on, tell me."

"Violet," says Eric, "Violet, Dad. She's the word, and she's the cra-
ziest, most generous steamroller I have ever met. A one-woman
band. The worldwide floral industry must have had a twenty percent
increase in revenues because of her alone this year. She's magical.
She paid for everything from soup to nuts, and I mean nuts. A private plane for the Rebbe, his gang, Luba, her family, the whole
Israeli contingent. The peonies, she insisted on peonies, which are
now out of season and had to be flown in from the four corners of
the earth. And the Rebbe approves of only one kosher caterer, and
then only if he brings his own crew and kitchen, which were
brought in piece by piece, cook by cook, and waiter by waiter, from
Brooklyn, so we now have an army of waiters here that has to be
redelivered to their homes all over New York. The woman is

amazing. She must really love you, because she certainly moved mountains for you. Della and I had to promise to tell no one but you, only you, and only if you pressed me. She cried when she told me that the Kanczuga Rebbe would officiate."

"She's not here, Eric? She didn't come? I didn't see her."

"She's here, Dad. I saw her standing at one of the tent entrances when the Rebbe married you. She's hard to miss, she's wearing an orange gown and the biggest yellow diamonds I've ever seen; she twinkles, she shines. She must have been avoiding you or maybe she's waiting for you to come to her, I don't know. Just look for a thousand points of light and you'll find her."

Before I can do much looking, though, the Rebbe collars me. I thank him for officiating so beautifully and for making the long trip. He makes light of his part in the event; he gives all the credit to Violet instead, and then wishes me all good things with Tatiana and Niki. "There must be much you want to say to Mrs. Finkel," he adds. "I think you will find her in the pergola where I left her a few minutes ago."

Years ago, at a spot where the lawn ends and the forest begins, I built the wooden pavilion for Ellen; she loved to sit and read there. By now it's getting dark, and only a bit of light from the back of the house illuminates the pergola. Violet is sitting alone, a bit hunched over, her shoulders wrapped in a bright orange silk shawl. She doesn't hear me walking in the grass; I call her name so as not to startle her. "Danny," she responds. She brushes away something on her face, then turns to me with a big smile. "Happy?" she asks.

"Thanks to you. I was really down after that so-called wedding in Lenox; then to come home to this incredible surprise, perfect in every detail . . . But no wonder, you produced it. It'll probably be days before I'm coherent enough to even begin to express my thanks—but why, Violet, why? Last time we spoke you almost bit off my head."

"Why not? Why shouldn't I be able to arrange at least one wedding without a single daisy? I was finally able to have my way, even though it was not Maria's wedding. It was yours. That's why."

I walk up to her and hug her tight. She must have been crying, her makeup is smudged. "Watch my hair," she complains, "and you're wrinkling my dress."

"Why?"

"Don't you know?" she asks. "Can't you imagine why? Life is funny, Danny boy. A lot of it is about timing, right or wrong. In my way I love you, you must know that. I began to love you the first night we met. I saw you standing there at your surprise party, looking all handsome and baffled, and right there and then—zap—I loved you. Hoping to speed up the relationship, I dragged you to Israel hoping to dazzle you with my good deeds and money. I figured I'd bag you, that we'd live happily ever after and golf our way into senility together. Even now, I don't know exactly what happened to me on that trip. It wasn't only the visit with the Rebbe; it was Maria, it was Jerusalem. Jerusalem seems to demand your help, your attention, your commitment. And at the Rebbe's I caught a glimpse of what I would call holiness. Look, I'm no fool, I know he's a human being like any other, but there is a commitment he has to acts of charity and kindness. For all my generous grants, that's what I've never had—a real commitment. If I'm ever going to find a way to make that commitment, I need to be free to do so. These last weeks in Europe put an end to my extravagant but tired, old lifestyle: the endless expensive indulgences, the pampering day after day you can command as long as you're paying for it through the nose. No more. In Abano I started playing around with one of the spa managers, a married man with six kids, the two of us splashing around in my pink marble Jacuzzi. I'm lying there with him on top of me, wondering what the hell am I doing there. I've got to find myself again—the real me, the Brooklyn me, the pre-money me, when I still had dreams. I have the potential to be a serious person, it's not too late. The Rebbe says that God waits for us to return until we've lived the last second of our lives, and I've got a lot of returning to do. You can't help me, Danny. You're made of different stuff. You don't need as much improvement as I do. You fell in love with Tatiana like a twenty-year-old, head over heels. Like a boy. It's amazing to see; sometimes I think that men never grow up, they just look older. You've stayed innocent in a funny way, experience hasn't made you cynical. You can still get carried away by a smile or a tear—I envy you that ability."

"But why the extravaganza? If you had bothered to come back here to attend the wedding, that alone would have been amazing enough."

"Because I love you, because we are special friends, because what else could I do for you that would stay with you always? At first, I wanted to stay away, to avoid the whole business, but that was wrong. This is my day, too; my best friend got married, and I was able to make the day even more memorable with my money, with my craziness. It was hard to organize from overseas, believe me, but I loved every irritating minute of it, because I was doing it for you. Is that a good enough answer?"

Tears are streaming down my cheeks. Violet is crying, too. In the increasing darkness we stand there crying together in the pergola. Then I take her into my arms. I embrace her briefly, somewhat formally, and she asks me for my handkerchief. "Two idiots," she says, dabbing her eyes, "two sentimental fools."

I don't deny it. I just hold her hand in mine.

"You know, Danny boy, we're going to end up together, eventually. First you'll have to raise Niki and be a good husband to Tatiana, and I'll have to become a damned saint, the best-dressed, most diamond-studded saint the world has ever seen. And then, when we're really old, who knows? You and I have got enough orneriness in us to outlive most people. We just might be sitting together on the verandah of a nursing home drooling into our bibs and holding hands, or maybe we'll be in wheelchairs with attendants, but somehow, somewhere, you and I will be together in the end, I believe that. So consider tonight's extravaganza an investment on my part. I made my honey happy in a big way, the payoff to come in twenty or thirty years. We'll have no teeth, and instead of sex we may have to wink at each other, but we'll be together, trust me."

Together, we walk silently back to the tent, now resounding with the spirited blare of Hassidic dance music. Before we enter, Violet whispers to me, "Later, make sure the florist delivers the flowers to the nearby hospital, as I arranged. I don't want them recycled so he can profit twice, not after what he charged me. And make sure that bum of a caterer delivers what will be a mountain of extra food to the Yeshiva in Monsey, I already arranged for a refrigerated truck. I don't want anyone to know I organized any of this, especially not Tatiana. Promise me."

I promise, and she hands me a folded piece of paper. "Don't lose it," she tells me. "It's my itinerary for the next year: phone numbers, faxes, everything. Just in case you find that you need me or miss me or something. Anything. Be in touch."

I'm barely in the tent, when Eric grabs me. "There you are, Dad, we've been looking for you everywhere. It's time for Tatiana and you to learn to fly." The Jewish dance music blares louder as Tatiana and

I are pulled into the middle of the dance floor, where we're each of us pushed onto a chair and lifted into the air by a group of young men. Someone throws us a napkin, we each grab an end, and to the band's exuberant wail we perform the traditional mock dance, both of us holding on for dear life to the bouncing chairs. Higher and higher we're raised; I duck when I'm near the top of the tent. Tatiana, half laughing and half scared, pulls on her end of the napkin. Now they've put Niki on a chair, up *he* goes; now Eric—our two boys join us in flight, the music is soaring along with our spirits, Tatiana is squealing with joy.

I'm laughing, I'm bouncing, I'm flying, but I do not fail to see Violet slip out of the tent with her chauffeur, who's carrying her orange silk scarf and a floral arrangement, while the caterer bows and scrapes behind them. My dear friend, my special friend, I wonder when will we speak again.

The men holding the four of us up seem to converge, and we all join hands with each other way up in the air, Eric and Niki and Tatiana and me, hanging on, happy together.

Reading Group Topics

The following are some, I hope, provocative questions to help stir a discussion of *Love With Noodles*. I would be happy to be a guest by phone (with sufficient advance notice) for any book club with six or more members who have read and are discussing the novel. Please contact Tina Ponzo, *tponzo@balfournyc.com*, to schedule a phone appearance at your book club meeting.

1. My inspiration for the novel came from an unlikely source—David Ben-Gurion. My family traveled to Israel frequently and were good friends with the Ben-Gurions. During one trip, Ben-Gurion invited me to his deceased wife's gravesite, remarking that "a woman shouldn't die before her husband—it isn't fair to either of them." Do you agree or disagree with this comment? What factors would cause being widowed to be more difficult for a man or a woman?

2. The protagonist, Dan Gelder, remembers his father saying that "Love is good but love with noodles is better." Noodles can mean wealth, companionship, beauty, or any other material consideration. Are these considerations more important or more likely to be seriously weighted in a second marriage?

3. Dan, an assimilated non-traditional Jew, has difficulty accepting his son's decision to marry a non-Jewish woman. His arguments against intermarriage are not rooted in religious practice. What do you think of his reasoning? Is there a better potential response that you can formulate?

4. What do you think should be the appropriate response of families and of the Jewish community as a whole to the increasing phenomenon of intermarriage?

5. The book gives the reader a glimpse into the lives of Jews on Manhattan's wealthy Upper East Side and describes some of the social dynamics. What characteristics are there in American Jewish life as described in the book which transcend particular locations and socio-economic status?

Acknowledgments

T he word "miracle" is often used loosely but I think it correctly describes the publication of a first novel by a sixty-five year old author. As in most miracles, a good deal of human intervention is required and I therefore would like to acknowledge with gratitude the efforts of my publisher, Will Balliett of Carroll & Graf Publishers, and of my literary agent, Kim Witherspoon of InkWell Management and her colleague, David Forrer, who all helped me immeasurably on the path to publication. I am also indebted to Billie Fitzpatrick, whose skilled editing added whatever finesse and polish exist in my work.

And I can never adequately thank Carolyn Starman Hessel, Executive Director of the Jewish Book Council, whose advice and encouragement were absolutely essential to my completion of this novel. Her enthusiasm for this book actually at times exceeded my own.

My daughter, Rebecca Sugar, was the first editor of my book and she and my sons Michael and John were among my severest critics together with Rex Alexander and Sonia Sorg, who typed and edited the manuscript many times. But it is my wife, Dr. Matta Freund, to whom I owe the greatest debt for her patience and good humor during the time in which I worked on this novel and for her belief that all the characters are truly fictional.